TEACHER EDITION

UNIT 4 Living Things Grow and Reproduce

Big Idea and Essential Questions

This Unit was designed to focus on this Big Idea and Essential Questions.

Big Idea

All living things have observable characteristics that allow them to be classified. Plants and animals pass these characteristics on to their offspring.

Essential Questions

L1 **How Are Living Things Grouped?**

L2 **What Is a Dichotomous Key?**

L3 **How Do Plants Grow and Reproduce?**

L4 **What Factors Affect Germination Rate?**

L5 **How Do Animals Grow and Reproduce?**

L6 **What Are Physical and Behavioral Adaptations?**

Professional Development

Houghton Mifflin Harcourt and **NSTA,** the **National Science Teachers Association,** have partnered to provide customized professional development resources for teachers using *ScienceFusion*.

The Professional Development Resources include

- Do-it-yourself resources, where you can study at your own pace
- Live and archived online seminars
- Journal articles, many of which include lesson plans
- Fee-based eBooks, eBook chapters, online short courses, symposia, and conferences

Access to the NSTA Learning Center is provided in the *ScienceFusion* Online Resources.

Printed in the U.S.A.

ISBN 978-0-547-69698-0

4 5 6 7 8 9 10 0877 20 19 18 17 16 15 14 13 12

4500380383 B C D E F G

Photo Credits

Front Cover: *crab* ©Mark Webb/Alamy; *geyser* ©Frans Lanting/Corbis; frog ©DLILLC/Corbis; *flask* ©Gregor Schuster/Getty Images; *rowers* ©Stockbyte/Getty Images.
Back Cover: *gecko* ©Pete Orelup/Getty Images; *bike* ©Jerome Prevost/TempSport/Corbis; *computer* ©Michael Melford/Getty Images; *landscape* ©Rod McLean/Alamy.

Unit Planning

Options for Instruction

Two parallel paths meet the unit objectives, with a strong **Inquiry** strand woven into each. Follow the **Print Path,** the **Digital Path,** or your customized combination of print, digital, and inquiry.

	LESSON 1	LESSON 2	LESSON 3
Essential Questions	**How Are Living Things Grouped?**	☑ Guided Inquiry **What Is a Dichotomous Key?**	**How Do Plants Grow and Reproduce?**
Print Path	☐ **Student Edition** **pp. 175–188** • Why Classify? • Classifying Living Things • Plants and Animals • Fungi and Protists • Bacteria and Archaea	☐ **Student Edition** **pp. 189–190** • Scaffolding for Inquiry	☐ **Student Edition** **pp. 191–204** • Tubes for Transport • No Seeds, Please! • Seed Power! • From Flower to Fruit to Seed • How Seeds Grow
Hands-On Inquiry	**Inquiry Flipchart** **p. 19** **How Does a Dichotomous Key Work?** ☐ Directed Inquiry **Grocery Grouping** ☐ Independent Inquiry	**Inquiry Flipchart** **p. 20** **What Is a Dichotomous Key?** ☐ Guided Inquiry	**Inquiry Flipchart** **p. 21** **Comparing Cones and Fruits** ☐ Directed Inquiry **Flowers in Hiding** ☐ Independent Inquiry
Digital Path	☐ **Digital Lesson** **Online Resources** Interactive presentation of lesson content	☐ **Virtual Lab** **Online Resources** Interactive scaffolded inquiry	☐ **Digital Lesson** **Online Resources** Interactive presentation of lesson content

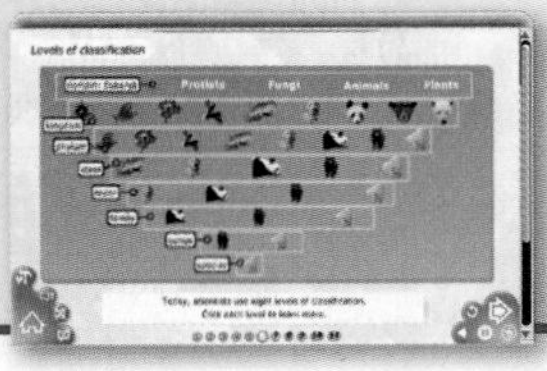

LESSON 4

Guided Inquiry

What Factors Affect Germination Rate?

☐ **Student Edition**
pp. 207–208
- Scaffolding for Inquiry

Inquiry Flipchart
p. 23

What Factors Affect Germination Rate?

☐ Guided Inquiry

☐ **Virtual Lab**
Online Resources
Interactive scaffolded inquiry

LESSON 5

How Do Animals Grow and Reproduce?

☐ **Student Edition**
pp. 209–222
- Have a Backbone?
- "Spineless" Invertebrates
- Communication Is Key
- Stages of Life
- It's Time for a Change

Inquiry Flipchart
p. 24

How Can You Model a Backbone?

☐ Directed Inquiry

How Do They Change?

☐ Independent Inquiry

☐ **Digital Lesson**
Online Resources
Interactive presentation of lesson content

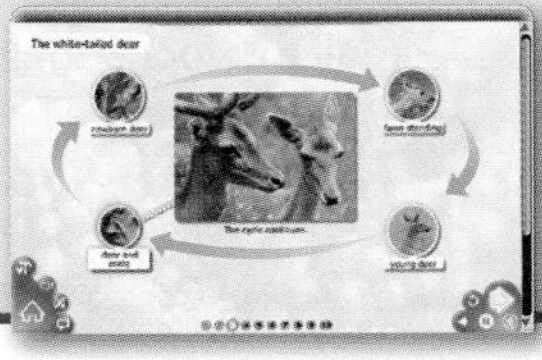

LESSON 6

What Are Physical and Behavioral Adaptations?

☐ **Student Edition**
pp. 225–240
- Adaptations
- Form and Function
- Eat or Be Eaten
- On Your Best Behavior
- The Circle of Life
- Living Things Change

Inquiry Flipchart
p. 25

Gobbling Up Your Greens

☐ Directed Inquiry

Animal Adaptations

☐ Independent Inquiry

☐ **Digital Lesson**
Online Resources
Interactive presentation of lesson content

OTHER UNIT FEATURES

People in Science, p. 223

S.T.E.M. Engineering and Technology, pp. 205–206B

Online Resources

Unit Assessment

Formative Assessment
Sum It Up! and Brain Check Student Edition, end of each lesson

Summative Assessment
Lesson Quizzes
Assessment Guide, pp. AG 38–AG 43

Unit 4 Review
Student Edition, pp. 241–244

Unit 4 Test
Assessment Guide, pp. AG 44–AG 48

Performance Assessment
SHORT OPTION: Teacher Edition, p. 243
LONG OPTION: Assessment Guide, pp. AG 49–AG 50

RTI Response to Intervention

RTI Strategies p. 173K

Online Assessment
Test-taking and automatic scoring
Banks of items from which to build tests

Planning for Inquiry

Use the following preview of Inquiry Activities and Lessons to gather and manage the materials needed for each lesson.

Activity	Inquiry and Design Process Skills Focus	Materials	Prep Tips, Troubleshooting, and Expected Results
Lesson 1 DIRECTED INQUIRY Flipchart p.19 A **How Does a Dichotomous Key Work?** **OBJECTIVE** Follow directions for an investigation to make and use a dichotomous key. 25–30 minutes pairs	• Compare • Classify/Order • Communicate • Infer	• blank dichotomous key	**Prep Tip** Display some classroom objects, and discuss ways that they can be grouped. Use this as a means to model how to make a dichotomous key. If pressed for time, provide blank dichotomous keys for students to complete, or start students out by doing the first branching together. **Troubleshooting** Reinforce that each branch must provide a clear choice for someone who has no idea or image of the final result. For example, a question on a key used to categorize foods could be *Is the food a type of meat?* If students have difficulty classifying some of their objects using the key, encourage them to think of other examples that have more distinct, obvious differences that can be utilized. **Expected Results** Students construct dichotomous keys that can be used by someone else to easily determine the identity of an object as described by its characteristics.
INDEPENDENT INQUIRY Flipchart p.19 B **Grocery Grouping** **OBJECTIVE** Plan and conduct an investigation to classify foods. 15–20 minutes individuals	• Compare • Classify/Order	• local referenced items	**Prep Tip** Having students keep a food journal for several days in advance of this activity will help them recall the foods they often eat. As a review, work as a class to develop a key for classifying types of literature or movies. **Expected Results** If students have not made a journal, provide magazines or reference books that display various kinds of food items for students to use to make their lists. Have students prepare the list of foods before thinking about organization. This will prevent them from thinking only of specific foods that are easily categorized. The purpose of the exercise is for them to be able to make groups from a list of objects. Limit the number of categories students identify to five or fewer to ensure that they have grouped several different foods in each category. **Expected Results** Students should be able to think of three or more categories in which they can classify all the foods they have listed.

Additional teaching support for all inquiry activities is available in **Online Resources.**

Notebook **Science Notebook Strategies**

- Lists of Kit-Supplied Materials
- Meeting Individual Needs
- Investigate More—Extensions and Variations
- and More!

Activity	Inquiry and Design Process Skills Focus	Materials	Prep Tips, Troubleshooting, and Expected Results
Lesson 2 INQUIRY GUIDED INQUIRY **Flipchart** p20 **Student Edition** pp. 189–190 **What Is a Dichotomous Key?** **OBJECTIVES** • Classify items based on characteristics they have or lack. • Use a dichotomous key to classify items. 30–45 minutes pairs	• Classify/Order • Observe • Record and Display Data • Compare	• 6 beans in a bag	**Prep Tip** Assemble a collection of six different beans. The beans should be distinguishable from one another but still share some common traits. For example, some beans may be round, while others are oval in shape. The beans may be various colors. Place the beans in cups or plastic bags so that students are forced to sort the beans after they receive them. You may wish to provide students with collections that are made up of different combinations of beans, allowing for greater variation among keys. **Troubleshooting** Make a display of all the beans with labels. This will allow students to easily name the beans in their keys. While the quantity of each type of bean in a collection can vary, there should only be six types of beans in each bag/cup. Remind students that their dichotomous keys must be clear enough so that another person can use it to identify each type of bean. **Expected Results** Students will devise a dichotomous key for collection of beans. Their keys should be decipherable by other students. Students should follow the prompts and record their responses on pages 189–190.

Go Digital! Virtual Lab

What Is a Dichotomous Key?

Key Inquiry Skills: Observe, Classify

Students develop and use dichotomous keys to classify three groups—primates, rain forest plants, and hand tools.

Planning for Inquiry (continued)

Activity	Inquiry and Design Process Skills Focus	Materials	Prep Tips, Troubleshooting, and Expected Results
Lesson 3 DIRECTED INQUIRY **Flipchart** p.21 **A Comparing Cones and Fruits** **OBJECTIVE** Follow directions for an investigation comparing the reproductive structures of gymnosperms and angiosperms. 20–30 minutes small groups	• Observe • Compare • Record Data • Infer	• pinecone • pine seeds • apple cross-section • apple seeds	**Prep Tip** You will need about ten apples for this investigation—five to slice in half and five from which you can remove the seeds. Prepare apples prior to class. Make sure that apple sections are sliced so that the seeds inside are visible. Coat the cut slices with lemon juice and keep them in a cool place to slow the darkening of the slices. Pine seeds, also known as pine nuts, are available in the produce department of most grocery stores. If possible, slice the pinecones in half to reveal a cross-section of these structures. **Caution!** Be aware of possible allergies. You may suggest that students wear gloves. **Troubleshooting** Cover work surfaces with paper towels or newspapers or have paper plates available on which students may place each object. If you cannot find pinecones with seeds intact on the cone scales, display photos or illustrations that clearly show the attached seeds. **Expected Results** Students should observe and draw the seed-bearing structures of gymnosperms and angiosperms. Their notes on the gymnosperm (pinecone) should indicate that seeds are attached to the outside of the cone scales with no covering. The seeds of the angiosperm (apple) are completely surrounded by the fruit.
INDEPENDENT INQUIRY **Flipchart** p.21 **B Flowers in Hiding** **OBJECTIVE** Research common examples of angiosperms. 45–60 minutes individuals	• Classify • Record Data	• research materials • local flowering plants	**Prep Tip** Identify resources for students to use in their research. Consider checking with a local florist or nursery for some of the plants students are likely to research. If possible, acquire samples of angiosperms for students to observe. **Troubleshooting** If students are unable to go outdoors, provide photos of a variety of plants both with and without flowers and cones. **Expected Results** Students should be able to identify and describe the forms of different angiosperms. Through their research, students should come to realize that almost all the plants surrounding them are angiosperms, even if the flowers of many of the plants are not readily apparent.

Additional teaching support for all activities is available in Online Resources.

Activity	Inquiry and Design Process Skills Focus	Materials	Prep Tips, Troubleshooting, and Expected Results
S.T.E.M. Engineering and Technology Flipchart p.22 **Mimicking an Adaptation** **OBJECTIVES** • Design a product that is based on a plant or animal adaptation. • Understand plant and animal adaptations. 15–25 minutes individuals	DESIGN PROCESS STEPS: 1 Find a Problem, 2 Plan and Build, 3 Test and Improve, 4 Redesign, 5 Communicate **1 Find a Problem** 2 Plan and Build 3 Test and Improve **4 Redesign** **5 Communicate**	• materials to be chosen by students	**Prep Tip** Provide students with background information about the use of biomimicry in product design. For example, engineers have been inspired by nature to design insect-like robots, competitive swimwear that simulates shark skin, and synthetic spider silk. Identify resources for students to use to identify and understand unusual plant and animal adaptations. **Expected Results** Students should be able to propose a design for a new product based on research of plant and animal adaptations.
Lesson 4 INQUIRY GUIDED INQUIRY Flipchart p.23 Student Edition pp. 207–208 **What Factors Affect Germination Rate?** **OBJECTIVES** • Observe and record how light and amount of water affect germination rate. • Infer what other factors may affect germination rate. 40–60 minutes small groups	• Plan and Conduct a Simple Investigation • Identify and Control Variables • Draw Conclusions	• 5 plastic cups • potting soil • plastic gloves • graduated cylinder • shoe box • bean seeds • water • ruler	**Prep Tip** Two weeks prior to the activity, sprout some bean seeds in a plastic bag. Allow the sprouts to die. You will use these sprouts in the Attention Grabber. Find two areas, one sunny, where cups can sit undisturbed for the duration of the activity. **Caution!** Water can make surfaces slippery. Have students notify you immediately of any spills. Students should wash their hands after this activity. **Troubleshooting** Place 4 cm of soil in the cups, and cover seeds with 2–3 cm of soil. Students should label cups A–E and place the same number of seeds in each cup. Review how to read a graduated cylinder. **Expected Results** All of the watered seeds are likely to germinate. However, only the seeds given the correct amount of water and light will grow well. Covered seeds will have spindly, unhealthy growth.

Go Digital! Virtual Lab

What Factors Affect Germination Rate?

Key Inquiry Skills: Control Variables, Design and Conduct a Simple Investigation, Predict

Students use a model of germinating seeds to experiment and determine the factors that affect the germination rate of seeds.

Planning for Inquiry (continued)

Activity	Inquiry and Design Process Skills Focus	Materials	Prep Tips, Troubleshooting, and Expected Results
Lesson 5 DIRECTED INQUIRY Flipchart p.24 **A How Can You Model a Backbone?** **OBJECTIVE** Students will model the structure and movement of a backbone. 15–20 minutes individuals	• Observe • Formulate or Use Models	• thick string (20 cm long) • 5 or more pieces uncooked wagon-wheel pasta per student • 5 or more gummy rings per student • paper clips	**Prep Tip** You will need a minimum of five pieces of both pasta and gummy rings per model, although students may use more. To save time, cut 20 cm lengths of string prior to class and tie a paper clip to one end of each string. Or tie a large knot in the end of the string so that the pasta does not slip off. Another alternative is to tie the string around a pencil or some other object. **Caution!** Be aware of possible allergies. Warn students not eat any foods used in the activity. Direct them to wash their hands following the activity. **Troubleshooting** It can be difficult to string pasta or other objects if the ends of the string are frayed or soft. Avoid this problem by tightly wrapping the end of the string with tape to make the string stiff like the end of a shoelace. **Expected Results** Students should make a workable model of a backbone that shows how the backbone is made up of stiff materials (pasta wheels) separated by softer materials (gummy pieces) that support and protect the spinal cord, yet allow for flexibility.
INDEPENDENT INQUIRY Flipchart p.24 **B How Do They Change?** **OBJECTIVE** Plan and conduct online research to learn which animals undergo incomplete metamorphosis and which undergo complete metamorphosis 45–60 minutes for initial research; additional time may be needed for students to complete their drawings individuals	• Compare • Gather Data • Record Data	• classroom resources • media resources	**Prep Tip** Identify possible sources for students to use for their research. To save time, have students complete their life cycle drawings outside of class. **Troubleshooting** Provide time for students to research insects from various sources. Encourage students to illustrate each insect's metamorphosis with as much detail as possible. Suggest students include labeling and notations so that another student might be able to use their work as a reference guide. **Expected Results** Students should identify insects that undergo each form of metamorphosis. Examples of insects that undergo incomplete metamorphosis are dragonflies, grasshoppers, cockroaches, cicadas, and mayflies. Insects that undergo complete metamorphosis include beetles, butterflies, ladybugs, bees, wasps, ants, and flies.

Activity	Inquiry and Design Process Skills Focus	Materials	Prep Tips, Troubleshooting, and Expected Results
Lesson 6 DIRECTED INQUIRY Flipchart p.25 **A Gobbling Up Your Greens** **OBJECTIVE** Follow directions for an investigation to observe how plant growth is affected when plants are trimmed. 20–40 minutes small groups	• Observe • Compare • Plan and Conduct a Simple Investigation • Draw Conclusions	• 6 small plant pots • potting soil • grass seeds • pinto beans • marigold seeds • scissors	**Prep Tip** Cover work surfaces with newspaper or paper towels. Identify an area where plants can be left undisturbed. If time is short, you may want to have students start this activity with plants that are already growing. If you do start with seeds, soak the seeds overnight in water or a liquid seed starter so that they will germinate more quickly. **Caution!** Warn students to take care using sharp instruments in the classroom. Have students notify you immediately of any spills. Water can make surfaces slippery, resulting in falls. Direct students to wash their hands after this activity. **Troubleshooting** Make sure that students do not trim the plants too aggressively. Plants should not be trimmed to less than half their original height. **Expected Results** Students will most likely find that the grass plant is best adapted to grazing. Most grasses will grow faster and become thicker after they have been trimmed, as long as they are not trimmed too close to the roots.
INDEPENDENT INQUIRY Flipchart p.25 **B Animal Adaptations** **OBJECTIVE** Plan and conduct an investigation to observe an animal and make note of its adaptations 30–60 minutes individuals	• Observe • Gather and Record Data • Plan and Conduct a Simple Investigation	• binoculars (optional)	**Prep Tip** Before students begin, have the class brainstorm a list of local animals that would be safe and easy to observe. Remind students of wildlife safety rules: Under no circumstances should they attempt to handle a wild animal. They should observe from a safe distance, staying as far away from the animal as possible so that their presence does not affect the animal's behavior. Students may wish to use binoculars for making their observations. **Caution!** Students should carry out their observations with an adult. **Troubleshooting** Students may also record their observations by using pictures or drawings. **Expected Results** Students should document their observations and provide an interpretation of any adaptations they notice.

Differentiated Instruction

Customize and Extend

You can extend and customize science instruction for your students using the following resources.

Leveled Readers

The **Science Leveled Reader Library** can be used to reinforce, enrich, and extend unit concepts. Use the following Leveled Readers with Unit 4.

BELOW-LEVEL

Classifying Living Things

Plant Growth and Reproduction

ON-LEVEL/ENRICHMENT

Classification

Plants and How They Grow

ABOVE-LEVEL/CHALLENGE

Discovery at Blue Moon Bay

The Life of an Oak Tree

An eight-page **Leveled Reader Teacher Guide** accompanies each reader. Each guide provides instructional strategies and three reproducible student worksheets for vocabulary, comprehension, and oral reading fluency.

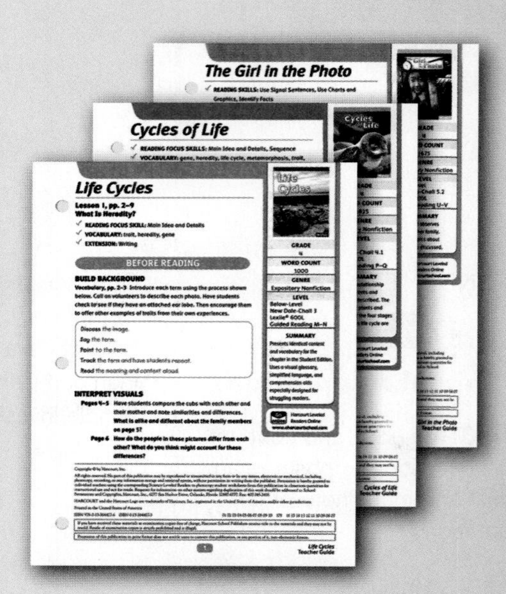

RTI Response to Intervention

Response to Intervention is a process for identifying and supporting students who are not making expected progress toward essential learning goals.

The following *ScienceFusion* components have the flexibility to be used to provide Core Classroom Instruction (Tier 1), strategic intervention (Tier 2), and intensive intervention (Tier 3).

Component	Location	Strategies and Benefits
Student Edition, Active Reading prompts Sum It Up, Brain Check	Active Reading throughout each lesson, Sum It Up and Brain Check at the end of each lesson	Student responses can be used as screening tools to assess whether intervention is needed.
Assessment Guide, Lesson Quizzes	AG 38–AG 43	Student responses can be used as screening tools to assess whether intervention is needed.
Inquiry Flipcharts	Inquiry Flipchart pp. 19, 21, 24, 25	Directed Inquiry for students who learn best through directed or teacher-led hands-on activities.
Teacher Edition, Unit Review Answer Strategies	TE pp. 241–244	Suggestions for intervention, guidance, and remediation for each review question.
Leveled Readers	TE p. 173J	Content support for students not meeting the learning needs during core classroom instruction.
Leveled Readers, Teacher Guides and Vocabulary, Comprehension and Fluency Worksheets	TE p. 173J	Direct insruction with small groups of students needing additional content at various readability levels.
Extra Support for Vocabulary and Concepts (online worksheets)	Online Resources	Support for individualized instruction with practice in essential content.
Online Student Edition with Audio	Online Resources	Provides learners with multiple-modality access to science concepts and information.
Interactive Digital Lessons and Virtual Labs	Online Resources	Provides individualized learning experiences. Lessons make content accessible through simulations, animations, videos, audio, and integrated assesment.

Differentiated Instruction

English Language Learners

Choose from these instructional strategies to meet the needs of English language learners. Suggestions are provided for adapting the activity for three proficiency levels. Point-of-use strategies also appear within unit lessons.

Unit Vocabulary

Lesson 1	Lesson 3	Lesson 5	Lesson 6
classification	nonvascular plant	vertebrate	adaptation
dichotomous key	vascular plant	invertebrate	instinct
domain	spore	life cycle	
genus	gymnosperm	complete metamorphosis	
species	angiosperm	incomplete metamorphosis	
	germinate		

Vocabulary Activity

Living Things Tic-Tac-Toe

Play variations of tic-tac-toe with the vocabulary words. Examples:

- Use pictures: students win the square if they say the word.
- Use words: have students select the correct picture.
- Use words: students must write or say a sentence that demonstrates the word's meaning.

Beginning	Intermediate	Advanced
Provide students with a 3 × 3 game board and a list of the vocabulary words. Assist students in writing words on their game boards. Note that students should fill in the squares of their boards with different words or with the same words but in different orders. Show a picture that represents a vocabulary word. Pronounce the word it represents, and have students repeat. Direct them to use a self-stick note to cover the word if it is present on their board.	Provide students with a 3 × 3 game board and a list of the vocabulary words. Have them write nine of the words in random order on their game boards. State a definition or give a description of a word. For example, *This kind of plant takes in water through its roots.* (vascular plant) Have students say the word and use a self-stick note to cover the word if it is present on their board.	Organize students into small groups. Provide each student with a 3 × 3 game board and a set of index cards on which the unit's vocabulary words have been written. Have them write nine of the vocabulary words on their boards in random order. Students can take turns drawing a card and stating a definition or giving a description of the word. After the word is identified, everyone who has the word on their board covers it with a self-stick note.

Model Concepts

Plant and Animal Adaptations

Organize students into small groups. Provide pictures of plants and animals in their natural environments. Pictures should clearly show the organisms' physical features or the animals' actions. Students will identify each organism's adaptations and discuss how the adaptations help with survival.

Beginning	Intermediate	Advanced
Have students circle the adaptations in the pictures. Provide a chart with two column heads: *Adaptation* and *How It Helps.* Have students name or draw the adaptation in the first column and use one or two words to describe in the second column how the adaptation helps the organism. For example: *lizard's long tongue/helps it catch food.* Assist students in writing one or two-word descriptions in the chart. Provide sentence frames for students to talk about the organisms: *A(n) _______ has _______. It can _______.*	Have students label the adaptations in the pictures. Then ask them to identify the plant's or animal's habitat and discuss how the adaptations help with survival. Provide sentence frames for discussion: *A(n) _______ uses its _______ to _______. A(n) _______ has a _______ that helps it _______.* Students can record their ideas in a chart in which they list the organism, its habitat, and adaptations. Ask students to share their ideas with the class.	Ask students to imagine they are an animal or plant and to write clues about their habitat and adaptations. For example: *I grow in the desert. I have sharp spines that protect me from predators.* Students should write clues for several plants and animals. Have them read their clues as other group members guess the plant or animal.

Model Inquiry Skills

Classify and Compare

Pair students or place them into small groups. Provide pictures of different plants and animals, such as those previously presented in the unit. For plants, include examples of vascular and nonvascular plants and angiosperms and gymnosperms. For animals, include different kinds of invertebrates and vertebrates. Students will classify and compare the plants and animals.

Beginning	Intermediate	Advanced
Provide labels on index cards, such as *vascular plant* or *mammal.* Ask: *Which pictures show a _______? Which animal is/has _______?* Assist students in matching the labels to the pictures. Note that labels may apply to more than one picture. Have students discuss their matches. Provide sentence frames: *These are _______. They are both _______. They both have _______. (animals, fish, fins)*	Provide labels on index cards, such as *vascular, nonvascular, vertebrate, invertebrate, alternation of generations, metamorphosis,* and so on. Have students match each label to as many pictures as they can. Encourage them to explain the groups they made. Provide sentence frames for support: *These are _______. They show _______. (nonvascular plants, alternation of generations)*	Provide labels, such as *angiosperm* and *vertebrate,* on index cards. Have students use the labels to group the pictures. Then ask students to describe how the plants and animals in each group they made are similar and different.

UNIT 4

How Living Things Grow and Reproduce

I Wonder Why

Use the images and the question to stimulate interest in the unit topic. Ask students to list the characteristics of mammals. Then have them read the text describing some of the echidna's unusual characteristics, including that it lays eggs. Have students speculate why this animal may be classified as a mammal.

Here's Why

Have students turn the page and read the response to the question. You may wish to share the following background with students.

Background

More About...

Echidnas

Echidnas are mammals native to eastern Australia and New Guinea. Sharp spines cover the backs and sides of echidnas, protecting them from predators. Echidnas have a diet of mainly termites and ants. Because of these characteristics, they are also known as *spiny anteaters.* Echidnas have long, narrow snouts and long tongues covered with sticky saliva that they use to lick up insects. Female echidnas lay one egg a year. The egg has a leathery shell, and it hatches in a pouch on the female's belly. The tiny, young echidna remains in the pouch for several weeks as it feeds on milk from its mother.

Professional Development **Science Background**

Use these keywords to access

- Professional Development from **The NSTA Learning Center**
- **SciLinks** for additional online content appropriate for students and teachers
- Teacher Science Background in the back of this Teacher Edition and in the Planning Guide

Keywords

animals
heredity
plants

UNIT 4

Here's why Scientists classify the echidna as a mammal, even though it lays eggs. Most mammals give birth to live young. When the echidna's eggs hatch, the young are tiny. They are no bigger than a lima bean!

In this unit, you will explore the Big Idea, Essential Questions, and Investigations on the Inquiry Flipchart.

Levels of Inquiry Key ■ DIRECTED ■ GUIDED ■ INDEPENDENT

Track Your Progress

Big Idea All living things have observable characteristics and pass them to their offspring.

Essential Questions

Science Notebook
Before you begin each lesson, be sure to write your thoughts about the Essential Question.

174 Unit 4

Big Idea and Essential Questions

Big Idea All living things have observable characteristics that allow them to be classified. Plants and animals pass these characteristics on to their offspring.

Post the Unit Big Idea on the board. Have students read the Essential Questions, which are also the titles of the lessons in this unit.

- Discuss how the Essential Questions can help keep them focused on the Big Idea of this unit.
- Have students read the Big Idea statement. The statement describes the main science concept they will be learning.
- Have students predict other ideas that will be taught in the lessons based on the titles, or have them give examples of pictures they expect to see.

Once they have completed all the lessons, they should have a better understanding of the Big Idea.

Essential Questions You may use the following Science Notebook strategy for working with the Essential Questions before students begin the unit or lessons in the unit.

- Strategies for Enduring Understandings, revisiting the Big Idea and Essential Questions are provided on page 241A.

Notebook Science Notebook

- Have students copy the Essential Questions into their Notebooks, leaving several writing lines between questions.
- Ask students to write responses to the Essential Questions. Urge them not to worry about whether their responses are correct; their ideas will change as they work in the unit. Assure them that they will be able to review and revise their answers at the end of the unit.
- Tips and strategies for using Science Notebooks are provided throughout this unit, in the Planning Guide, and in Online Resources.

Go Digital

For a complete digital curriculum and resources that provide full coverage of the objectives for this unit, see Online Resources for this program.

Options for Inquiry

FLIPCHART 

Students can conduct these optional investigations at any time before, during, or in response to the lesson in the Student Edition.

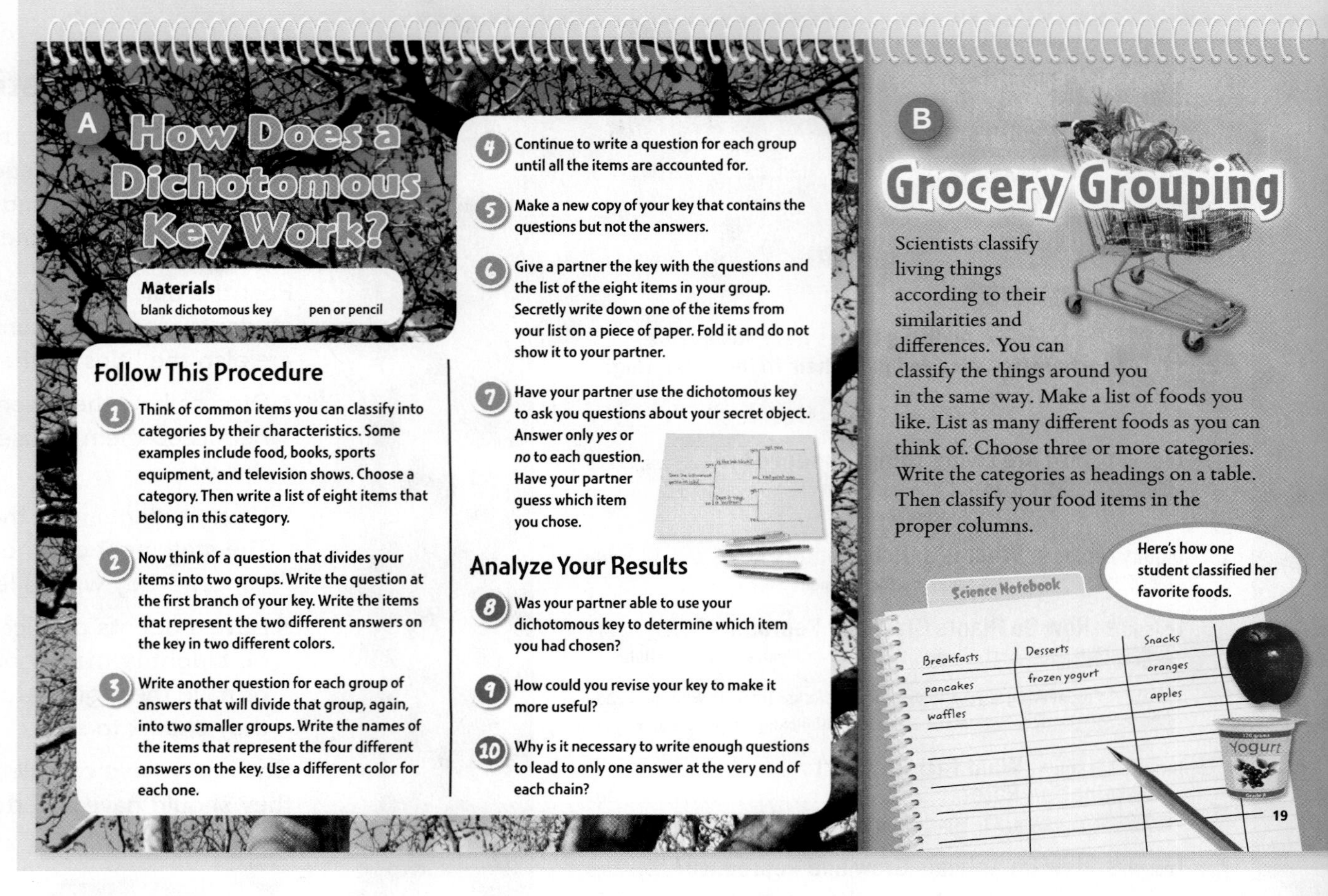

Directed Inquiry

A How Does a Dichotomous Key Work?

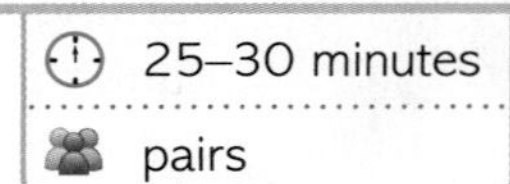
25–30 minutes
pairs

Prep and Planning Tips

Make sure that students understand that each branch must provide a clear choice that can be answered only one or two ways. For example, if the chart is categorizing foods, one of the questions could be *Is this a meat?* This format should be used in place of a question such as *What is the food made of?* or *Is the food a meat colored red, brown, or white?* Reinforce that each branching should provide a clear choice that could be used by someone who has no idea or image of the final result.

Expected Results

Students should construct dichotomous keys that can be used by another student to easily determine the identity of an object as described by its characteristics.

Independent Inquiry

B Grocery Grouping

15–20 minutes
individuals

Prep and Planning Tips

See the Planning for Inquiry page for more information. Having students keep a food journal for several days in advance of this activity may help them quickly recall the foods they often eat.

Science Notebook

Students can use the sample Science Notebook page shown as a model for categorizing the foods they identify. Before they make their table, have them first make a list of foods. Then have them determine and list the categories. After they make the table with correct heads, they can return to their list and use different colored pencils to circle the foods that fit in each category. This step will aid them in transferring the data from the lists to the table.

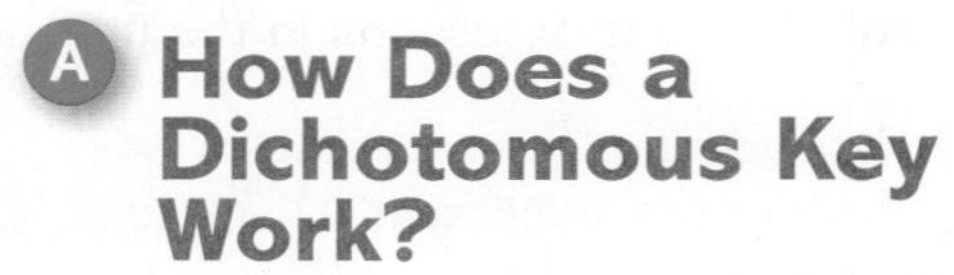

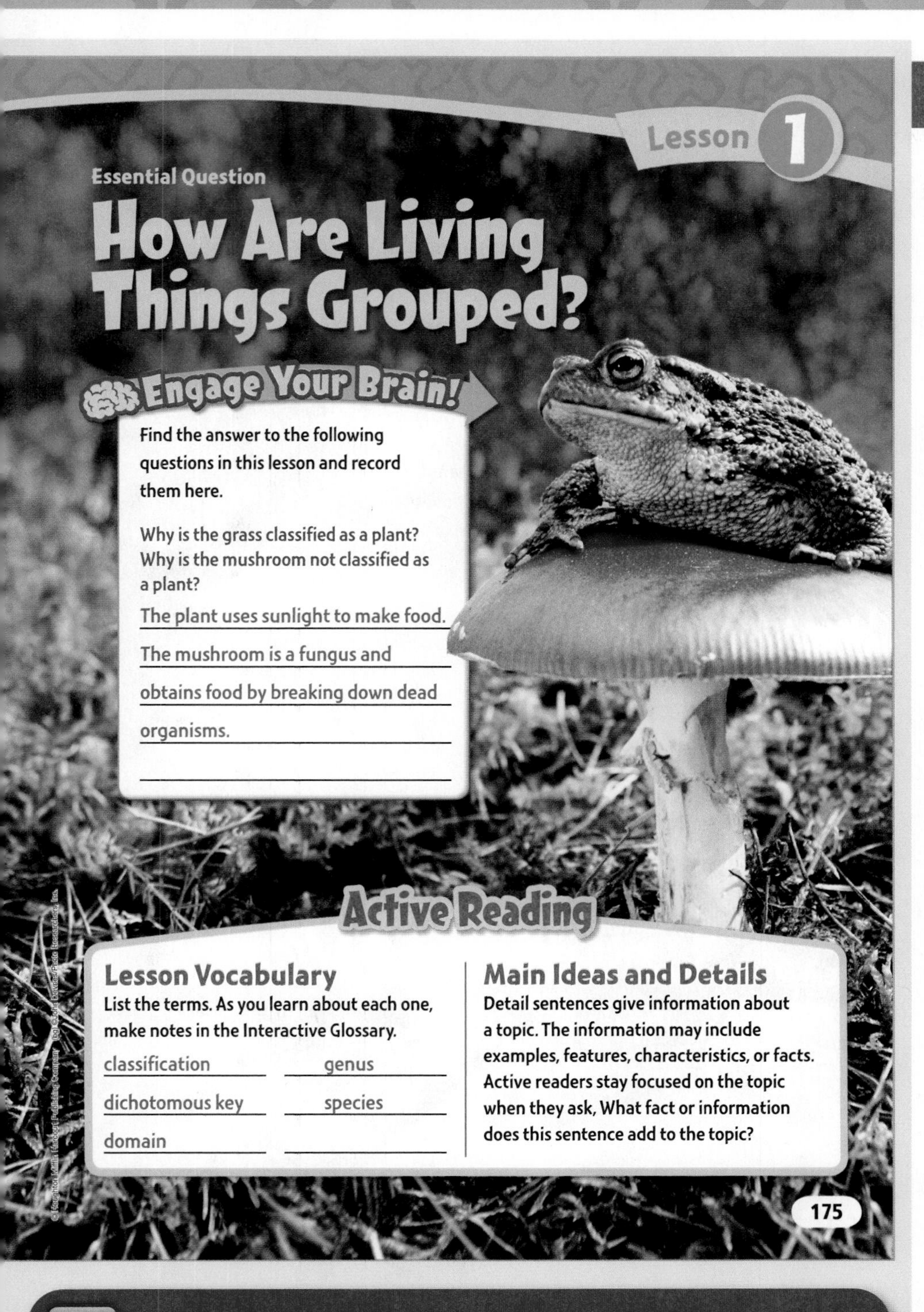
Lesson 1

Essential Question

How Are Living Things Grouped?

Engage Your Brain!

Find the answer to the following questions in this lesson and record them here.

Why is the grass classified as a plant? Why is the mushroom not classified as a plant?

The plant uses sunlight to make food. The mushroom is a fungus and obtains food by breaking down dead organisms.

Active Reading

Lesson Vocabulary

List the terms. As you learn about each one, make notes in the Interactive Glossary.

classification | genus
dichotomous key | species
domain

Main Ideas and Details

Detail sentences give information about a topic. The information may include examples, features, characteristics, or facts. Active readers stay focused on the topic when they ask, What fact or information does this sentence add to the topic?

175

Go Digital

An interactive digital lesson is available in the Online Resources. It is suitable for individuals, small groups, or may be projected or used on an interactive white board.

1 Engage/Explore

Objectives

- Identify characteristics used to classify a group of objects.
- Describe the basic characteristics of the six kingdoms of organisms.
- Describe how scientists classify living things.

Engage Your Brain!

Have students make a list of the characteristics of the plants and the mushroom shown in the photo. Focus on the color of the two types of organisms and what these differences might mean. Record students' ideas as they answer the questions *Why is the grass classified as a plant? Why is the mushroom not classified as a plant?* Remind students to record their final answers to the questions when they find them on the fourth spread of this lesson where fungi are described.

Active Reading Annotations

Remind students that active readers "make texts their own" by annotating them with notes and marks that help with comprehension. Encourage students to use pencil, not pen, to make annotations and to feel free to change their annotations as they read. The goal of annotation is to help students remember what they have read.

Vocabulary and Interactive Glossary

Remind students to find and list the yellow highlighted terms from the lesson. As they proceed through the lesson and learn about the terms, they should add notes, drawings, or sentences in the extra spaces in the Interactive Glossary.

2 Explain

Notebook Generate Ideas

Read the introductory text together, and have students brainstorm lists of characteristics of birds and insects, focusing on how they are the same and different.

Active Reading

Remind students that the main idea may be stated in the first sentence, or it may be stated elsewhere. To find a main idea, active readers ask, What is this paragraph mostly about?

Interpret Visuals

Use the idea of grocery organization to help students understand how classification is applied from very broad to specific categories. **If you are out shopping, in which kind of store would you choose to buy peanut butter?** grocery store **How are items organized in the grocery store?** in general categories—dairy, produce, frozen foods, and so on **Where would you first look for peanut butter?** with canned goods **How would you narrow the search?** Look in the aisle that contains jams, jellies, and peanut butter, then look for my specific brand.

Explain that the graphic organizer shows the broadest groups that scientists use to classify organisms. Domains are like choosing the grocery store from among many stores. Kingdoms are like the general categories in the store. Have students look for the *Domain* and *Kingdom* tags as they read the lesson.

Develop Inquiry Skills

INFER **What might happen if you asked to be sent a bird of paradise?** You might receive a bird when you wanted a plant; both organisms have the same common name.

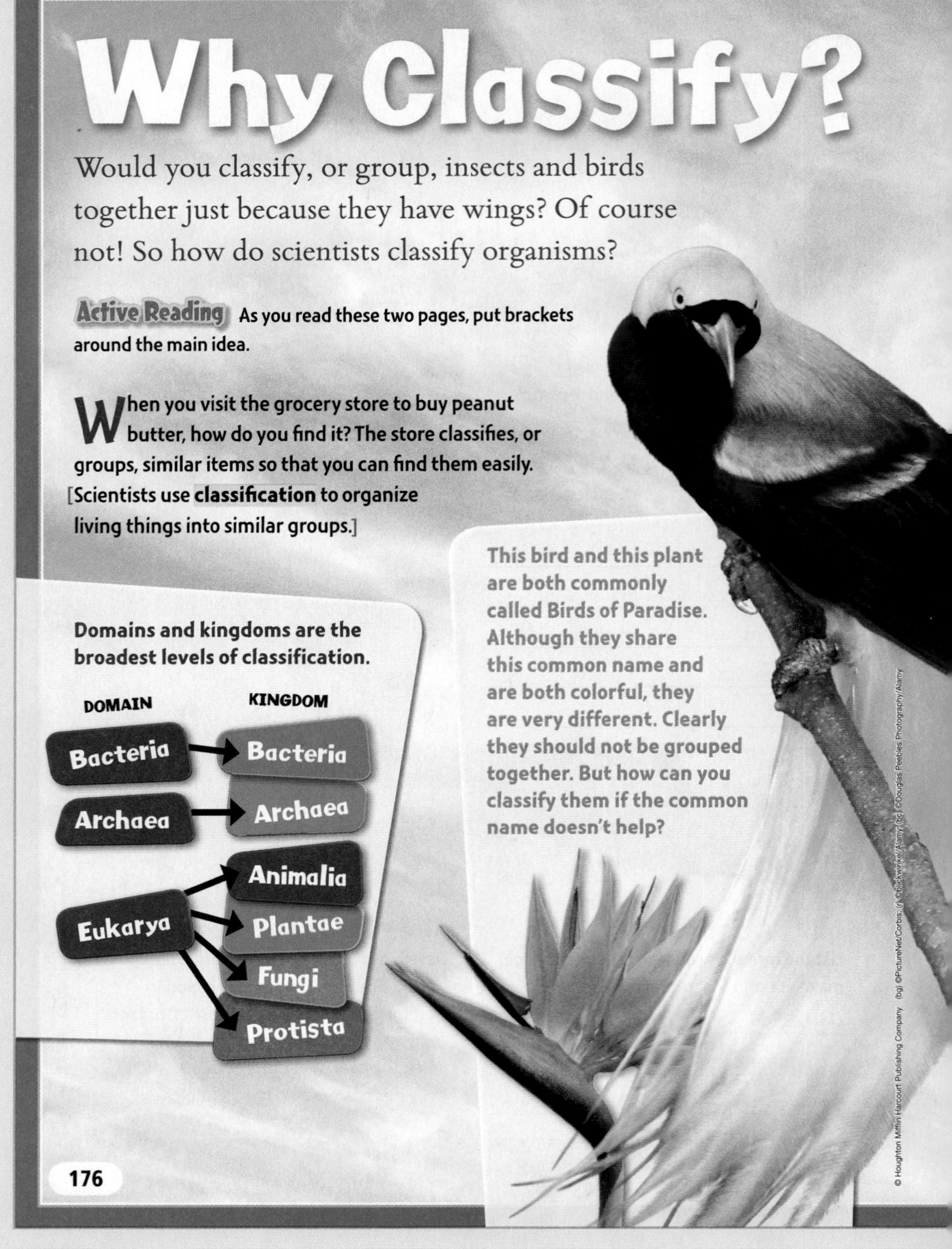

Why Classify?

Would you classify, or group, insects and birds together just because they have wings? Of course not! So how do scientists classify organisms?

Active Reading As you read these two pages, put brackets around the main idea.

When you visit the grocery store to buy peanut butter, how do you find it? The store classifies, or groups, similar items so that you can find them easily. [Scientists use **classification** to organize living things into similar groups.]

Domains and kingdoms are the broadest levels of classification.

This bird and this plant are both commonly called Birds of Paradise. Although they share this common name and are both colorful, they are very different. Clearly they should not be grouped together. But how can you classify them if the common name doesn't help?

176

Writing Connection

Narrative Have students write a short paragraph describing how they organize a general category of objects in their home, such as coats and jackets. Have them include specifics on how to determine the identity of a specific object in the group, such as their own jacket. The paragraph can be descriptive or written as a story. Suggest they make a dichotomous key to illustrate how, through process of elimination, a person unfamiliar with their home could find the specific object.

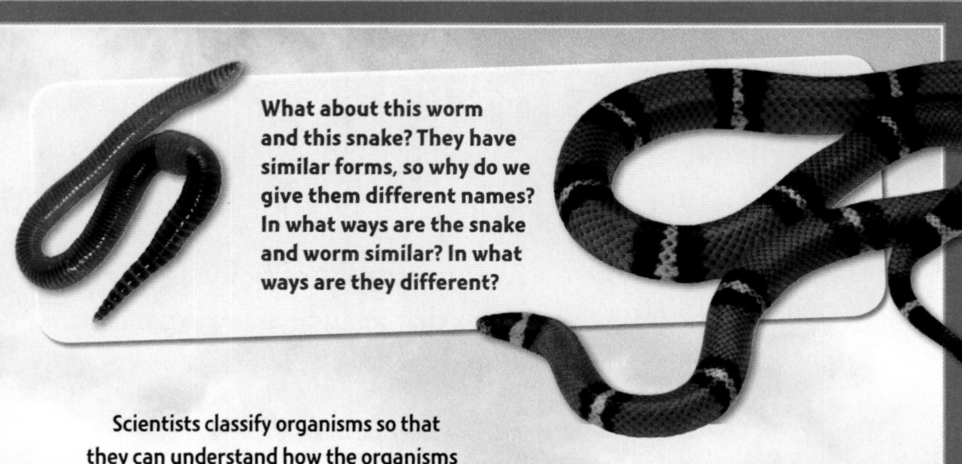

What about this worm and this snake? They have similar forms, so why do we give them different names? In what ways are the snake and worm similar? In what ways are they different?

Scientists classify organisms so that they can understand how the organisms are related. Cell type, cell structure, and genetic information are three types of information used to classify organisms. Other features used to classify organisms include shape, size, and symmetry.

Scientists use different tools to identify and record data about differences in organisms. These differences can be used to identify an organism. A **dichotomous key** [di•KOT•uh•muhs KEE] is a chart with many choices that guide you to the name of the thing you want to identify. You can make a dichotomous key to identify all kinds of things.

Using a Dichotomous Key

Fill in the dichotomous key below to help someone determine which type of shoe he or she is observing.

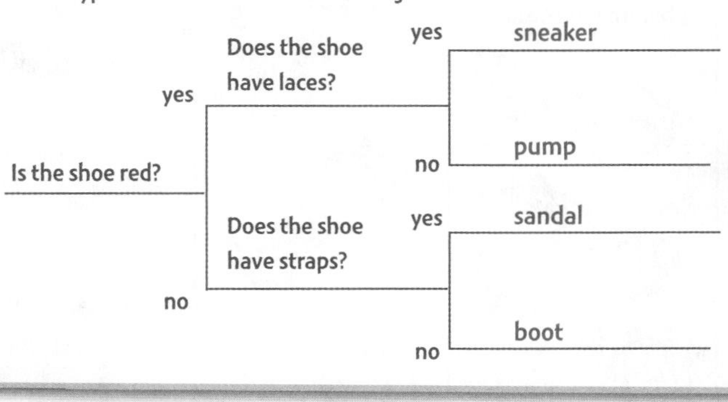

sandal
sneaker
boot
pump

177

English Language Learners

Multiple-Meaning Words The word *key* is commonly used to describe an object that unlocks doors. However, this word has several meanings. The word *key* can also be used to describe anything that helps to decipher or discover something. A dichotomous key is an example of this meaning. Other examples are map keys and keys used to break a secret code. A third meaning of *key* is as an indication of central importance, as in *key idea*.

Develop Science Vocabulary

classification Point out that *classification* is the act of organizing things into different groups, or classes, for a purpose. Have students identify several ways that classification is used in a school. Examples might include classifying students into grades (3rd, 4th, 5th), classifying content into different subjects (math, science, social studies), and classifying rooms by use (cafeteria, gym, library).

dichotomous key Explain that *dichotomous* means "divided into two parts," and a key is something that helps to decode or unlock something. Together the two words describe a tool that branches into segments in order to help people identify things.

Interpret Visuals

As an aid for students as they complete the Interactivity, draw and label each of the four types of shoes on the board: sneaker, pump, boot, sandal. Suggest that students write the name of each shoe that satisfies the question asked at each branch. For example, after the question *Is the shoe red?* students would write *pump* and *sneaker* next to *yes,* and *sandal* and *boot* next to *no.* Have students continue recording the types of shoes that answer each question as they move through the key.

Notebook Summarize Ideas

Direct students to think about the main idea they identified on this page. Ask them to find two details in the spread that support the main idea. Have students use both the main idea and two details to summarize, either orally or in writing, what they have learned about classification.

2 Explain (continued)

Notebook Generate Ideas

Direct students to the classification-table graphic at the bottom of these two pages. Ask them to describe what they think the graphic explains. Tell them to write down any questions they have about it. Then have them read through these two pages.

Active Reading

Remind students that living things may be grouped into categories according to specific characteristics. As a way to remember facts about living things in general, active readers focus on the characteristics of specific categories.

Interpret Visuals

Assist students in interpreting the visual of the classification graphic. Have them trace the classification of the camel as you read, and lead the class through the different levels.

Develop Science Concepts

Which classification level is the most general and includes the largest variety of organisms? domain **Which classification level is the most specific?** species **How many different types of organisms have the same species?** Only one. The species level is so specific that it includes only one type of organism.

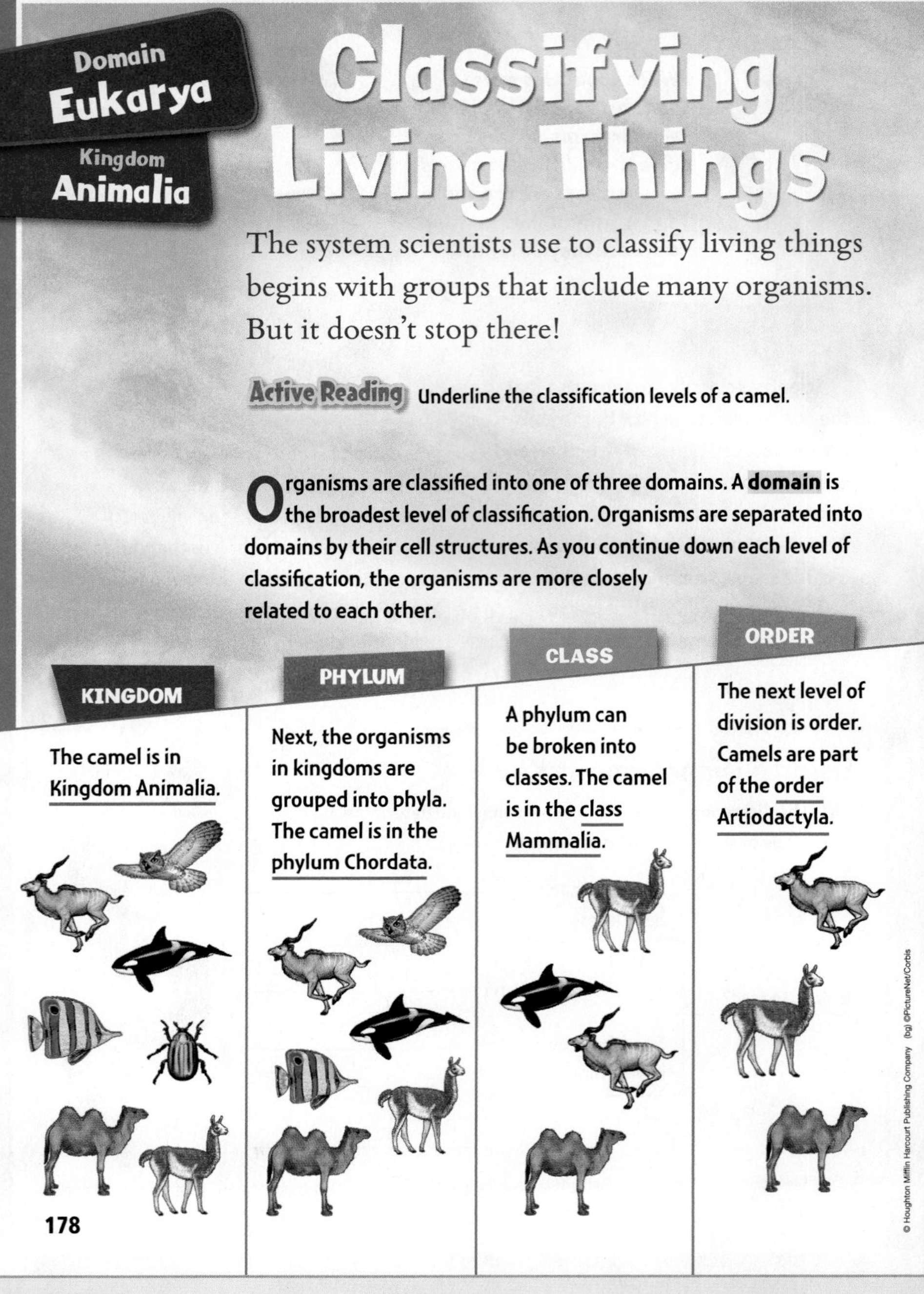

Domain Eukarya

Kingdom Animalia

Classifying Living Things

The system scientists use to classify living things begins with groups that include many organisms. But it doesn't stop there!

Active Reading Underline the classification levels of a camel.

Organisms are classified into one of three domains. A **domain** is the broadest level of classification. Organisms are separated into domains by their cell structures. As you continue down each level of classification, the organisms are more closely related to each other.

KINGDOM

The camel is in Kingdom Animalia.

PHYLUM

Next, the organisms in kingdoms are grouped into phyla. The camel is in the phylum Chordata.

CLASS

A phylum can be broken into classes. The camel is in the class Mammalia.

ORDER

The next level of division is order. Camels are part of the order Artiodactyla.

178

Differentiation — Leveled Questions

Extra Support

Why are there no plants shown on this page? This page shows the classification of animals. Plants do not belong to the kingdom Animalia.

Challenge

Are animals that belong to the same species exactly the same? Explain. Animals that belong to the same species are similar in most characteristics. However, all organisms have individual variations that make them unique.

The organisms to the right are commonly called sea stars, but scientists classify them separately. They are all in Kingdom Animalia. These marine animals have bony skeletons, but they do not have a backbone. They all belong to the Echinoderm phylum. The true sea star at top belongs to the class Asteroidea. The brittle star and basket star are similar to the true sea star, but they differ from it in important ways. They are classified into the class Ophiuroidea.

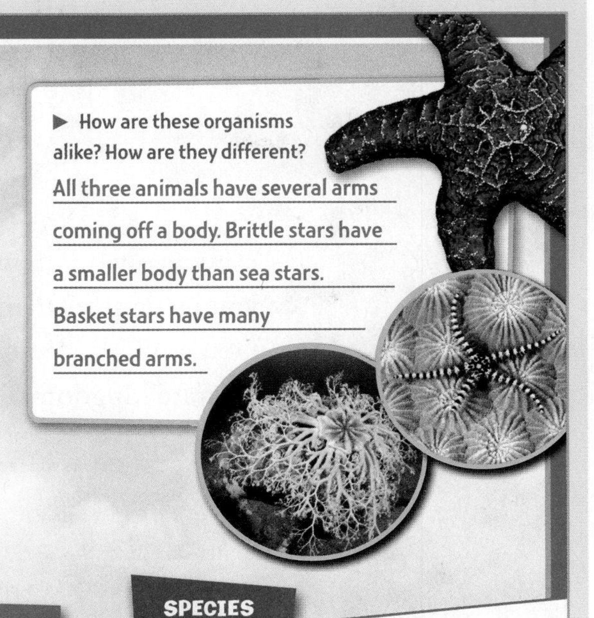

► How are these organisms alike? How are they different?

All three animals have several arms coming off a body. Brittle stars have a smaller body than sea stars. Basket stars have many branched arms.

FAMILY

Orders can be further divided into families. Camels belong to the family Camelidae.

GENUS

A **genus** is a subdivision of a family. This camel belongs to the genus *Camelus.*

SPECIES

Finally, organisms are classified by species. **Species** are unique organisms. This camel belongs to the species *dromedarius.*

The two-part scientific name for the camel is *Camelus dromedarius.* As you can see, the scientific name is made of the genus and species names. The first letter of the genus name is always capitalized, but the species name is not. This two-part name is based on a system developed by the scientist Carolus Linnaeus in the 1700s.

179

English Language Learners

Latin Names Point out that the genus and species names given to all organisms are typically said to be Latin in origin. However, not all names given are based on real Latin words. Many are based on Greek words or even on the names of people. However, the names are all "Latinized" for conformity. Suggest that students make a display of photos of their favorite animals labeled with the animals' scientific names. Remind them to use proper capitalization.

Develop Science Vocabulary

domain Direct students to review the graphic organizer on the previous spread. Point out that the three domains are Bacteria, Archaea, and Eukarya. Stress to students that all organisms on Earth belong to one of these three domains.

genus Review with students that an organism's scientific name is the genus and species. Share that the scientific name for humans is *Homo sapiens.* Write this scientific name on the board.

species Point out that the species is the last level of classification that makes one organism different from another. Ask the students to identify which parts of the scientific name *Homo sapiens* is the genus and which is the species.

Interpret Visuals

Before they complete the Interactivity, have students examine the photos and read the descriptions of the sea stars. **What levels of organization do these organisms share?** Domain Eukarya, Kingdom Animalia, Phylum Echinoderm (or Echinodermata) **At what point do their classifications diverge?** at class **Would these organisms have the same species name? Explain.** No; these are different organisms. Even if they were in the same genus, they would have different species names.

Notebook Summarize Ideas

Ask students to summarize the levels by which organisms are classified. Ask them to list the order of the levels of classification, and to use the terms *general* and *specific* in their summaries. Sample answer: Organisms are classified into categories that begin very general and then become more specific. The order, from general to specific, is domain, kingdom, phylum, class, order, family, genus, species.

2 Explain (continued)

Notebook Generate Ideas

Have the class preview these two pages by reading the title and looking at the images and captions. Point out the classification tags that indicate that these pages are about organisms in Kingdom Animalia and Kingdom Plantae, which are both members of Domain Eukarya. Have students make lists of common characteristics of organisms in these two kingdoms. Record their ideas on the board.

Active Reading

Remind students that some text segments state information essential to understanding a topic. Active readers identify and focus on these text segments as a way to deepen their understanding of the topic.

Interpret Visuals

After students read the text about plants, have them look at the plant photos and read the captions. **Which characteristics are used to classify plants?** presence of vascular tissue; whether they produce seeds; if they produce seeds, whether they produce them in fruits or cones

Develop Inquiry Skills

COMPARE **How are plants that have vascular tissues and those that do not have vascular tissues the same?** All plants are multicellular and use light from the sun to make food. **How are they different?** Plants with vascular tissue have long tubes that transport materials throughout the plant. Plants without this tissue must absorb materials like a sponge.

Domain Eukarya

Kingdom Plantae

Plants and Animals

How many different plants and animals can you recognize? Plants and animals are both in Domain Eukarya, but they are grouped into separate kingdoms.

Active Reading As you read these two pages, underline the parts of the text that explain how plants and animals are classified.

There are more than 320,000 species of plants. Plants are made up of many cells and use sunlight to make food. Some plants are very large, while other plants may be tiny. Scientists classify plants according to the structures they have and how they use those structures to live.

Some plants have vascular tissue. Vascular tissue consists of long, narrow tubes that transport materials throughout the plant. Other plants just absorb the materials they need, like a sponge absorbs water.

Plants are also classified by the way they reproduce. Some plants produce seeds in fruits, while others produce seeds in cones. Some plants don't produce seeds at all! All of these characteristics are used to classify plants.

This conifer is a vascular plant. It produces seeds on cones, can grow tall, and lives for many years.

Mosses do not have vascular tissue. They grow low to the ground and absorb nutrients in a sponge-like manner.

Some plants use flowers to reproduce. Flowering plants make up the largest number of species in Kingdom Plantae.

180

Differentiation — Leveled Questions

Extra Support

Which type of organism, plants or animals, is made up of many cells? Both plants and animals are made up of many cells.

Challenge

In what different ways do plants produce seeds? Some plants produce seeds in fruits, while others produce seeds in cones. Some plants do not produce any seeds.

Most animals are made of multiple cells and cannot make their own food. Animals are often divided into two main groups. Animals that have backbones are called vertebrates. Vertebrates include fish, birds, reptiles, amphibians, and mammals. Animals without backbones are invertebrates. Invertebrates include insects, worms, jellyfish, and sponges.

Vertebrates make up only about 5% of the animal population on Earth. Approximately 95% of Earth's animals are invertebrates!

Within these two main groups, animals are further classified according to their body structures, how they take in oxygen and digest food, and many other factors. What do you think some of these other factors could be?

Do the Math!

Use Fractions

Mammals account for about $\frac{1}{10}$ of all vertebrates. Birds account for about $\frac{1}{6}$ of all vertebrates. Together, what fraction of vertebrates is made up of mammals and birds?

$\frac{3}{30} + \frac{5}{30} = \frac{8}{30} = \frac{4}{15}$

181

English Language Learners

Prefixes Explain that the word *invertebrate* means "not a vertebrate." The word is made by adding the prefix *in–* to the word ***vertebrate***. Reinforce how adding *in–* to the beginning of words causes them to take on the opposite meaning. Examples: *in*considerate, *in*correct

Have students make lists of words beginning with *in–*, record a definition for each term, and then use a dictionary to confirm meanings.

Develop Inquiry Skills

CLASSIFY **What structure helps scientists divide animals into two main groups?** the presence or absence of a backbone **Which animals shown are vertebrates?** frog, chicken, lion

OBSERVE **You have discovered a new organism. You know that it is either a plant or an animal. What characteristic could help you classify the organism?** Sample answer: If the organism uses light to make food, it is most likely a plant. If the organism consumes plants or other organisms for food, it is an animal.

Develop Science Concepts

Suggest students look at the lists they made in Generate Ideas as they brainstorm factors by which animals are classified. Some factors include how they reproduce, whether they maintain a constant body temperature, and type of body covering.

Do the Math!

Use Fractions Remind students that to add fractions, the denominator must be the same. Convert $\frac{1}{10}$ to $\frac{3}{30}$ and $\frac{1}{6}$ to $\frac{5}{30}$ Now add the numerators. The total is $\frac{8}{30}$. Reduce this fraction by dividing numerator and denominator by two, resulting in a final answer of $\frac{4}{15}$.

Notebook Summarize Ideas

Ask students to list, either orally or in writing, the different ways that plants and animals are classified. *plants: vascular/nonvascular, seeds/no seeds, flowers/cones; animals: vertebrate/invertebrates; body structures; digestion*

2 Explain (continued)

Notebook Generate Ideas

Have the class preview these two pages by reading the title and looking at the images and captions. Point out the classification tags at the top of the pages. **How are the classifications of fungi and protists the same?** They are both classified under Domain Eukarya. **How are they different?** They are classified into different kingdoms: Kingdom Fungi and Kingdom Protista.

Active Reading

Remind students that authors compare and contrast events, objects, and ideas when pointing out ways they are alike and different. Active readers remember similarities and differences because they focus on the events, objects, and ideas being compared.

Develop Science Concepts

Encourage students to find examples of each of the differences they box as they complete the Active Reading. For fungi, they may box the word *size*. They could point out that yeasts are microscopic, while mushrooms are large enough to pick out of the ground. Share that the largest living organism on Earth is thought to be a specimen of the fungus *Armillaria ostoyae* found in the Malheur National Forest in the Blue Mountains of eastern Oregon. The fungus is estimated to cover over 2,200 acres (890 hectares) and to be at least 2,400 years old.

Develop Inquiry Skills

CLASSIFY **A mushroom grows out of the ground like a plant. Why is it not classified as a plant?** A mushroom does not use light to make food as a plant does. **How does a mushroom get food?** It feeds on dead or decaying materials.

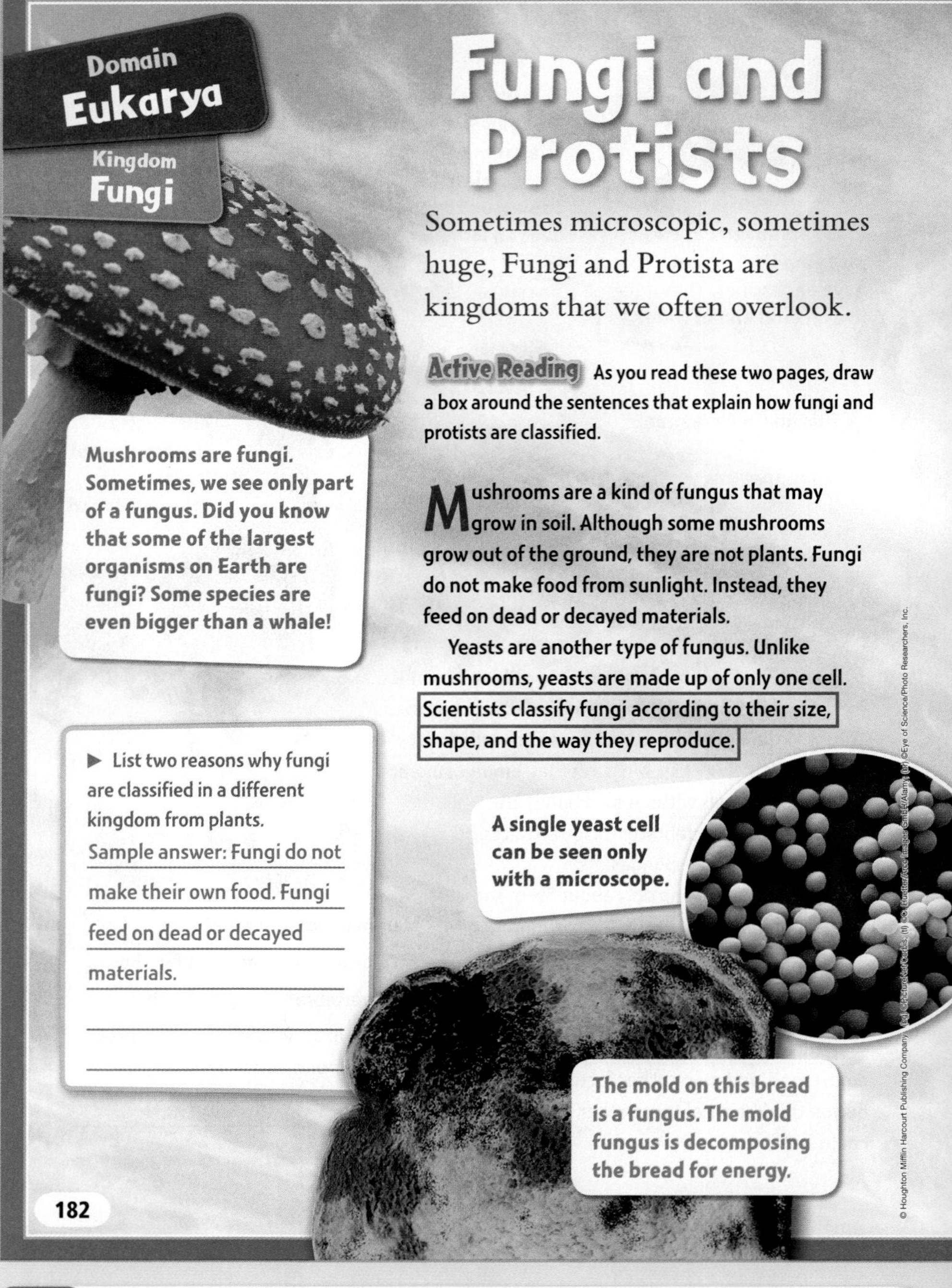
Domain Eukarya

Kingdom Fungi

Fungi and Protists

Sometimes microscopic, sometimes huge, Fungi and Protista are kingdoms that we often overlook.

Active Reading As you read these two pages, draw a box around the sentences that explain how fungi and protists are classified.

Mushrooms are a kind of fungus that may grow in soil. Although some mushrooms grow out of the ground, they are not plants. Fungi do not make food from sunlight. Instead, they feed on dead or decayed materials.

Yeasts are another type of fungus. Unlike mushrooms, yeasts are made up of only one cell. Scientists classify fungi according to their size, shape, and the way they reproduce.

Mushrooms are fungi. Sometimes, we see only part of a fungus. Did you know that some of the largest organisms on Earth are fungi? Some species are even bigger than a whale!

▶ List two reasons why fungi are classified in a different kingdom from plants.

Sample answer: Fungi do not make their own food. Fungi feed on dead or decayed materials.

A single yeast cell can be seen only with a microscope.

The mold on this bread is a fungus. The mold fungus is decomposing the bread for energy.

182

Math Connection

Solve a Problem Yeasts reproduce by budding. During budding, a yeast cell splits into two cells. Then the two cells split, making four cells.

Ask students to determine how many yeast cells would result from five buddings if you started with only one cell. Students should be able to calculate that if yeast cells double in number with every budding, there will be 32 cells after the yeast splits five times.

$2 \times 2 \times 2 \times 2 \times 2 = 32$

Protists

Kingdom Protista is very diverse.
How would you classify these protists?

The single-cell amoeba can form a structure that allows it to move or reach out to capture food.

This brown algae is large and looks similar to a plant. It lives in water and performs photosynthesis.

Euglena is a single-celled protist. Like plants, it has structures that allow it to make food from sunlight.

A paramecium moves using hair-like structures on the outside of its one-celled body. Movement allows it to sense and capture prey.

Kingdom Protista is probably the most diverse kingdom within Domain Eukarya. Protists may look or act like plants, fungi, or even animals! Most protists are made up of only one microscopic cell, but some kinds of protists live in large colonies that look like a single organism.

Protists have developed various ways to move. Some form structures they use to drag themselves across surfaces. Other protists have hair-like structures they use to move around in water. Many protists don't move at all.

Within Kingdom Protista, scientists have traditionally classified organisms according to whether they are most like plants, animals, or fungi. Plant-like protists use sunlight to make food. They are classified according to size and color. Animal-like protists are able to move and capture prey. Fungus-like protists grow and feed like fungi.

183

English Language Learners

Irregular Plurals The words *fungus* and *fungi* are confusing for students who are learning English. Typically, plurals are formed by adding *s* or *es* to the end of the word. However, in the case of *fungi*, the singular *fungus* is transformed by changing *us* to *i* to form the plural. Other examples of words that form plurals in this way include octopus/octopi, cactus/cacti, and alumnus/alumni. Have students practice pronouncing both forms of these words.

Misconception Alert

Some students may think that protists are types of bacteria, or that they are very similar to bacteria. Point out that although many protists are single-celled like bacteria, protists and bacteria are classified into different domains. This means that protists are as different from bacteria as plants and animals are different from bacteria.

Develop Science Concepts

What are the three types of protists? plant-like, animal-like, and fungi-like protists **When is an organism classified as a protist?** An organism classified within Domain Eukarya and that cannot be classified into another kingdom is classified as a protist.

Interpret Visuals

Have volunteers choose one of the protists shown on this page. Ask the volunteers to identify which type of protist they have chosen and to describe the characteristic that makes it animal-like, plant-like, or fungi-like. Sample answer: The paramecium is an animal-like protist. It is able to move and capture prey like an animal.

Summarize Ideas

Have students think of one sentence that summarizes the characteristics of fungi, and another that summarizes the characteristics of protists. Have them share their summary sentences, either orally or in writing.

2 Explain (continued)

Notebook Generate Ideas

Have the class preview these two pages by reading the title and looking at the images and captions. Point out the classification tags at the top of the pages. **How does classification of bacteria compare to that of plants, animals, fungi, and protists?** Bacteria are in their own domain. Plants, fungi, animals, and protists are all classified as different kingdoms in Domain Eukarya. Ask them to think about how different bacteria and archaea are from each other. Lead students to understand that plants are more similar to protists than to bacteria, or that animals are more similar to fungi than to archaea. You may wish to provide a line of questioning that stimulates them to think about how different bacteria and archaea are from each other and from other organisms.

Active Reading

Remind students that signal words show connections among ideas. Words and phrases that signal contrast include *unlike, different from, but,* and *on the other hand.* Active readers remember what they read because they are alert to signal words.

Misconception Alert

Students may be confused as to why bacteria and archaea are classified differently from each other and from other organisms. Explain that although bacteria and archaea appear similar to us, they have very basic differences that cause them to be classified differently. Most of these differences are chemical in nature.

Domain **Bacteria**

Kingdom **Bacteria**

Bacteria and Archaea

Did you know that bacteria are some of the simplest living organisms? While some types of bacteria are harmful, other types are quite helpful!

Active Reading As you read these two pages, draw boxes around words that signal contrasts.

There are more bacteria on Earth than any other living thing. Bacteria are found almost everywhere. They are microscopic and cover the surfaces of everything you see. They can live on humans and other organisms—and even inside them, too!

Bacteria can cause disease and pollute lakes and streams, but they can also be helpful. Bacteria are used to make foods such as yogurt and cheese. We even have bacteria in our bodies that help us digest food! Bacteria are classified according to their shape, size, how they get food, and whether or not they use oxygen.

Some of the foods that you may eat are made using bacteria.

The cyanobacteria in this stream are reproducing quickly, causing a bloom. In a bloom, all of the oxygen in the water may be used up, causing other organisms to die.

184

Math Connection

Solve a Problem Bacteria cells reproduce by splitting into two cells. Each of the resulting cells then splits. This results in a doubling of the population of bacteria each time they split. Thus, one bacterium can reproduce to make millions of bacteria cells in a short time. Use this problem to illustrate this concept: Suppose you clean your desktop, leaving only one bacterium cell. If this cell can split once every minute, how many cells will there be in ten minutes? ($2 \times 2 \times 2 \times 2 \times 2 \times 2 \times 2 \times 2 \times 2 \times 2 = 2{,}048$)

Archaea are single-celled organisms similar to bacteria. However, the structures and genetic material of Archaea and bacteria are different, so they are classified in separate domains.

Archaea live in extreme environments and get energy from unusual resources. Some archaea are found in springs where temperatures are so high that nothing else can survive there. Some archaea get energy from ammonia or sulfur gas. Most archaea are classified according to their chemical structure or genetic material.

Domain
Archaea

Kingdom
Archaea

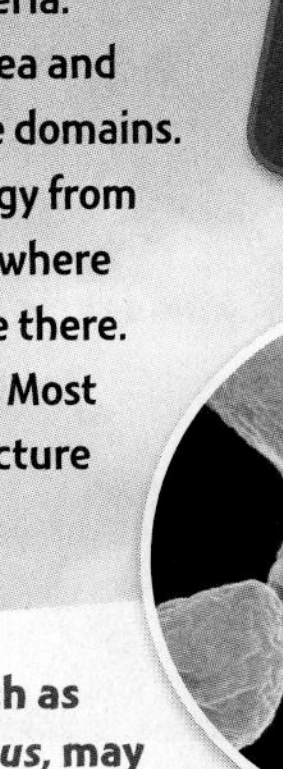

Archaea, such as this *Sulfolobus*, may look like bacteria, but these single-celled organisms live in extreme environments—for example, in this hot spring in Yellowstone National Park.

▶ Use the information in this lesson to fill out the table below.

Kingdom	Description of Kingdom	Example
Animalia	made up of many cells; do not make their own food	**Canary**
Plantae	made up of many cells; use sunlight to make food	**Pine tree**
Fungi	feeds on dead or decaying matter	**Bread mold**
Protista	classified as whether they look like plants, animals, or fungi	Possible answer: Paramecium
Bacteria	single cell; can be useful	Possible answer: Cyanobacteria
Archaea	single cell: lives in extreme environments	Possible answer: *Sulfolobus*

185

Writing Connection

Daily Journal Have students keep a journal in which they record each instance in which they are interacting, or seeking to avoid interacting, with bacteria. For example, students could keep track of the number of times they eat foods such as yogurt, wash their hands to remove dirt and germs, ensure safe food preparation, encounter smells while emptying the kitchen garbage can or cleaning out old foods from the refrigerator, and so on. Have students share their entries with the class.

Develop Inquiry Skills

EXPERIMENT Ask students to consider how they could determine whether bacteria are present on a surface. Obtain several sterile petri dishes with the nutrient agar. Have students use cotton swabs to rub surfaces in the classroom and then swab the surface of the agar. They should use a separate swab and dish for each surface. Direct them to seal the dishes with tape and label each dish with the surface tested. Ask students to record their predictions of what will happen in their Science Notebooks. Keep the petri dishes in a dark, warm place for several days and then observe. Have students compare the results with their predictions. Students should note which dishes grow more bacteria, and record the results in their Science Notebooks.

Develop Science Concepts

Are all bacteria harmful? Explain. No; bacteria are used to make foods such as yogurt and cheese, and they help us digest our food.
How are the cyanobacteria in the stream and the archaea in the hot spring the same and different? They both are in water environments. The bacteria, which belong to Domain Bacteria, live in normal temperature water. The archaea, which belong to Domain Archaea, live in extreme temperatures.

Notebook Summarize Ideas

Use the Interactivity table on this page as an opportunity for students to summarize the lesson. Explain that they must fill in the missing kingdoms, provide a general description of the organisms in each kingdom, and complete the *Example* column. Suggest that students compile their descriptions and examples into a class list that summarizes the characteristics of all the kingdoms.

3 Extend/Evaluate

Sum It Up!

- Suggest that students review the Interactivity on the previous page before they complete Sum It Up! This Interactivity provides a good summary of the kingdoms discussed in the lesson.
- Post a list of the six kingdoms that students must identify on this page for use as a reference.
- Encourage students to jot down notes that describe the organism shown in each photo. They can compare the notes to the descriptions of the kingdoms throughout the lesson to help them determine which kingdom is a good match.
- Have students use the Answer Key to check their answers when they are finished. Tell students to correct any wrong answers so they can use this page to study for tests.
- Encourage students to ask for help with any concepts about which they are still unclear.

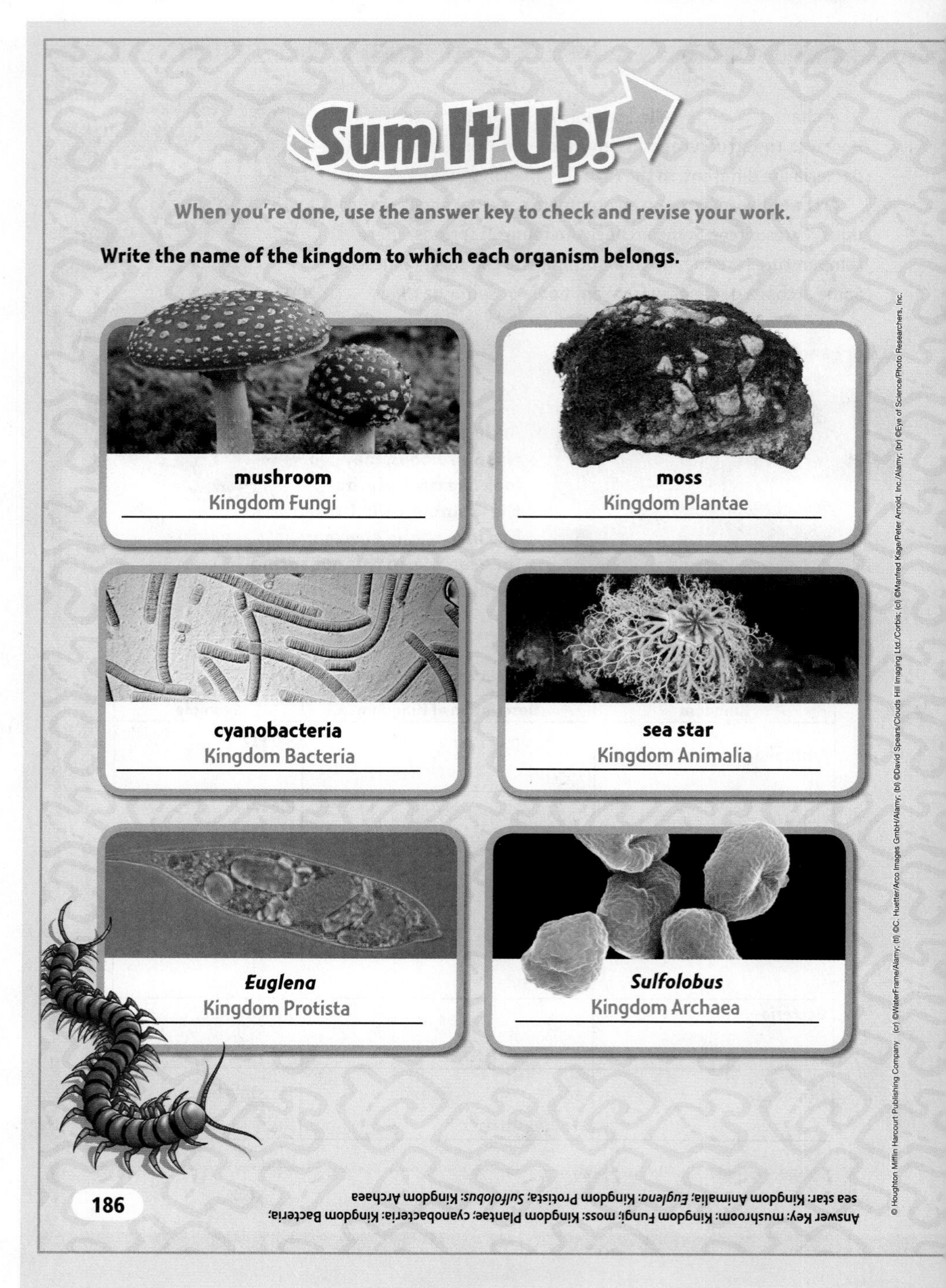

Sum It Up!

When you're done, use the answer key to check and revise your work.

Write the name of the kingdom to which each organism belongs.

mushroom
Kingdom Fungi

moss
Kingdom Plantae

cyanobacteria
Kingdom Bacteria

sea star
Kingdom Animalia

Euglena
Kingdom Protista

Sulfolobus
Kingdom Archaea

186

Answer Key: mushroom: Kingdom Fungi; moss: Kingdom Plantae; cyanobacteria: Kingdom Bacteria; sea star: Kingdom Animalia; *Euglena*: Kingdom Protista; *Sulfolobus*: Kingdom Archaea

Lesson 1

Name ______________________

Word Play

1. Use the clues to help you unscramble the words below.

1. nomaids — domains — The three broadest groups used for classification
2. gunif — fungi — The kingdom that includes yeasts and mushrooms
3. iclsifastinoca — classification — The organization of living things into categories
4. espsice — species — The name that identifies a unique organism
5. snuge — genus — The first part of the scientific name of an organism
6. stoprtia — protista — The kingdom that includes *Euglena*
7. minkdog — kingdom — The classification level that comes after domain

187

Answer Strategies

Word Play

1. If necessary, have students look back through the lesson to find the definitions of any words they cannot unscramble. Provide a word list for students who are struggling.

   As a challenge, ask students to make their own scrambled Word Play using these words and their own definitions, or with new words from the lesson.

Assessment

Suggested Scoring Guide

You may wish to use this suggested scoring guide for the Brain Check.

Item	Points
1	35 (5 points per item)
2	20
3	15
4	10
5	20
Total	100

Lesson Quiz

See Assessment Guide, p. AG 38.

3 **Extend/Evaluate** (continued)

Answer Strategies

Apply Concepts

2. It may help to lead a class discussion to summarize the concept of classification. Ask in general terms how organisms are classified. Students should understand that scientists classify organisms according to structures and functions and that they look for similarities and differences.
3. Encourage students to recall the definitions and classifications of animals from their memories in order to make the drawing. Students may review the lesson on animals.
4. Have students examine the pictures one at a time and identify each organism shown. Then have them choose the plant graphic. If students cannot identify each type of organism, encourage them to supply as much information in a description as possible and use that information to decide.
5. Students may wish to use any notes they made in answering question 4 to compose their answer. Encourage students to use complete sentences as they write a comprehensive answer that explains their choice.

Take It Home!

Students may wish to write on index cards the names of kingdoms and an example of an organism in each kingdom. They can then carry the cards on their walk.

Apply Concepts

2 Explain how and why scientists classify organisms.

Scientists classify organisms according to their shapes, sizes, and other features. Classification allows scientists to identify important characteristics about organisms and determine how the organisms are related.

3 Draw an organism that would be classified as an animal.

Students should draw a picture of any animal.

4 Circle the organism that would be classified as a plant.

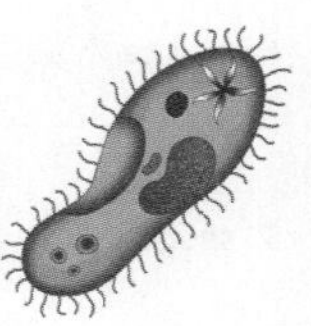

5 Explain why you chose the organism you circled. What characteristics would cause it to be classified this way?

Sample answer: It has leaves, produces a flower for reproduction, has roots and a stem, grows out of the ground, and uses the sun to produce food.

Take It Home! Share what you have learned about classification with your family. Take a walk with an adult and name the kingdoms of the organisms you see.

Make Connections

Easy

Art Connection

Make Your Own Classification Table

Assign students to make a simple illustrated classification table. Have them draw a table and divide it into seven sections. Tell them to label each section with a different kingdom and draw in the box an example of an organism that belongs to that kingdom.

Average

Writing Connection

Narrative

Tell students that scientists must explore to learn about new organisms before classifying the organisms. Ask students to imagine they are scientists who have found a new life form. Tell them to write about what they would do to determine how to classify it. Encourage them to use their imaginations and include details.

Average

Health and Physical Education Connection

Classifying Diseases

Students are often confused as to which diseases are caused by bacteria. Direct students to list some common illnesses and then look up which are caused by bacteria and which are caused by viruses or other pathogens. Explain that only diseases caused by bacteria can be treated with antibiotics.

Challenging

Social Studies Connection

Archaea in Extreme Environments

Ask students to do research to find an example of archaea that live in an extreme environment. Then have them make a poster including some facts and photos that show the location and the organisms.

Guided Inquiry

FLIPCHART  P. 20

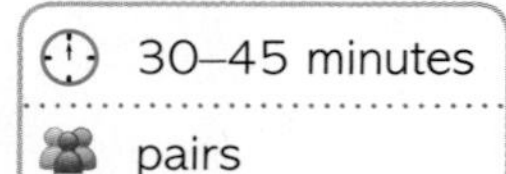
30–45 minutes
pairs

Students should follow the directions on the Flipchart. The accompanying Lesson Inquiry pages in the Student Edition provide scaffolding for guided inquiry.

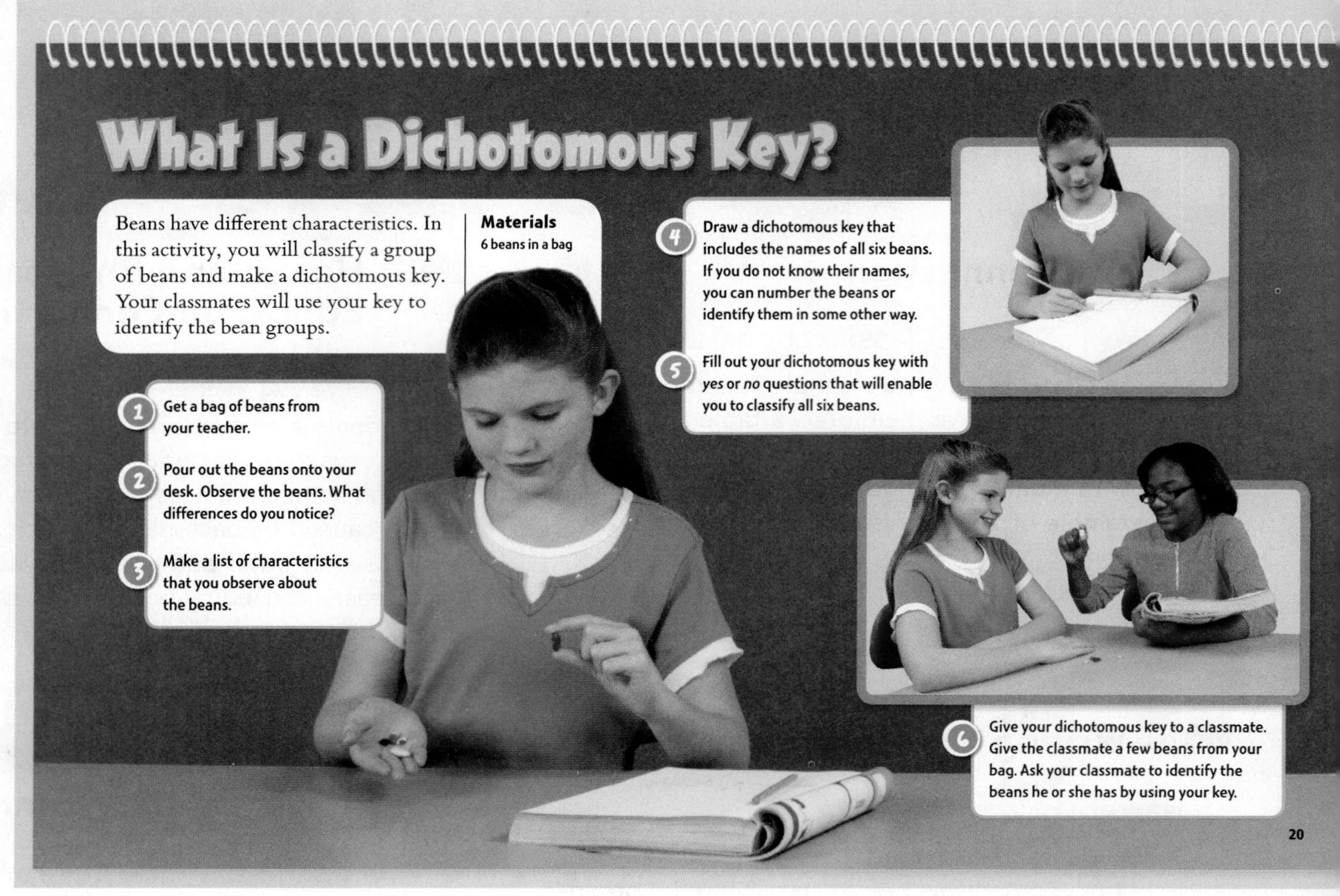

Inquiry Skills Focus Classify/Order, Observe, Record and Display Data, Compare

Objectives

- Classify items based on characteristics they have or lack.
- Use a dichotomous key to classify items.

Prep and Planning Tips

See the Planning for Inquiry page for more information.

Prior to the activity, prepare a bag of beans for each student. Any six differently shaped or colored beans can be used. The sample key is based on a kidney bean, a lima bean, a black bean, a black-eyed pea, a lentil, and a navy bean. This assortment of beans should enable students to readily identify distinguishing characteristics that they can use to construct their keys.

You may wish to provide students with collections that are made up of different combinations of beans, allowing for greater variation among keys.

Expected Results

Students should make and use a dichotomous key that can be used to identify different types of beans.

1 Engage/Explore

Attention Grabber

Poll the class on what snack they would like to eat, such as popcorn. Tell students that you have their snack inside a bag, and reveal an item such as green beans. When students protest, ask how they know that green beans are not popcorn. What if, for example, other people called green beans *popcorn*? Now ask them to describe popcorn instead of just naming it. Explain that scientists make dichotomous keys based on descriptions in order to identify items so that there are no misunderstandings based on names.

Preview Activity

Before beginning the investigation, have students review the directions on the Inquiry Flipchart and the accompanying Student Edition response pages. Then have them complete the response page as they follow directions on the Flipchart.

Name ______________________

Essential Question

What Is a Dichotomous Key?

Set a Purpose

What will you learn from this investigation?

Sample answer: I will learn how to make and use a dichotomous key.

Think About the Procedure

Why are the beans you are given different from one another?

You use classification to identify different items. The beans must be different so that they can be sorted by their differences.

Record Your Data

In the space provided, make your dichotomous key using the bean characteristics you identified.

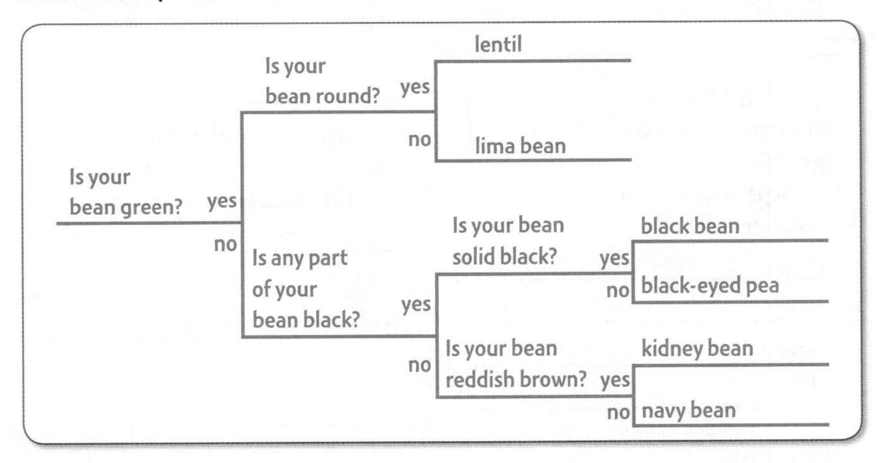

Go Digital

An interactive digital lesson is available in Online Resources. It is suitable for individuals, small groups, or it may be projected or used on an interactive white board.

1 Engage/Explore (continued)

Guide the Investigation

Develop Inquiry Skills

CLASSIFY/ORDER Be sure that students interpret the data and use the dichotomous key correctly. They may be tempted to split the beans into too many groups instead of using yes/no branches to whittle them down. Also, be sure to mention that some branches can go on longer than other branches. Each branch of the dichotomous key should end in one specific bean type.

OBSERVE As students observe the beans, ask: **What characteristics can you use to classify the beans?** Sample answer: size, shape, color

RECORD AND DISPLAY DATA **What format will you use to present your classification?** a dichotomous key

FORMULATE AND USE MODELS Demonstrate the format of a dichotomous key by showing how the characteristics are listed and then branch off according to the characteristic chosen. Invite students to examine the blank dichotomous key and ask any questions to clarify how it is used. **How is information recorded and displayed in a dichotomous key?** Characteristics are described and organized into *yes* or *no* branches.

COMPARE **Which things are you comparing in this exercise?** different kinds of beans

2 Explain

Develop Inquiry Skills

DRAW CONCLUSIONS Remind students of the Attention Grabber that kicked off this lesson. Suggest they use that experience to explain why it is important to be very specific when determining criteria for classifying living things.

ANALYZE AND EXTEND Discuss students' responses to the items.

1. Discuss why scientists look at many examples of an organism before generalizing its characteristics. Explain that individuals have variations that may be outside the norm for the species as a whole.
2. Ask students to evaluate the various keys based on how well they were able to use each key to identify a specific bean.
3. Play a game of "What Am I?" in which students ask questions in order to identify an object. Discuss how each question helped eliminate certain categories, narrowing the result until the object could be identified.
4. To illustrate how scientists might classify an organism, ask students to list some of the characteristics they might use to identify a golden-haired Labrador retriever.

3 Extend/Evaluate

5. Accept reasonable responses. Students might ask, "If you make different dichotomous keys for the same objects, will you always be able to identify each object?" Discuss with them how they could find answers to their questions.

Assessment

Lesson Quiz
See Assessment Guide, p. AG 39.

Draw Conclusions

Scientists classify and organize living things based on how they are similar or different from one another. Why is it important for scientists to use the same characteristics to classify living things?

Sample answer: Scientists must use the same characteristics to make their classification consistent. This helps ensure that the scientists are describing the same living things.

Scientists must be very specific when describing living things. Why might scientists want to avoid using terms such as *small, big, heavy,* and *light* when classifying living things?

Sample answer: These terms are not precise or exact. Scientists must use terms with specific, agreed-upon definitions that can be applied in a consistent manner by many people.

Analyze and Extend

1. **Which characteristics did you use to classify the beans? Which characteristics did your classmates use?**

   Sample answer: I used color and shape to classify my beans. My classmates used color and size to classify their beans.

2. **Compare charts with a classmate. Was one chart easier to use than the other chart?**

   Sample answer: My classmate based his key on size, which was confusing unless you had a ruler.

3. **How might grouping and classifying things, rather than just describing them, make it easier for others to identify the things?**

   Sample answer: If things have been classified into groups, it is easier to tell others about each thing by naming the group the thing belongs to.

4. **How was the dichotomous key you made to classify beans different from dichotomous keys scientists use to classify organisms?**

   Sample answer: Scientists' dichotomous keys probably have more questions.

5. **What other questions would you like to ask about how scientists use dichotomous keys?**

   Sample questions: How long is the longest dichotomous key ever made? What are other characteristics that scientists include in dichotomous keys?

190

Differentiated Inquiry

Easy

A Simple Key

Have students choose four different writing tools from their desks and make a simple dichotomous key that can be used to identify the items they chose. The key should branch twice and end with four different descriptions. Have students trade keys with a partner and have the partner use the key to identify one of the objects.

Easy

Identify Candy

Students may have difficulty understanding how to make a good dichotomous key if they have not successfully used one.

Make a simple dichotomous key using something familiar, such as different types of candy.

Ask students to choose one of the candies randomly from a bag. Then have them identify the candy using the dichotomous key. When students can successfully identify several candies, have them try the other activities again.

Average

Compare Two Dichotomous Keys

Research to find two different dichotomous keys used by scientists to identify something.

Compare the keys. How are they similar? How are they different? Write a brief summary of the two keys.

Challenging

Use a Scientific Dichotomous Key

Research to find a scientific dichotomous key that can be used to identify plants or other organisms in your environment.

Take the key and use it to find and identify an organism in your yard or school environment.

Describe the challenges and success you had in using the key.

Options for Inquiry

FLIPCHART 

Students can conduct these optional investigations at any time before, during, or in response to the lesson in the Student Edition.

Gymnosperms and angiosperms both make seeds for reproduction. How are their seeds similar? How are they different?

Materials
- pinecone
- pine seeds
- apple half section
- apple seeds

Follow This Procedure

1. Pine trees are gymnosperms. Observe the pinecone and the pine seeds.
2. In your Science Notebook, draw and label the structures you observe.
3. Apple trees are angiosperms. Observe the apple half section and the apple seeds.
4. In your Science Notebook, draw and label the structures you observe.
5. Make notes on anything interesting that you observe. Include these details in your drawings and notes:
   - the appearance of the seeds
   - where the seeds are found in the apple and cone
   - the surroundings of the seeds in both structures
   - the labels *gymnosperm* and *angiosperm*

Analyze Your Results

6. How are the seed structures between gymnosperms and angiosperms similar? How are they different?
7. What structure protects pine seeds? What structure protects apple seeds?
8. Which of these structures do you think is more effective at protecting the seeds? Why?

B **Flowers in Hiding**

There are many more species of angiosperms than gymnosperms. Take a look around your neighborhood. You will probably see grass and trees, as well as shrubs and other plants. How many of them have flowers? Even if you don't observe flowers, the plants may bloom at some point during the year. Do research to identify and learn about three common angiosperms. Identify the plants by name, and draw what they each look like with and without their flowers. Record your drawings and notes in an *Angiosperm Journal* section in your Science Notebook.

Here's how one student recorded his observations.

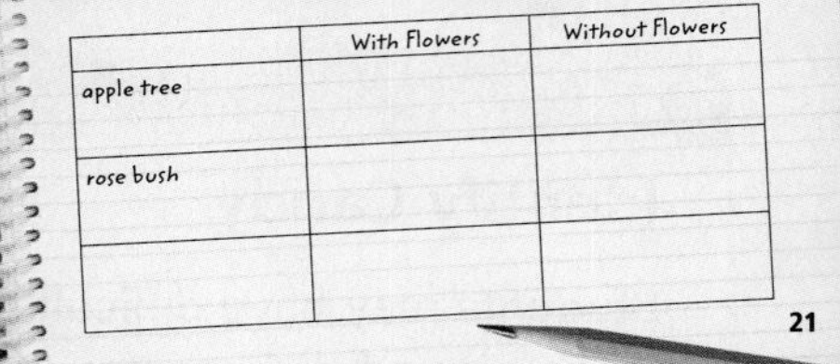
Science Notebook

	With Flowers	Without Flowers
apple tree		
rose bush		

21

Directed Inquiry

A Comparing Cones and Fruits

 20–30 minutes

 small groups

Prep and Planning Tips

You will need about ten apples for this investigation—five to slice in half and five from which you can remove the seeds. Slice the apples prior to class.

Pine seeds, also known as pine nuts, are available in the produce department of most grocery stores. If possible, slice the pinecones in half so that students may observe a cross-section of these structures as well. If you cannot find pinecones that still have seeds on the cone scales, you may wish to display pictures that clearly show how the seeds attach to the cones.

Expected Results

Students should observe and draw the seed-bearing structures of both gymnosperms and angiosperms. Their notes on the gymnosperm (pinecone) should indicate that the seeds are attached to the outside of the cone scales with no covering. The seeds of the angiosperm (apple) are completely surrounded by the fruit.

Independent Inquiry

B Flowers in Hiding

45–60 minutes

individuals

Prep and Planning Tips

See the Planning for Inquiry pages for more information. Identify suitable resources for students to use in their research.

Science Notebook

Students can use the Science Notebook page shown on the Flipchart as a model for recording their findings. Encourage them to include drawings of both the general plant structure and details of flowers and fruits. Challenge students to include at least one plant that does not have obvious flowers, such as grass plants, oak or maple trees, or many shrubs.

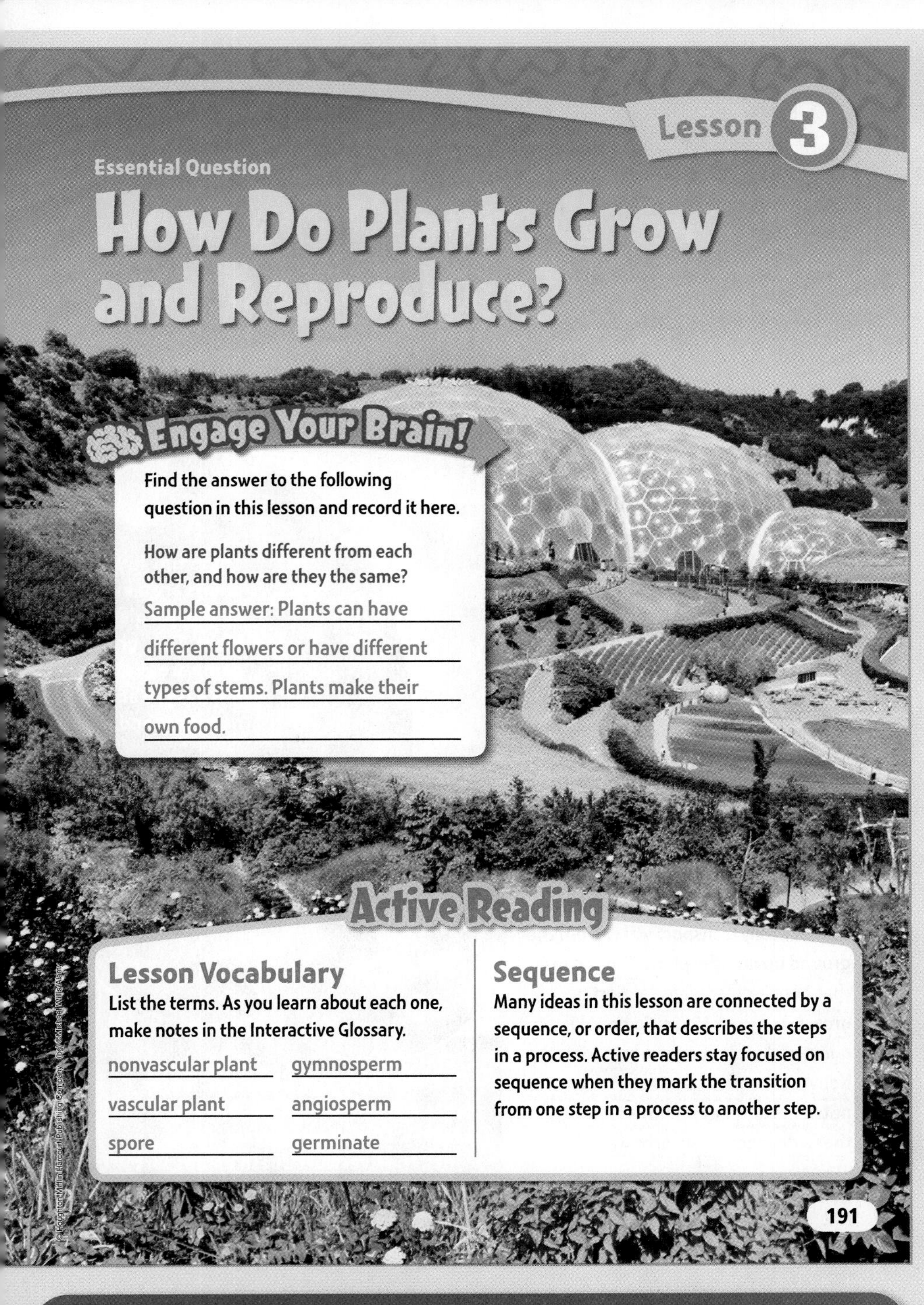

Lesson 3

Essential Question

How Do Plants Grow and Reproduce?

Engage Your Brain!

Find the answer to the following question in this lesson and record it here.

How are plants different from each other, and how are they the same?

Sample answer: Plants can have different flowers or have different types of stems. Plants make their own food.

Active Reading

Lesson Vocabulary

List the terms. As you learn about each one, make notes in the Interactive Glossary.

nonvascular plant	gymnosperm
vascular plant	angiosperm
spore	germinate

Sequence

Many ideas in this lesson are connected by a sequence, or order, that describes the steps in a process. Active readers stay focused on sequence when they mark the transition from one step in a process to another step.

191

Go Digital

An interactive digital lesson is available in the Online Resources. It is suitable for individuals, small groups, or may be projected or used on an interactive white board.

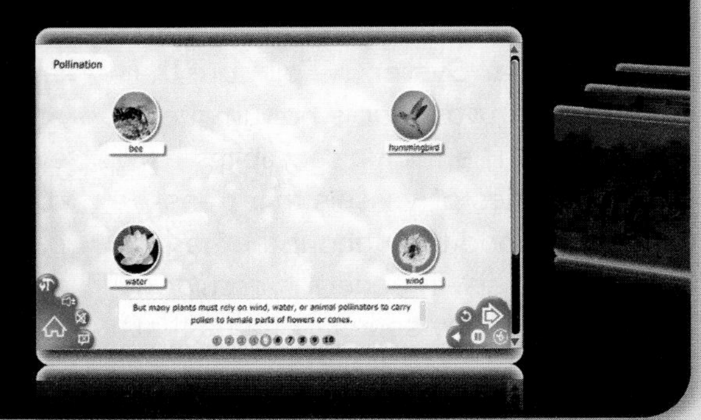

1 Engage/Explore

Objectives

- Know the reproductive structures of some vascular plants.
- Describe fertilization and seed development in plants.
- Explain the life cycle of simple plants.

Engage Your Brain!

Explain that the domes in the photo are part of the Eden Project. This project, located in Cornwall, England, is built on a former clay mine and includes the world's largest greenhouses in which plants from all over the world are grown.

Ask students to observe the different plants in the photo and think about different plants they are familiar with. To organize thinking, have the class make a list of differences and similarities on the board. Remind students to record their final answer to the question when they find it in this lesson.

Active Reading Annotations

Remind students that active readers "make texts their own" by annotating them with notes and marks that help with comprehension. Encourage students to use pencil, not pen, to make annotations and to feel free to change their annotations as they read. The goal of annotation is to help students remember what they have read.

Vocabulary and Interactive Glossary

Remind students to find and list the yellow highlighted terms from the lesson. As they proceed through the lesson and learn about the terms, they should add notes, drawings, or sentences in the extra spaces in the Interactive Glossary.

2 Explain

Notebook Generate Ideas

Ask students to preview these pages by looking at the images. Ask them to compare and contrast the two plants they see. Be sure they understand that the photo shows an enlarged image of the liverworts, and that the pepper plant is shown smaller than actual size.

Active Reading

Remind students that authors compare and contrast events, objects, and ideas when they point out ways they are alike and different. Active readers remember similarities and differences because they focus on the events, objects and ideas being compared.

Develop Science Concepts

What are vascular tissues, and what do they do? They are tubes that run throughout a plant and transport materials.

Which plant is the vascular plant? the nonvascular plant? The pepper plant is a vascular plant; the liverwort is a nonvascular plant.

Compare the relative sizes of these two plants. The pepper plant is larger. Vascular plants tend to be larger because the vascular tissue allows them to take up water and transport it throughout the plant, no matter how large it is. Nonvascular plants must absorb water from the environment, so they must remain small in order to stay moist.

Develop Inquiry Skills

COMPARE **The cells in the center of a club moss carry water; the cells on the outside carry food. What vascular plant structures do these two groups of cells resemble?** The center cells resemble xylem, and the cells on the outside resemble phloem.

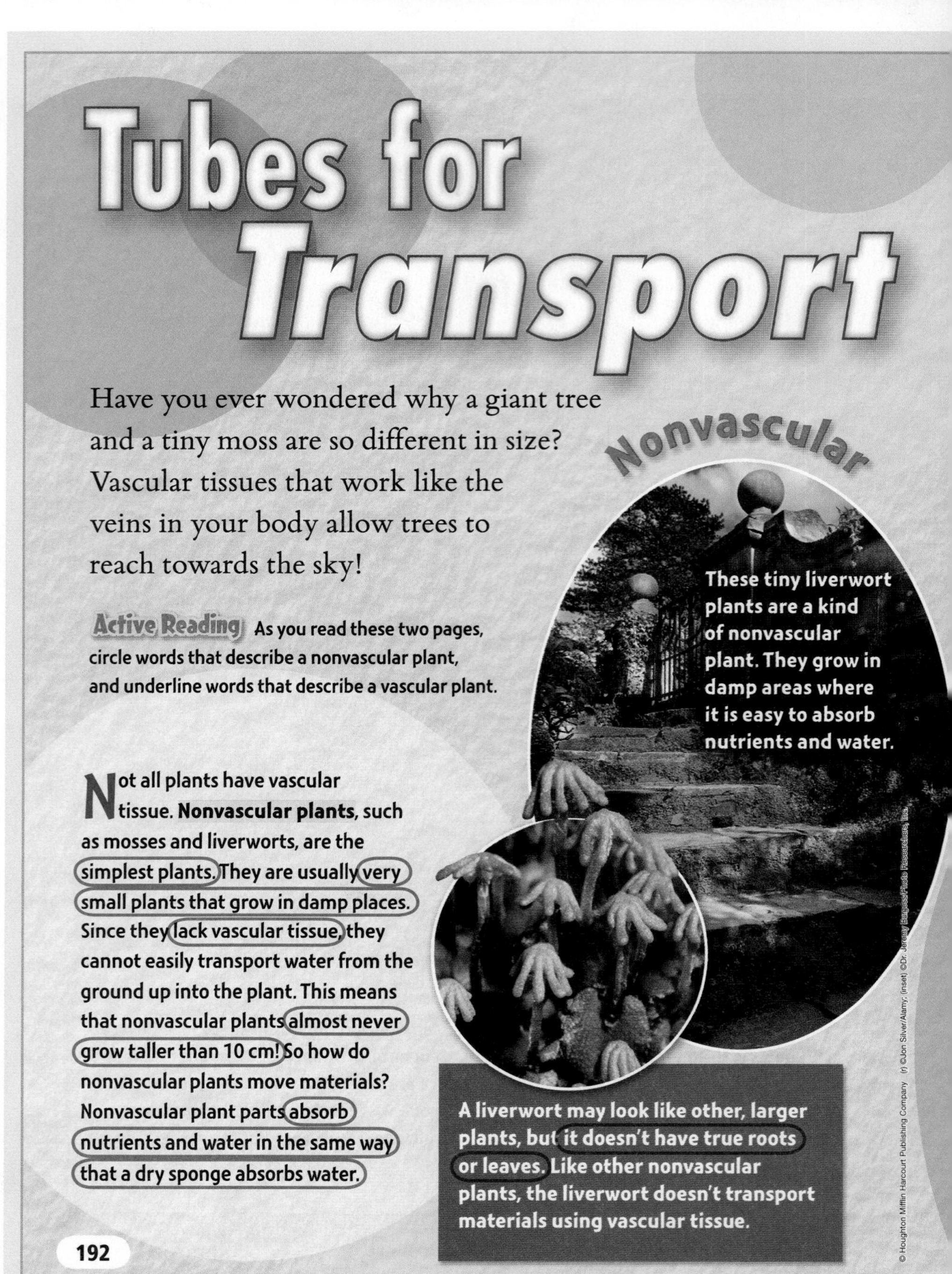

Tubes for Transport

Have you ever wondered why a giant tree and a tiny moss are so different in size? Vascular tissues that work like the veins in your body allow trees to reach towards the sky!

Active Reading As you read these two pages, circle words that describe a nonvascular plant, and underline words that describe a vascular plant.

Nonvascular

Not all plants have vascular tissue. **Nonvascular plants**, such as mosses and liverworts, are the simplest plants. They are usually very small plants that grow in damp places. Since they lack vascular tissue, they cannot easily transport water from the ground up into the plant. This means that nonvascular plants almost never grow taller than 10 cm! So how do nonvascular plants move materials? Nonvascular plant parts absorb nutrients and water in the same way that a dry sponge absorbs water.

These tiny liverwort plants are a kind of nonvascular plant. They grow in damp areas where it is easy to absorb nutrients and water.

A liverwort may look like other, larger plants, but it doesn't have true roots or leaves. Like other nonvascular plants, the liverwort doesn't transport materials using vascular tissue.

192

English Language Learners

Vascular Systems Point out that the term *vascular* is not unique to plants. The term also applies to the series of vessels that transport blood throughout the bodies of animals. In general, *vascular* refers to any series of tubes that carry fluids throughout the body of an organism. The vascular system of humans and plants are different in structure, but they perform the same function—they transport materials throughout the organism.

When you look at a very tall tree, you are looking at a vascular plant. If the tree takes in water from the soil with its roots, how does the water get to the leaves at the top? **Vascular plants** have vascular tissues that allow them to move water, nutrients, and sugars across long distances. Tiny tubes in vascular tissues move water and nutrients up a plant the same way that you pull up water when you drink through a straw. Most of the plants around us, including trees, grasses, and shrubs, are vascular plants.

Do the Math!

Find the Average

A grouping of moss plants has the following height measurements: 9 cm, 5 cm, 8 cm, 11 cm, and 7 cm. A grouping of pepper plants has the following height measurements: 55 cm, 65 cm, 48 cm, 52 cm, and 60 cm. Calculate the averages, and compare the heights of the vascular and nonvascular plants.

Nonvascular (moss) =

$(9 + 5 + 8 + 11 + 7) \div 5 = 8$ cm;

Vascular (pepper plants) =

$(55 + 65 + 48 + 52 + 60) \div 5 = 56$ cm

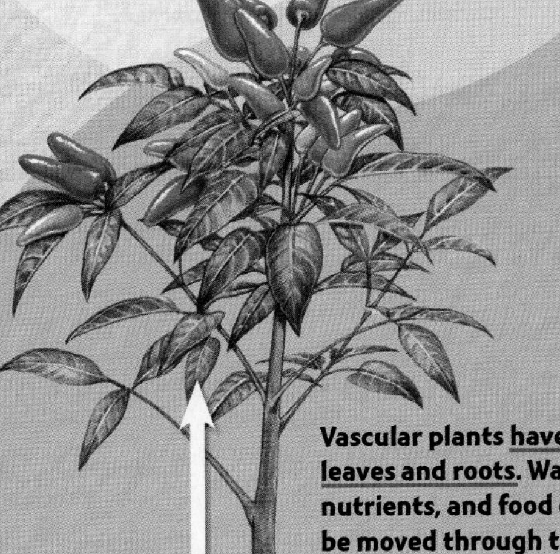

Vascular plants have true leaves and roots. Water, nutrients, and food can be moved through the vascular tissue to other plant parts as needed.

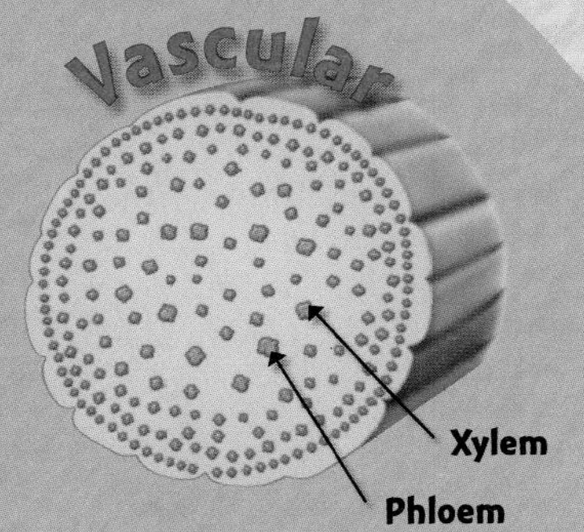

If you cut away a section of vascular tissue, you would see two kinds of smaller tubes. *Xylem* carries water and nutrients from the roots to all the other parts of the plant. *Phloem* carries sugar from the leaves to the rest of the plant.

193

Writing Connection

Write an Article Ask students to write an article comparing how vascular and nonvascular plants move materials. Suggest that students write an outline as the first step in writing their articles. Their finished articles should include information about how each type of plant gets water and nutrients, how these materials move through the plant, and the relative sizes of the plants.

Develop Science Vocabulary

nonvascular plants Remind students that the prefix *non–* means "not." So a nonvascular plant is one that is not vascular.

vascular plants Reinforce that a vascular plant has tissues that move materials throughout the plant. Have students recall the purpose and structure of vascular tissue when they define this term.

Do the Math!

Find the Average

Remind students that to find the average of a group of data, you add the values and then divide the total by the number of items added. **How many plants are you adding in each group?** five **How will you use this information to find the averages?** I will divide each total by five.

Interpret Visuals

Invite students to look at the graphic of the vascular tube cross-section. Explain that it shows a cutaway view of the tubes that move materials through a vascular plant. Reinforce that xylem carries water and other materials absorbed by the roots. Phloem carries the sugars that the plant uses for food from the leaves to other plant parts. Share that an easy way to remember which tube carries which materials is that both *food* and *phloem* start with the initial sound *f*.

Notebook

Summarize Ideas

Have students think about how they would use the contrasting characteristics they learned on these pages to identify whether a plant they discovered is a nonvascular plant or a vascular plant. Have students summarize the steps they would take to classify such a plant either orally or in writing.

2 Explain (continued)

Notebook Generate Ideas

Have students preview these pages by looking at the two reproduction graphics. Ask them to describe how the graphics are connected to the introductory paragraph on the page.

Active Reading

Remind students that sequence, or order, is important in text that describes the development of an idea or the steps in a process. Active readers stay focused on sequence when they mark the transition from one stage of an idea or step in a process to another.

Interpret Visuals

Have students examine the diagram of the moss life cycle. Explain that mosses, liverworts, and ferns have two forms, or phases, in their life cycle.

What happens if a moss spore lands in a good location when it shoots out of the capsule? It grows into the "leafy" form of the moss plant.

If mosses don't have roots, what keeps them in place? Structures that act like roots anchor them to the ground.

How do scientists know that these structures are not roots? Mosses are nonvascular plants. These structures do not have tubes that move water from them to other parts of the plant.

English Language Learners

Microscopic Explain that moss pods, which contain spores, are tiny but visible to the unaided eye. Individual spores themselves, however, are microscopic. They are too small to see with the unaided eye. Then remind students that the prefix *micro–* means "very small." *Scope* means "to look at" and refers to instruments for looking at objects. Objects that are microscopic are only visible through a microscope.

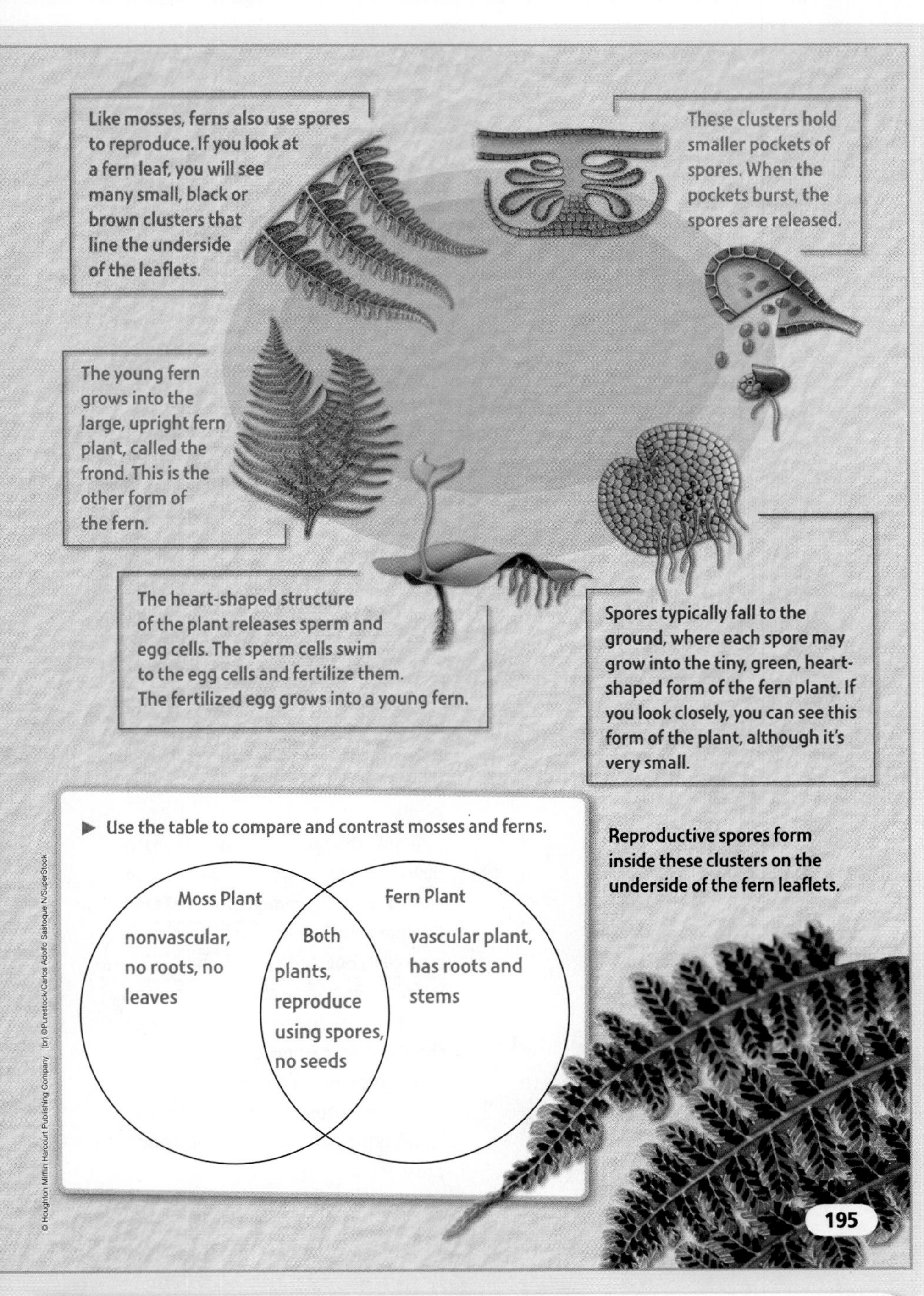

Develop Science Vocabulary

spore Point out that spores are used in reproduction for other organisms, such as fungi, as well as plants. Spores are not the product of the union of an egg cell and a sperm cell.

Misconception Alert

Students may continue to confuse spores with seeds, as both grow into a new plant. Explain that a spore is made up of only one cell, while a seed is made up of many cells and many parts. Though the pods that contain spores are visible to the unaided eye, individual spores are typically microscopic.

Develop Inquiry Skills

COMPARE **How are the two plants shown on these pages similar in classification?** They are both simple plants that do not use seeds to reproduce.

CLASSIFY **How do the classifications of the moss and the fern differ?** The moss is a nonvascular plant; the fern is a vascular plant.

Notebook Summarize Ideas

Before students work on the Interactivity, have students review the two life cycle diagrams and then summarize, the similarities of the life cycles of mosses and ferns. Then have students fill in the Venn Diagram with what they have learned.

Differentiation — Leveled Questions

Extra Support

What do these life cycles have in common? They both reproduce without using seeds; they are both plants.

Challenge

Why is there no specific starting or stopping point in the graphics showing plant reproduction? These processes occur in a cycle. There is no real beginning or end.

2 **Explain** (continued)

Generate Ideas

Have the class preview these two pages. Direct them to read the title and to look at each picture. Ask: **How do the pictures and captions help you understand more about seeds?** Record their ideas on the board.

Active Reading

Remind students that authors compare and contrast events, objects, and ideas when they point out ways they are alike and different. Active readers remember similarities and differences because they focus on the events, objects and ideas being compared.

Develop Science Vocabulary

gymnosperms Reinforce that the word part ***gymnos*** comes from the Greek and means "naked." Have students compare the pictures of the gymnosperm seeds on this page with those of the pomegranate on the facing page. Then have students describe a "naked" seed as opposed to one that is covered.

angiosperms The word part *angio* comes from a Greek word for *vessel,* and *sperm* comes from the Greek word for *seed.* When put together, *angiosperm* means "a seed in a vessel." The "vessel" is the ovary in which the seeds develop.

Develop Inquiry Skills

COMPARE **In what ways are seeds better than spores for reproduction?** Seeds have coverings that protect them and allow them to rest until the environment is right for growth. Spores do not have these structures and must sprout soon after landing in a moist environment.

Seed Power!

You have probably seen many types of seeds, and even eaten some! How are seeds different from spores?

Active Reading As you read these two pages, circle the phrases that describe gymnosperms. Draw boxes around phrases that describe angiosperms.

These pinecones are part of a gymnosperm. This gymnosperm produces seeds on cones. The smaller male cones produce *pollen.* The larger female cones contain eggs within structures called *ovules.*

Some plants grow from seeds instead of spores. Seeds have an advantage over spores for multiple reasons. Spores need to stay moist and sprout soon after being released, but seeds do not. A seed has a covering that protects it, enabling the seed to rest in an environment for years until conditions are right for sprouting. Scientists have grown plants from seeds that are hundreds, and even thousands, of years old!

Plants that do not produce seeds in flowers are called **gymnosperms.** The word *gymnosperm* means "naked seed." Gymnosperm seeds have a protective seed coat, but the seeds are not enclosed by fruit. There are a few gymnosperms that don't produce seeds in cones, but these are uncommon.

Cone-producing plants, called conifers, are the most common gymnosperms. Conifers include pine, fir, spruce, and cedar trees.

The fertilized ovule on each scale of a female pinecone becomes a seed.

196

Differentiation — Leveled Questions

Extra Support

What are gymnosperms? Gymnosperms are plants that do not produce seeds in flowers. They include evergreen trees and shrubs that have green needles instead of leaves.

Challenge

You see two types of cones growing in the same pine tree. What are you observing? the male cones, which are small and produce pollen, and the female cones, which are large and produce the ovules

▶ The shapes below are an orange, a watermelon, and a green bean. Draw seeds for each one and explain why you drew them where you did.

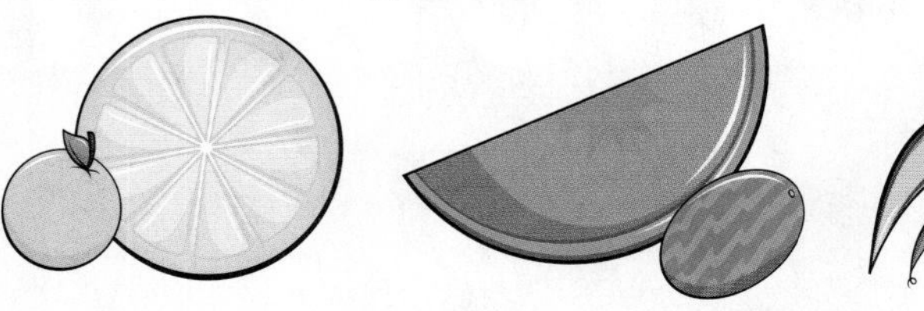

I drew the seeds in the fruits because angiosperm seeds are often enclosed in a fruit.

Gymnosperms aren't the only plants that produce seeds. **Angiosperms** are plants that produce seeds in flowers. More than 85% of the total species of plants on Earth are angiosperms. Think of the plants that grow near your school. Do you think that most of these are gymnosperms or angiosperms?

Some angiosperm seeds have an advantage over gymnosperm seeds. Since angiosperm seeds are often enclosed in a fruit, they are easily spread when animals eat the fruits. Gymnosperm seeds may also be spread by animals, but typically fall to the ground and grow where they land.

This pomegranate tree produces flowers. The flowers produce sperm and eggs that unite to become seeds within the fruit.

Writing Connection

Seed Plant Journal Direct students to keep a journal in which they note every plant, fruit, or seed they encounter over the course of one day. Remind students that plants are used as a resource for making cloth and lumber as well as for food. Have them use the data they collect to write a paragraph detailing how seed-bearing plants affect their lives.

Misconception Alert

Many students may think that green beans and tomatoes and similar structures are "vegetables" and not fruits. Explain that structures that produce seeds are all fruits. To clarify this concept, have students do research and make a list of all the fruits they can find. Examples include peanuts, beans, coconuts, squash, pumpkins, and avocados.

Develop Science Concepts

Reinforce the concepts on these two pages by asking the following questions.

How do angiosperms differ from gymnosperms? Angiosperms produce seeds in flowers. Gymnosperms produce seeds on cones.

The gymnosperm seeds shown on these pages have wings. Why are wings a helpful adaptation? The wings can catch the wind and allow the seeds to be carried away from the parent plant.

Interpret Visuals

If possible, bring in samples of the fruits shown in the Interactivity. Have the students examine an orange half and a slice of watermelon and open up a green bean to find the seeds.

Notebook Summarize Ideas

Ask for a volunteer to come to the board and draw a picture of a gymnosperm, including the cone structures. Ask for a second volunteer to draw a picture of an angiosperm, including flowers or fruit. Have students use the drawings to help them summarize these pages either orally or in writing.

2 Explain (continued)

Notebook Generate Ideas

Discuss with students the different types of flowers and seeds they are familiar with. Ask them to consider how flowers and seeds from different plants are the same and different. Make a class list of questions students have about seeds and flowers. Then return to these questions after completing these pages.

Active Reading

Remind students that informational text contains many facts. Active readers process informational text with deliberate speed that enables them to focus on and retain the facts presented. Underlining facts helps active readers focus more readily.

Develop Science Concepts

Direct students to look at the diagram of the flower and read the text describing the flower parts. Reinforce what they have learned with the questions that follow.

What is the male part of the flower called, and what does it produce? The anther is the male part. It produces pollen, which contains sperm.

What are the female parts of the flower called, and what do they do? The stigma collects pollen. The ovary contains eggs in ovules.

What must happen before seeds can develop? The flower must be pollinated, and the pollen must fertilize the ovules.

What changes occur as the seeds develop? The ovules develop into seeds, and the ovule wall becomes a seed coat. The ovary develops into the fruit.

From Flower to Fruit and Seed

Many angiosperms use flowers to reproduce. Do you know how flowers form fruit?

Active Reading As you read these two pages, circle the names of the parts of a flower.

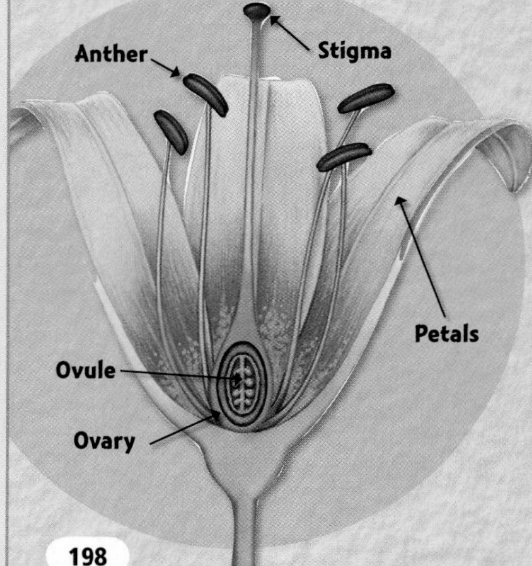

Although you might think of flowers as big and colorful, many flowers are tiny and hard to spot. For example, did you know that grasses grow flowers? Oak trees and maple trees do, too!

Typical flowers have both male and female reproductive parts. A male part, the *anther*, produces pollen grains, which contain sperm. The female parts include the *stigma* and the *ovary*, which contains eggs in ovules.

Flowers that are colorful or fragrant produce sticky nectar that some animals eat. As an animal gathers nectar, pollen may stick to its body. As the animal moves from flower to flower, it transfers pollen to the stigmas of these flowers. This is called pollination.

After pollen lands on a stigma, sperm from the pollen move down to the ovules within the ovary. Fertilization occurs when a sperm cell unites with the egg inside each ovule. The ovules develop into seeds, and each ovule wall becomes a seed coat. The ovary surrounding the ovules becomes a fruit.

198

English Language Learners

Ovary Tell students that the term *ovary* is used in reference to both plants and animals to describe a place where the female egg is produced for reproduction. Although the structures are very different from each other, they serve the same purpose. Have students point to the image of the ovary on the page and say the word aloud.

Math Connection

Pumpkin Averages Pumpkins come in all sizes and average between 100 and 700 seeds each. Provide the following data to students, and have them find the mean (422), median (429), and mode (none) of the data.

Pumpkin	Number of Seeds
1	173
2	587
3	258
4	663
5	429

Misconception Alert

Many people are confused by the concept of seedless fruits. Explain that seedless fruits, such as watermelon, have been bred so that the seeds do not fully develop within the fruit. All seedless fruits are grown from cuttings of stems and leaves instead of seeds.

Interpret Visuals

Before students complete the Interactivity, have them review the visuals on these two pages. **Why is there a bee shown on these pages?** Bees are one of the organisms that spread pollen and help with fertilization. **What happens after a bee visits a flower?** Pollen sticks to the stigma, enters the ovary, and fertilizes the ovules.

Students may think that fruits are produced by flowers. Make sure that students understand that flowers don't *make* fruits, they *become* fruits. Reinforce this idea using "Pumpkin Seed Development." Have students add numbers (1, 2, 3, 4) to the stages shown. Point out that in stage 2, the flower is changing into the fruit. In Stage 3, only a small part of what were the flower petals are still visible on the developing fruit.

Notebook Summarize Ideas

Have students draw a flower and label its parts. Direct them to indicate which part of the flower produces pollen (sperm), and which part produces eggs. Then have students summarize, either orally or in writing, how flowers become seeds.

2 Explain (continued)

Notebook Generate Ideas

Before beginning this lesson, ask students to read the title and look over these pages. Next, ask them to explain what they think happens during the process of germination. Have the class then read the pages.

Active Reading

Remind students that sequence, or order, is important in text that describes the development of an idea or the steps in a process. Active readers stay focused on sequence when they mark the transition from one stage of an idea or step in a process to another.

Develop Science Concepts

Why are the protective coverings on seeds an advantage? The coverings keep the embryo inside safe when environmental conditions are poor.

When does the seed begin to germinate? when conditions are good for growing, usually in the spring

What would happen if a seed had to germinate immediately after it was released from a plant? Many seeds would not be successful, because it is likely they would be germinating when weather conditions were not good for plant growth.

Tell students that many seeds can germinate after remaining dormant for hundreds or even thousands of years. Two of the oldest seeds to germinate were a date palm seed that scientists estimate had been dormant for 2,000 years, and an Asian water lotus seed that was successfully germinated after 1,200 years.

How Seeds Grow

Once a seed is released, it can sit and rest for a long time. But when conditions are right, look out! The seed sprouts and grows into a new plant.

Active Reading As you read these two pages, write numbers next to captions to show the order of events.

What happens to seeds when they are released in cold or dry weather? Seeds have a hard outer coat that protects them. The coat allows a seed to rest until the environment is right for growing. Many plant seeds rest during winter and then **germinate**, or start to grow, when the conditions are right in the spring and the ground becomes warm and moist.

This avocado seed contains an embryo that will grow into a new plant. In avocados, the embryo is mostly made up of two *cotyledons*. These embryonic leaves provide energy for the emerging plant. The embryo and cotyledons are surrounded by a protective seed coat.

plants not shown to scale

A dormant seed lies in the soil when the environment is not suitable for a plant to grow.

When conditions are right, the seed germinates. The embryo absorbs water and breaks through the seed coat. A stem grows upward and a root grows downward.

Cotyledons provide extra energy for growth. Roots grow denser.

200

English Language Learners

Germinate Have English learners look up the definition of *germinate* to find its nonscientific meanings. *Germinate* can be used to describe anything that grows or develops or comes into existence. Often it is used to describe the development of an idea or a project. Write several sentences using the term in a nonscientific way and point out how the scientific meaning and general meanings are similar.

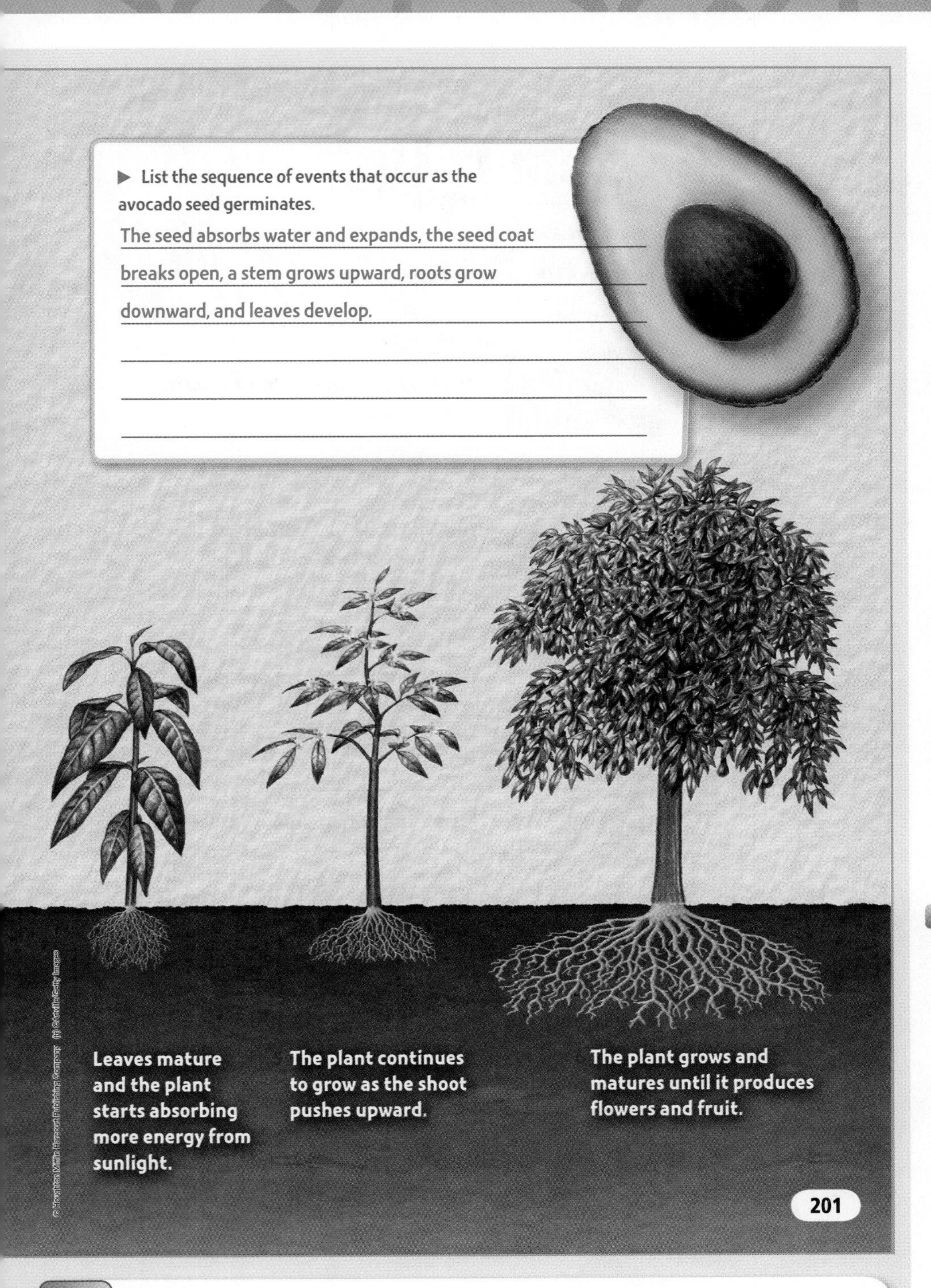

Develop Science Vocabulary

germinate Encourage students to use context clues to determine the meaning of the word *germinate.* Explain that another word for *germinate* is *sprout.*

Interpret Visuals

Encourage students to use germination and growth sequence as a guide for completing the Interactivity. Suggest that they underline the important details they wish to include.

Why doesn't a seed need sunlight to germinate? Sunlight is necessary for photosynthesis. The embryo gets the food it needs from food stored in the cotyledons. So sunlight is not necessary to make food until the stem emerges from the ground and the food stored in the cotyledons is used up.

At what point in the germination of the seed is it able to get water? when the roots form

Notebook Summarize Ideas

Ask students to summarize these two pages by drawing their own visual sequence of germination. Encourage them to use an example of one of their favorite plants in their sequence.

Differentiation — Leveled Questions

Extra Support

What does a germinating plant use for food before it starts making its own? A germinating plant uses food stored in the cotyledons.

Challenge

What would likely happen to a plant that germinates in a dark location? It would grow as long as there was food in the cotyledons. After that, the plant would likely die because it has no light, which it needs to make food.

3 Extend/Evaluate

Sum It Up!

- Encourage students to review the photos and illustrations in the lesson as they complete Sum It Up!
- Remind students to read the direction line so that they are clear about what they are being asked to provide.
- Allow students to work in pairs if they have difficulty. You may wish to provide these students with a word bank for their reference. Have them review the material independently to ensure that they understand the concepts.
- As an extension of the activity, have students add new terms and draw visuals to go with the terms.
- Have students use the Answer Key to check and correct their answers. Encourage students to ask for help with any concepts about which they are still unclear.

When you're done, use the answer key to check and revise your work.

Write the term that matches each photo and caption.

1 
nonvascular
The type of plant that must grow in damp places

2 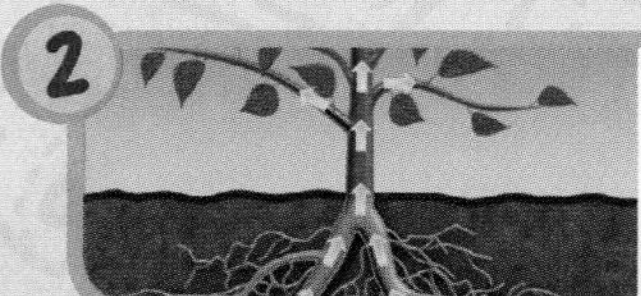
vascular
The type of tissue that can transport materials throughout the plant

3 
capsule
The structure that contains spores in mosses

4 
flower
The structure that produces seeds in angiosperms

5 
cone
The structure that produces seeds in gymnosperms

6 
seed
A reproductive structure that stays protected before germinating

202

Answer Key: 1. nonvascular 2. vascular 3. capsule 4. flower 5. cone 6. seed

Brain Check

Lesson 3

Name ____________________

Word Play

1. Use the words in the box to complete the puzzle.

Across

7. This becomes the seed on a cone scale or a flower
8. A plant that doesn't have true leaves or roots and doesn't grow tall
10. The male part of a flower

Down

1. A plant with tissue that can transport materials throughout the plant
2. What a plant does when it sprouts from a seed
3. A type of plant that produces flowers to make seeds
4. A reproductive structure that stays protected before germinating
5. Leaves that provide food for a germinating plant
6. A type of plant that produces seeds within a cone
9. A reproductive structure a fern grows from

Answers: 1 Down VASCULAR; 2 Down GERMINATES; 3 Down ANGIOSPERM; 4 Down SEED; 5 Down COTYLEDONS; 6 Down GYMNOSPERM; 7 Across OVULE; 8 Across NONVASCULAR; 9 Down SPORE; 10 Across ANTHER

gymnosperm* angiosperm* germinates* nonvascular* vascular*
spore* **seed** **anther** **cotyledons** **ovule**

* Key Lesson Vocabulary

203

Answer Strategies

Word Play

1. Tell students that one good strategy for solving Word Play exercises is to read the clue and then try to think of possible answers before looking at the crossword space. If they can come up with one or more possible answers and then check the crossword boxes, they can often confirm that one of their guesses is the correct answer.

Assessment

Suggested Scoring Guide

You may wish to use this suggested scoring guide for the Brain Check.

Item	Points
1	50 (5 points per item)
2	20
3	10
4	10
5	10
Total	100

Lesson Quiz

See Assessment Guide, p. AG 40.

3 Extend/Evaluate (continued)

Answer Strategies

Apply Concepts

2. Encourage students to try to draw the sequence on their own. Then have them review the lesson to find the illustrated sequence and check their answer against it. Have students revise their graphic as needed.
3. Ask students to think about the question and break it down into two parts. First they need to know which type of plant produces a seed in a fruit (angiosperms). Second, they need to be able to identify an example of that plant (the flowering tree).
4. Have students review the life cycle of the fern in the lesson. Make sure that students understand the difference between the structures that produce spores and the structures that produce sperm and egg cells. As a follow-up, you might have students draw and label both structures.
5. If possible, you can extend this question to make it hands-on by providing samples of male and female cones and allow students to handle and observe the cones as they write their answers.

Take It Home!

Suggest that students keep a weekly log of their plant's growth. Students may wish to sketch the plant in their weekly observation.

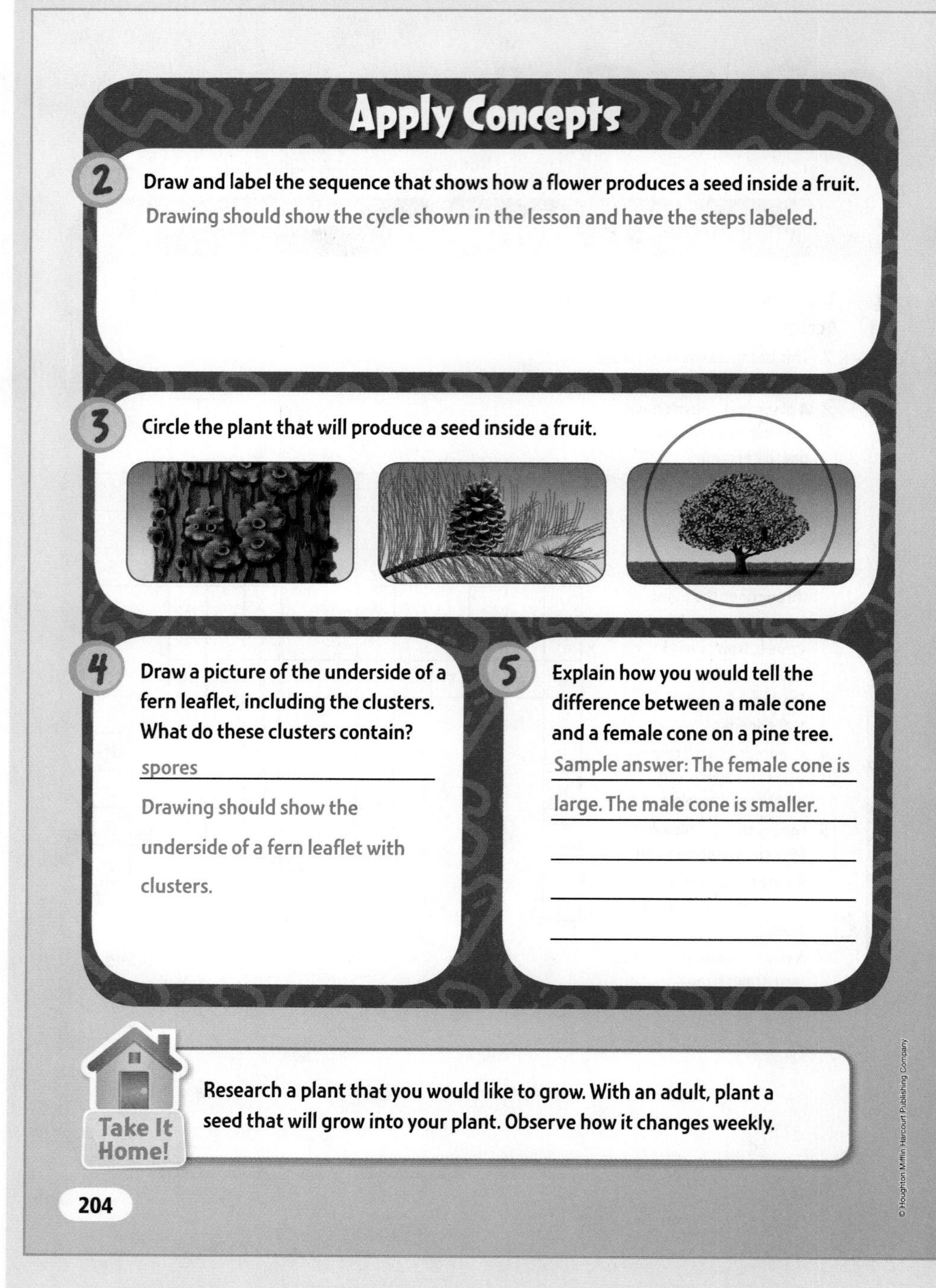

Make Connections

Easy

Art Connection

Expressing with Plants

Challenge students to make artistic renditions of their favorite plant. They can use pencils, paints, sculpture, or any other media to produce their work. Have them use the knowledge they've gained from this lesson to feature some specific plant structures in their work.

Average

Math Connection

Germination Rates

Explain that scientists calculate seed germination as a percentage by using this formula: number of seeds germinated/total seeds × 100. Have students practice determining seed germination percentages by providing sample data that includes the number of total seeds and the number that germinated. Then turn the calculations around and have students determine the number of plants that have germinated based on the percentage and the total number of seeds.

Average

Writing Connection

Dinosaurs and Plants

Tell students that the Mesozoic Era, when dinosaurs roamed Earth, was a time of rapid evolution for plants. At the beginning of the Mesozoic, gymnosperms dominated the environment. The landscape was filled with conifers, ginkgoes, and cycads. By the end of the Mesozoic, angiosperms started to appear and flourish. Have students research pictures and descriptions of Mesozoic Era plants. Then students should make visual displays that show the plants' forms and explain how the plants were important to the diets of dinosaurs.

Challenging

Social Studies Connection

Flowers for All Occasions

Ask students to think about the roles that flowers play in the lives of humans. Ask them to research the roles of flowers in social activities such as weddings or the traditional ceremonies of ancient civilizations. Have students give brief presentations about what they learn.

S.T.E.M.

Engineering and Technology

Objectives

- Understand that technological systems are designed to meet people's needs and improve quality of life.
- Describe how an object or process functions.
- Determine the role of technology in the work of scientists.

Generate Ideas

Notebook

Ask students to think about a recent trip to a zoo or wildlife park. Have them recall whether the animals were wearing tracking devices. Direct them to the pictures shown on this page to help them generate ideas.

Background

- Tracking devices are attached to animals in order to help scientists record, monitor, and understand their needs and behaviors. These devices are especially useful in learning about animals that migrate long distances or live in remote areas.
- GPS technology has made it easier to study the movements of animals. Observing wildlife with remote cameras also allows scientists to learn how animals behave without the need for human interference.

Develop Inquiry Skills

DRAW CONCLUSIONS To help students answer the Interactivity, have them talk about the variety of animal body sizes, shapes, and parts and the different ways in which animals move. **Why would a bird need a different tracking device than a dolphin?** Sample answer: Birds fly and dolphins swim, so the devices attached to them need to work well in the air or in water. Also, a dolphin does not have a leg or a wing to fasten a tracking device to.

S.T.E.M.

Engineering & Technology

How It Works:

Tracking Wildlife

Tracking animals helps scientists learn the animals' patterns of movement. Researchers fit animals with a variety of devices that send back information. Mammals often wear tracking collars. Toads can wear tracking belts. Fish can swallow tiny devices that work inside their bodies!

This lion is fitted with a GPS collar. Sometimes collars like these also have cameras that send back video.

Tracking devices are attached to marine animals with glue or suction cups. The collars send signals to GPS satellites, enabling scientists to locate and track the collars over time.

Troubleshooting

Describe how an animal's body, its movement, and its environment determine the design of a tracking device.

Answers will vary but should reflect understanding of the practical necessities of a device in relation to an animal and its environment.

205

continued

Animal tracking devices help scientists understand the behaviors of animals within their natural habitats.

Choose an animal. Draw a diagram of how a tracking device might be attached to the animal. Explain how the device is attached and what information it captures.

Answers will vary based on the animal the student chooses.

Research an animal species that has been studied using a tracking device. Which kind of device was used? What kind of data did it gather, and what did scientists learn about the species?

Answers will vary based on the animal the student chooses.

Build On It!

Rise to the engineering design challenge—complete **Make a Process: Mimicking an Adaptation** in the Inquiry Flipchart.

Build On It!

In **Mimicking an Adaptation**, the design challenge associated with this lesson, students use the steps of the engineering design process to design a product based on a plant or animal adaptation. See the pages that follow.

Other opportunities to apply the design process appear throughout the *Inquiry Flipchart*.

Develop S.T.E.M. Concepts

DESIGN CRITERIA As students consider the first Interactivity, remind them that each device is designed to fit a specific kind of animal and to work appropriately in its habitat. Explain to students that tracking devices should not exceed three percent of an animal's weight. The devices should not interfere with natural movement or behaviors.

RESEARCH Before students complete the second Interactivity, compile a master list of different animals that have been studied using tracking devices. Use the Internet or other sources to help generate the list.

- **How did the information scientists learned about the animal help animals of that species survive?** Sample answer: Scientists learned the location of the nesting place of a group of sea turtles, and this knowledge helped people better protect that area.

Notebook Summarize Ideas

Direct students to summarize the characteristics of an animal species that scientists must consider when designing tracking devices. Guide students in a discussion about what scientists have learned from tracking wildlife.

Engineering and Technology

FLIPCHART 

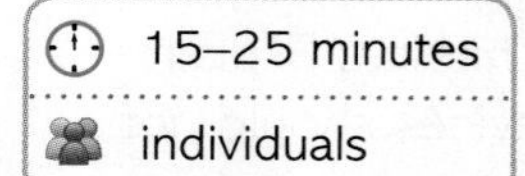

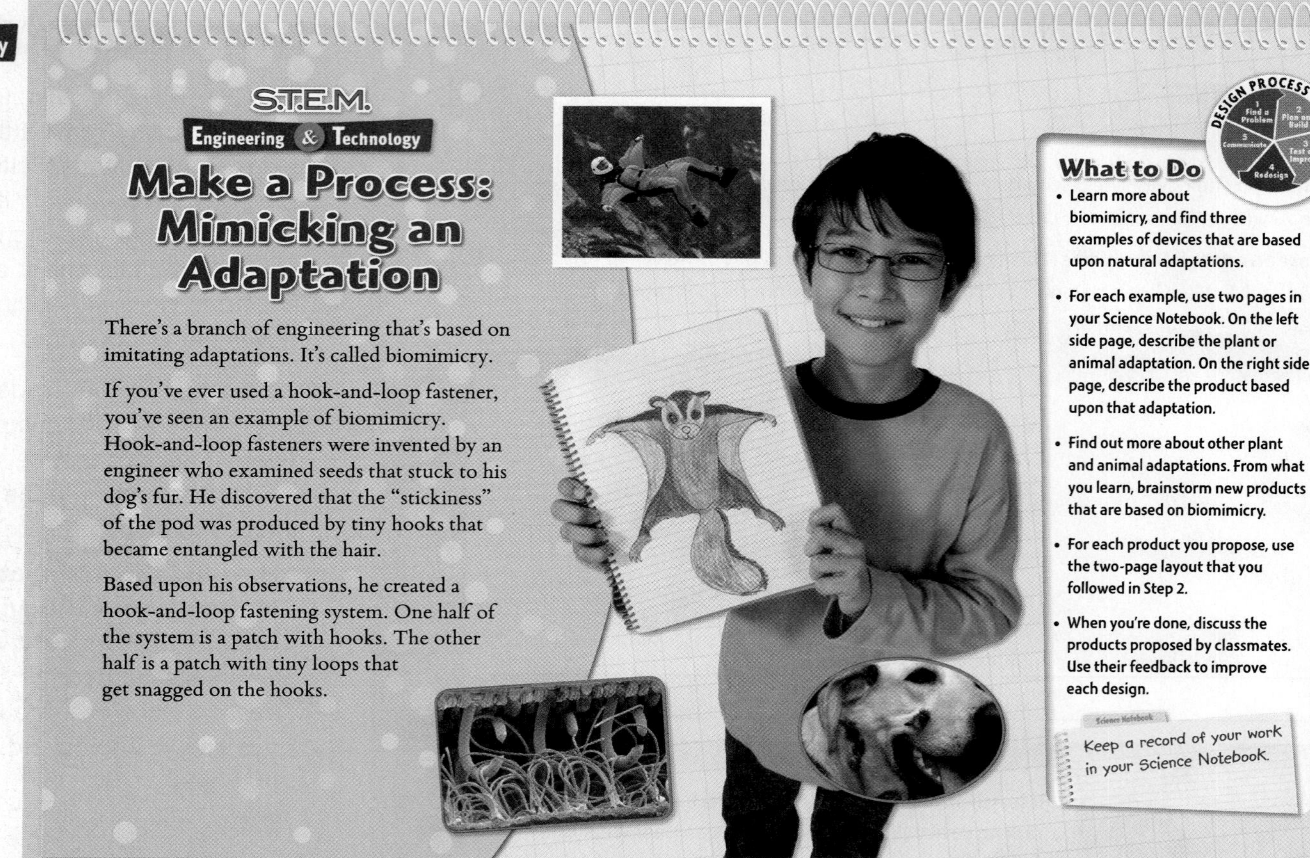

Objectives

- Use the five steps of the design process to design a product that is based on a plant or animal adaptation.
- Understand plant and animal adaptations.

Prep and Planning Tips

- Provide students with background information about the use of biomimicry in product design. For example, engineers have been inspired by nature to design bug-like robots, competitive swimwear that simulates shark skin, and synthetic spider silk.
- Identify resources for students to use to identify and understand unusual plant and animal adaptations.

Expected Outcomes

Students should be able to propose a design for a new product based on research of plant and animal adaptations.

1 Engage/Explore

Attention Grabber

Pass around a shoe or other object that uses the hook-and-loop fastening system. Encourage students to fasten and unfasten the closure. At the same time, pass around burrs that have hooks as a method of seed dispersal. Provide hand lenses so that students can see the hooks and loops on the tape and compare them with the hooks on the burrs.

Preview Activity

Before beginning the activity, have students review the directions on the Engineering and Technology Flipchart page. You may wish to have students review the lesson on the engineering design process earlier in this program.

Guide the Activity

Develop Inquiry Skills

INFER **Why might a scientist draw inspiration from nature when designing a new product?** Sample answer: There are a huge variety of adaptations in nature. These adaptations have solved problems such as dispersing seeds, allowing movement through water and air and over land, and trapping prey. Understanding how these adaptations work can help scientists meet human needs and solve human problems.

Strategies for Success

Provide ample time for students to learn about biomimicry and the many products that have been inspired by plant and animal adaptations. Students may also benefit from sharing the drawings they made in their Science Notebook.

Before students consider the design for their product, have the class make a list of unusual plant and animal adaptations that they have identified in their research. Students can use this list to inspire ideas of possible new products.

Science Notebook

During the Activity Encourage students to research plants and animals that are adapted to life in extreme environments, such as the Arctic tundra or near a hydrothermal vent on the ocean floor. Have students list the adaptations that allow organisms to survive in these environments and consider how each adaptation might be adapted to make a useful product. If possible, show video clips of some unusual plant and animal adaptations.

2 Explain

Develop the Engineering Design Process

1. **FIND A PROBLEM** Invite students to brainstorm a list of some everyday problems that might be solved using biomimicry. Examples include pencils that always need sharpening, the TV remote that needs to be found, or a pet that needs to be fed while a family is on vacation.

3. **TEST AND IMPROVE** Have students record their product and the adaptation that inspired it in their Science Notebooks. Students can trade their ideas with a partner for feedback.

4. **REDESIGN** Bring the class together, and share results. Were some products better than others at incorporating adaptations? Allow students time to make improvements to their designs.

3 Extend/Evaluate

Quick Check

Discuss with students what they learned as they went through the design process. Ask: **Why did you select a particular plant or animal adaptation as your inspiration? What made it useful? How can you imagine people using your product?**

Science Notebook

After the Activity Review students' notebooks for the double-page drawings and notes they took on products based on animal adaptations. Students should have included similar drawings and notes describing their own ideas for one or more products. Look for evidence of revisions based on feedback received when they presented their ideas to the class.

Hooks and Catches Give students a hand lens and samples of both halves of the hook-and-loop fabric fastening system. Direct students to observe the hooks and catches of the system and draw a diagram of it in their Science Notebook.

Wingsuit Flying Show students pictures or videos of athletes participating in the extreme sport of wingsuit flying. Then have students apply the concept of biomimicry to the stretched wing structures found in modern-day flying squirrels (shown on the Flipchart) and extinct pterosaurs.

Guided Inquiry

FLIPCHART P. 23

40–60 minutes

small groups

Students should follow the directions on the Flipchart. The accompanying Lesson Inquiry pages in the Student Edition provide scaffolding for guided inquiry.

Inquiry Skills Focus Plan and Conduct Simple Investigations, Identify and Control Variables, Draw Conclusions

Objectives

- Observe and record how light affects germination rate.
- Observe and record how amount of water affects germination rate.
- Infer what other factors may affect germination rate.

Prep and Planning Tips

See the Planning for Inquiry page for more information.

- Make sure students do not cover seeds with more than 3 cm of soil. They should place the same number of seeds in each of the cups.

Expected Results

All of the bean seeds given water are likely to germinate in either location. However, only the seeds given the correct amount of water and placed in light will grow well. The germinated seeds growing under the shoe box will have growth that is spindly, indicating that these plants are unhealthy.

1 Engage/Explore

Attention Grabber

Show students a sealed plastic bag containing bean seeds that sprouted in the bag two weeks earlier. Pass the bag around the classroom and have students brainstorm reasons why the seedlings are now dead or dying. Students may ask: Where was the bag kept? Was it in the dark? Did you add water? Was the bag always kept closed? Students may suggest that the seedlings are dying because they did not have light, air, or soil or because they had too much water. Use the discussion to spark students' curiosity about what plants need to grow.

Preview Activity

Before beginning the investigation, have students review the directions on the Inquiry Flipchart and the accompanying Student Edition response pages. Then have them complete the response pages as they follow directions on the Flipchart.

Inquiry Flipchart page 23

Lesson 4 INQUIRY

Name ____________________

Essential Question

What Factors Affect Germination Rate?

Set a Purpose

Why is it important to know the factors that affect germination?

Sample answer: People use plants for many things, and so it is important for people to know how to grow plants effectively.

Think About the Procedure

Which two factors are you testing in this activity?

Cups A and B will test how light affects germination rate. Cups C, D, and E will test how water affects germination rate.

Record Your Data

In the space below, make a table to record your observations.

Students should make tables in which they can record the germination rates of the seeds in the five different cups.

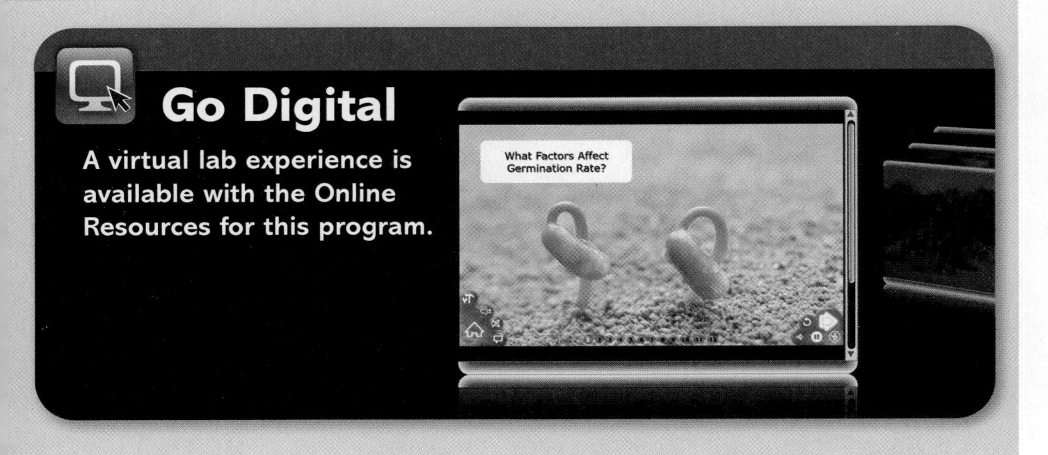

Guide the Investigation

Develop Inquiry Skills

IDENTIFY AND CONTROL VARIABLES

Explain to students that they are essentially doing two different experiments in this investigation. In each experiment, they will be changing only one thing. The factor that they change is called a *variable*.

What is the variable in Step 3 of the experiment? the amount of light the seedlings receive

How will you make sure the seeds in one cup get more light than the seeds in the other cup? I will place one cup under a box so no light can reach it, and I will place the other cup in an area with light.

What is the variable in Step 4 of the experiment? the amount of water the seeds receive

How will you make sure the seeds in the three cups get the correct amount of water? I will add no water to cup *C*; each day I will add 40 mL and 80 mL of water, respectively, to cups *D* and *E*.

PREDICT **What do you think will happen to the seeds?** Answers will vary. Some students may suggest that all of the seeds that got water will germinate, but only the seeds with light and an appropriate amount of water will grow into healthy plants.

GATHER AND RECORD DATA Discuss with students how they will make a table and then record their results.

At a minimum, students' data tables should have five rows—a row for each cup. Students should have a column for each day they make observations. The date should be recorded in that column.

2 Explain

Develop Inquiry Skills

DRAW CONCLUSIONS Remind students to revisit their predictions and to draw conclusions about whether the data they gathered supported their predictions. Remind students to consider the results of experiments objectively and honestly.

ANALYZE AND EXTEND Discuss students' responses to the items.

1. Have students consider all of the preparations they did to the seeds before starting their experiment. For example, they first filled the cups with soil. Then they sprinkled only a certain amount of soil on top of the seeds. Ask students why these steps were important.
2. Remind students that they should change only one thing in their experiment (the tested variable). Tell them that they should explain precisely how they would change the tested variable (e.g., how much soil they will use in each experimental condition).

3 Extend/Evaluate

3. Accept reasonable answers. Some students may ask questions about factors or conditions that affect the rate at which a different kind of seed might germinate.
4. Students should take measurements and keep records. These records will help you judge the accuracy of their summaries.

Assessment

Lesson Quiz

See Assessment Guide, p. AG 41.

Draw Conclusions

Which plants grew the most? Which plants grew the least?

Sample answer: Plants A and C grew the least. Plants B and E grew the most.

How does light affect seed germination?

Sample answer: The seeds with access to sunlight germinated fastest and grew more than the seeds with little or no sunlight.

How does water affect seed germination?

Sample answer: The seeds given the most water germinated and grew the fastest.

Analyze and Extend

1. **What other factor do you think might affect germination?**

   Sample answer: The depth the seed is placed in the soil might affect germination.

2. **How could you test this factor?**

   Sample answer: I could place seeds on top of the soil, under 5 cm of soil, and under 10 cm of soil to see which seeds germinated first.

3. **What other questions would you like to ask about germination rates?**

   Sample answer: Will flowers grow bigger if they get more water each day?

4. **Choose one question you wrote and investigate it. Write a summary of your investigation.**

   Answers will vary. Approve the procedure for each investigation before it is conducted and verify the accuracy of the summary.

Differentiated Inquiry

Easy

Investigate Temperature

- Encourage students to repeat the seed-sprouting experiment at home, except with a new variable: temperature.
- Have students place one cup of seeds in a refrigerator and another cup of seeds under a shoe box at room temperature. Both cups should be given water daily.
- Ask students to report their results.

Easy

Do Germinated Seeds Need Soil to Grow Well?

- Ask students whether they think germinated seeds need soil to grow well. Then have them conduct an experiment to find out.
- Students place germinated bean seeds in a cup filled with soil, and then place the same number of germinated seeds between two moist paper towels. Place both groups of seeds in a shaded area, keep moist, and observe for several days.
- Ask students to report their results.

Average

Observe a Life Cycle

- Have students grow a fast-growing flowering plant, such as a rapid-cycling *Brassica* plant.
- Students should water and observe the plant every day. Encourage students to take a photograph or draw a picture of the plant during their observations.
- Ask students to use their photographs or drawings to make a poster about the plant's life cycle.

Challenging

Which Type of Soil?

- Have students use an online encyclopedia or nonfiction books from the school library to research different types of soil (clay, silt, sand, or mixtures thereof).
- Students should form a hypothesis about which type of soil bean seeds would sprout and grow best in.
- Next, have students prepare mixtures that represent at least three different soil types.
- Students should conduct an experiment by trying to sprout and grow bean seeds in the different soil mixtures.
- Ask students to report their results.

Options for Inquiry

FLIPCHART P. 24

Students can conduct these optional investigations at any time before, during, or in response to the lesson in the Student Edition.

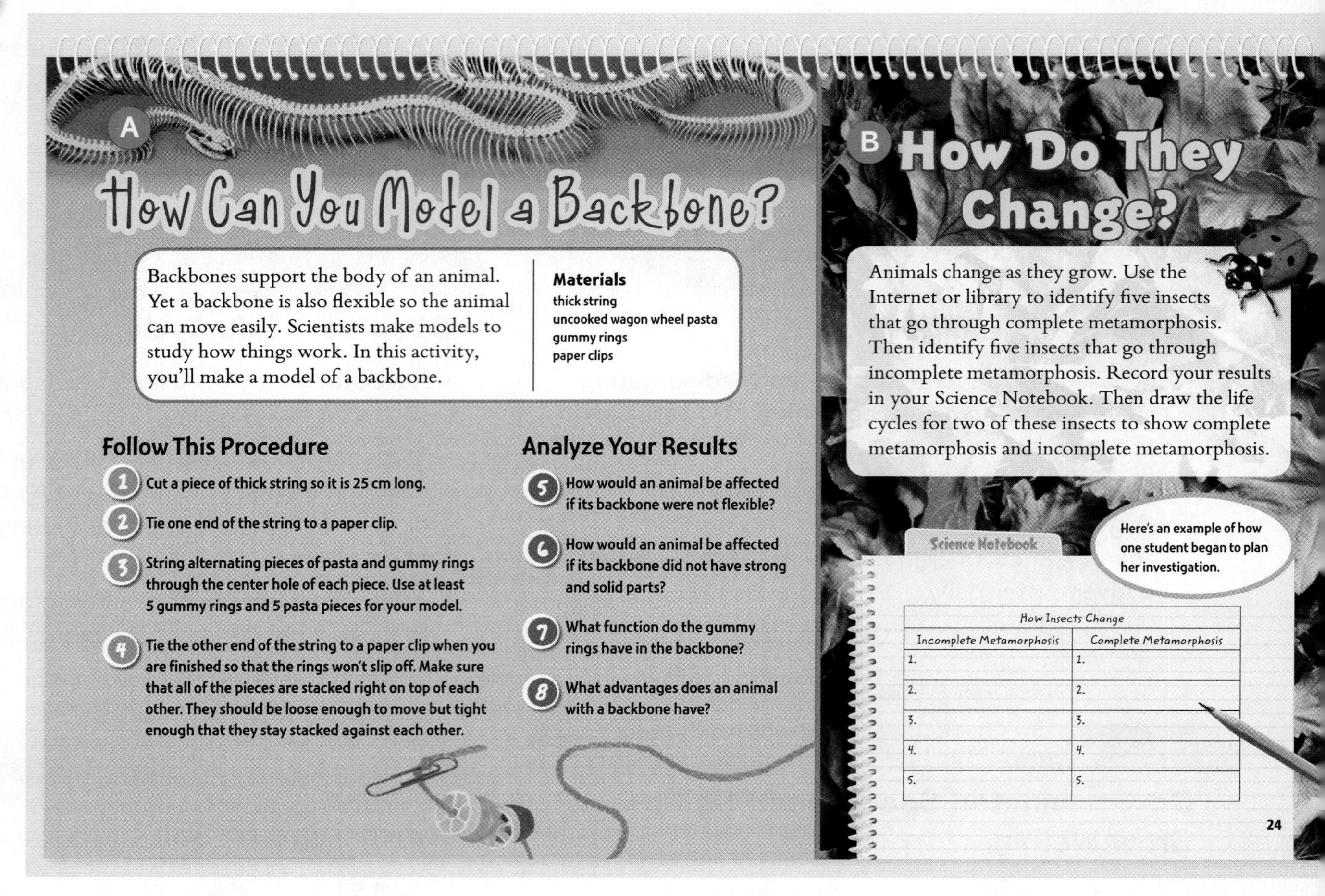

A **How Can You Model a Backbone?**

Backbones support the body of an animal. Yet a backbone is also flexible so the animal can move easily. Scientists make models to study how things work. In this activity, you'll make a model of a backbone.

Materials
thick string
uncooked wagon wheel pasta
gummy rings
paper clips

Follow This Procedure

1. Cut a piece of thick string so it is 25 cm long.
2. Tie one end of the string to a paper clip.
3. String alternating pieces of pasta and gummy rings through the center hole of each piece. Use at least 5 gummy rings and 5 pasta pieces for your model.
4. Tie the other end of the string to a paper clip when you are finished so that the rings won't slip off. Make sure that all of the pieces are stacked right on top of each other. They should be loose enough to move but tight enough that they stay stacked against each other.

Analyze Your Results

5. How would an animal be affected if its backbone were not flexible?
6. How would an animal be affected if its backbone did not have strong and solid parts?
7. What function do the gummy rings have in the backbone?
8. What advantages does an animal with a backbone have?

B **How Do They Change?**

Animals change as they grow. Use the Internet or library to identify five insects that go through complete metamorphosis. Then identify five insects that go through incomplete metamorphosis. Record your results in your Science Notebook. Then draw the life cycles for two of these insects to show complete metamorphosis and incomplete metamorphosis.

Science Notebook

Here's an example of how one student began to plan her investigation.

How Insects Change

Incomplete Metamorphosis	Complete Metamorphosis
1.	1.
2.	2.
3.	3.
4.	4.
5.	5.

24

Directed Inquiry

A How Can You Model a Backbone?

15–20 minutes
individuals

Prep and Planning Tips

- Make sure that you have enough wagon wheel pasta and gummy rings for the exercise. It will require a minimum of five pieces of both pasta and gummy rings per model, although students may use more.
- To save time, cut 20 cm lengths of string prior to class and tie a paper clip to one end of each piece of string. If paper clips are not available, tie a large knot in the end of the string so that the pasta does not slip off.

Expected Results

Students should make a workable model of a backbone that shows how the backbone is made up of stiff materials (pasta wheels) separated by softer materials (gummy pieces) that support and protect the spinal cord, yet allow for flexibility.

Independent Inquiry

B How Do They Change?

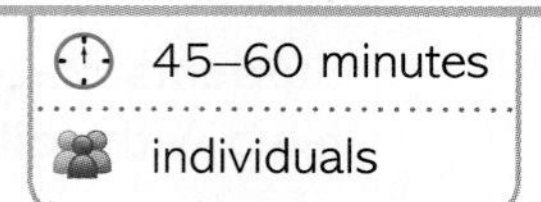

Prep and Planning Tips

Identify possible sources for students to use for their research. Students will need additional time to complete their drawings.

Notebook

Science Notebook

Students can use the sample Science Notebook page as a model for recording data from their initial research. Remind students that even though they are to identify ten insects—five that undergo incomplete metamorphosis and five that undergo complete metamorphosis—they are only to draw the life cycles of two insects in each category. Suggest that students sketch the stages of the life cycles in their Science Notebooks.

Go Digital

An interactive digital lesson is available in the Online Resources. It is suitable for individuals, small groups, or may be projected or used on an interactive white board.

1 Engage/Explore

Objectives

- Describe how vertebrates and invertebrates are classified, and identify members of each group.
- Recognize that animal growth involves life cycles.
- Identify the stages of complete and incomplete metamorphosis.

Engage Your Brain!

Ask students to think about the different forms that animals take as they grow. Have students describe how they can recognize if an animal is young or old. Direct students to these descriptions to formulate initial answers to the questions *How are these organisms similar? How are they different?* Remind students to record their final answer to the question when they find it in the lesson.

Active Reading Annotations

Remind students that active readers "make texts their own" by annotating them with notes and marks that help with comprehension. Encourage students to use pencil, not pen, to make annotations and to feel free to change their annotations as they read. The goal of annotation is to help students remember what they have read.

Vocabulary and Interactive Glossary

Remind students to find and list the yellow highlighted terms from the lesson. As they proceed through the lesson and learn about the terms, they should add notes, drawings, or sentences in the extra spaces in the Interactive Glossary.

2 Explain

Notebook Generate Ideas

After students preview the title, photographs, and introductory sentences on these pages, direct them to reach around and feel the bone running up the middle of their backs and necks. Explain that, like all of the living things shown on these two pages, they have a backbone. Share that another term for organisms that have backbones is *vertebrates*.

Active Reading

Remind students that the main idea may be stated in the first sentence, or it may be stated elsewhere. To find a main idea, active readers ask, What is this passage mostly about?

Interpret Visuals

Ask students to look at the snake backbone. **What is a backbone made of?** A backbone is made up of a series of bones that are joined together in a line or rod shape.

What purpose does a backbone serve? A backbone gives support to an animal and provides protection.

How could you test to see if an animal has a backbone or not? You could look or feel along the back of an animal to see if it has a hard structure running along the middle of its back.

HAVE A BACKBONE?

How are birds and fish similar? They have backbones! What other animals have backbones?

Active Reading As you read this page, underline the main idea.

Animals differ so much that you may wonder what factors scientists could ever use to classify them. One of the major factors that scientists use when classifying animals is whether an animal has a backbone. **Vertebrates** are animals with backbones. Look at the different vertebrates on these pages. Find other factors that scientists may use to classify these animals.

Most backbones are made up of bones that are linked together, as you can see in the snake backbone above.

Fish are vertebrates that live in water. They use gills to take in oxygen present in water.

Frogs are amphibians. Amphibians are vertebrates with smooth skin. Most amphibians live part of their lives on land and part in water.

210

Differentiation — Leveled Questions

Extra Support

Which types of vertebrates might you find in water? fish and amphibians

Challenge

Some people are born with some of the bones in their backbones fused together. What problem might this cause? These people might have trouble moving, since the flexibility of their backbone is diminished.

A snake is a reptile. Reptiles are vertebrates with scaly skin. Most reptiles live on land and some live in water.

Because the bones are separate and linked, as opposed to one solid bone, backbones are flexible. Flexibility allows vertebrates to move easily.

Vertebrates can be grouped into five classes: mammals, birds, reptiles, amphibians, and fish. Even though most of the animals you can name are probably vertebrates, these animals make up only about 4.5% of all animal species!

Mammals are vertebrates that have hair or fur on their bodies. Young mammals drink milk from their mothers' bodies.

Draw a Vertebrate

This dog is a vertebrate. Draw in the body part that causes it to be classified in this way. What did you draw?

Students should draw a segmented backbone on the dog.

a backbone

Birds are vertebrates with feathers and wings. Most birds can fly.

211

Math Connection

Solve a Problem Remind students that scientists classify animals into two large groups—vertebrates and invertebrates. If only 4.5% of Earth's animal species are vertebrates, what percent are invertebrates ? 100% – 4.5% = 95.5% 95.5% of animal species are invertebrates.

Develop Science Vocabulary

vertebrate Tell students that a backbone is also known as a spine. Have them practice substituting the word *spine* for the word *backbone* in sentences in the text.

Develop Science Concepts

What are the five types of vertebrates shown on these two pages? reptiles, amphibians, birds, fish, and mammals

Are most animals on Earth classified as vertebrates? No; only about 4.5% of Earth's animals are vertebrates.

Interpret Visuals

If students have difficulty completing the Interactivity, direct them to the images of the snakes. Suggest they visualize where the backbone is placed inside the snake. Remind them of where their own backbone is. Then direct them to draw a backbone on the dog.

As an extension, show photographs of the skeletons of different vertebrates. Work together as a class to identify which part of each skeleton is the backbone.

Notebook Summarize Ideas

Ask students to summarize the information on these pages by stating the definition of *vertebrate*, either orally or in writing. Suggest they list in their Science Notebooks the five different types of vertebrates shown, along with descriptions and examples of each.

2 Explain (continued)

Notebook Generate Ideas

Ask students to preview the section by reading the title, introductory text, and captions. Explain that every organism shown is an invertebrate. Have students brainstorm the characteristic they all have in common. (They all lack backbones.)

Active Reading

Remind students that signal words show connections among ideas. *For example* and *for instance* signal examples of an idea. *Also* and *in fact* signal added facts. Active readers remember what they read because they are alert to signal words.

Develop Science Concepts

Explain that scientists classify invertebrates by whether they have tissues, whether they have a body cavity, and what type of body cavity they have. Other characteristics they examine are body symmetry and whether their bodies are segmented.

As students review the photos, make sure they understand that the marine sponge is not a plant or a rock, but is instead a simple invertebrate that is anchored to the sea floor.

Why are all the animals shown on these pages classified as invertebrates? They do not have backbones.

You are standing in a field. Are you likely to be surrounded by more vertebrates or more invertebrates? Invertebrates; they make up about 95.5% of animal species.

What do some invertebrates use for support in place of a backbone? Shells and hard skins or hard covering

Which type of animal is most the most numerous on Earth? insects

"SPINELESS" INVERTEBRATES

Spider

About 95.5% of all animals lack backbones! What kind of animals could these be?

Active Reading As you read these two pages, circle the clue words that signal a detail such as an example or an added fact.

Animals without backbones are **invertebrates**. Invertebrates vary from very simple sponges to complex insects. Invertebrates fill the coral reefs in the oceans and break down dead matter in soil. Some invertebrates even serve as food for humans!

The simplest invertebrates are corals, sponges, and jellyfish. You are probably familiar with earthworms. Earthworms are invertebrates that break down materials in soil.

Mollusks, such as the whelk, are more complex. Many mollusks have a shell that protects their soft bodies. Squid are mollusks that have internal shells. Octopi are mollusks that do not have shells at all.

Whelk

Marine sponge

212

Math Connection

Symmetry One way scientists classify organisms is on the basis of symmetry. Vertebrates and arthropods are generally bilaterally symmetrical—the left side is a mirror image of the right. Many echinoderms have radial, or five-part symmetry. Sponges often have no symmetry and are called asymmetrical. Challenge students to find out about the symmetry of different invertebrates. Have them draw different animals and indicate their lines of symmetry. Have students share their drawings with the class.

Do the Math!

Analyze Data

Number of Species of Some Invertebrates (estimated)	
Mollusks	85,000 species
Arachnids	102,000 species
Crustaceans	47,000 species
Insects	1,000,000 species

Use the table to answer the questions.

If you were to find an invertebrate, what type of invertebrate would it most likely be? Why?

insect; There are many more insect species than any other kind of invertebrate.

How many more species of this type are there than all of the other listed invertebrates combined?

1,000,000 – 234,000 = 766,000

The reef lobster is a crustacean.

Echinoderms, such as sea urchins and sea stars, are invertebrates that live in salt water. When fully grown, they have body parts in multiples of five.

The largest group of invertebrates is the *arthropod* group. Arthropods have body parts in segments. The arthropod group includes crustaceans, spiders, and insects. *Crustaceans* have hard exterior shells and five pairs of jointed limbs. Spiders have two body segments and eight legs. Insects have antennae, jaws, and three body segments. There are more insect species on Earth than all other animal species combined.

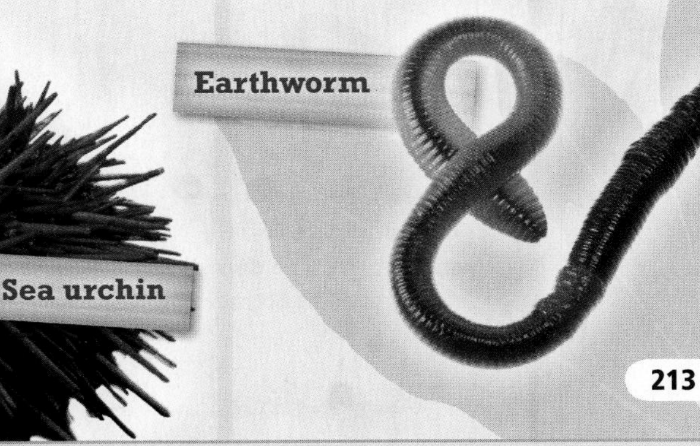

Earthworm

Sea urchin

213

Writing Connection

Write a Description Suggest that students research how invertebrates with hard outer skeletons, such as crabs and lobsters, shed and replace their skeletons as they grow. Have students illustrate the stages that these animals go through and include extended captions that describe how this process, called molting, works.

Develop Science Vocabulary

invertebrate Point out that the word *invertebrate* is simply the word *vertebrate* with the prefix *in–* at the beginning. Remind students that adding the prefix *in–* to a word makes it an antonym with the opposite meaning. For example, *inactive* is the opposite of *active,* and *involuntary* is the opposite of *voluntary*.

Do the Math!

Analyze Data

As students read the first question, ask for suggestions about to how to solve the problem. Review the approximate number of the different types of invertebrates listed in the table. Point out that the number of insect species is far more than all other types of invertebrates put together. Have students use this information to solve the problem.

Make sure that students understand that the second problem has multiple parts. They must use the answer to problem 1 (insects) as a starting point. Next, they must add up the number of species that are *not* insects. 85,000 + 102,000 + 47,000 = 234,000 Finally, they must subtract the number of "other" species from the number of insect species. 1,000,000 – 234,000 = 766,000

Notebook Summarize Ideas

Have students summarize these two pages using an idea web graphic organizer. Direct students to write the main idea at the top of the chart and then to draw lines from the main idea in which they can write details. Suggest that they include a detail box for each group discussed on this page: simplest invertebrates (sponges, corals, jellyfish, earthworms), mollusks, echinoderms, and arthropods (crustaceans, spiders, insects).

2 **Explain** (continued)

Notebook Generate Ideas

Have students brainstorm answers to this question: **If you could not speak to one another, how could you share information?** Point out that animals cannot talk, but they have other means of communicating.

Develop Inquiry Skills

INFER **Why is it important for animals to communicate with one another?** Animals must communicate to find mates, to convey the location of food sources, to signal danger, and to mark territory.

Which senses are used by animals for communication? Animals use sound, touch, smell, and visual cues to communicate.

Interpret Visuals

Direct students to study the trail of ants on this page. Point out that the ants are following each other in a line. Ask if students have observed this behavior in nature. **How are the ants on this page able to follow long, invisible pathways to a food source and then back home?** They are leaving invisible chemicals that give off a scent that can be recognized and followed by other ants.

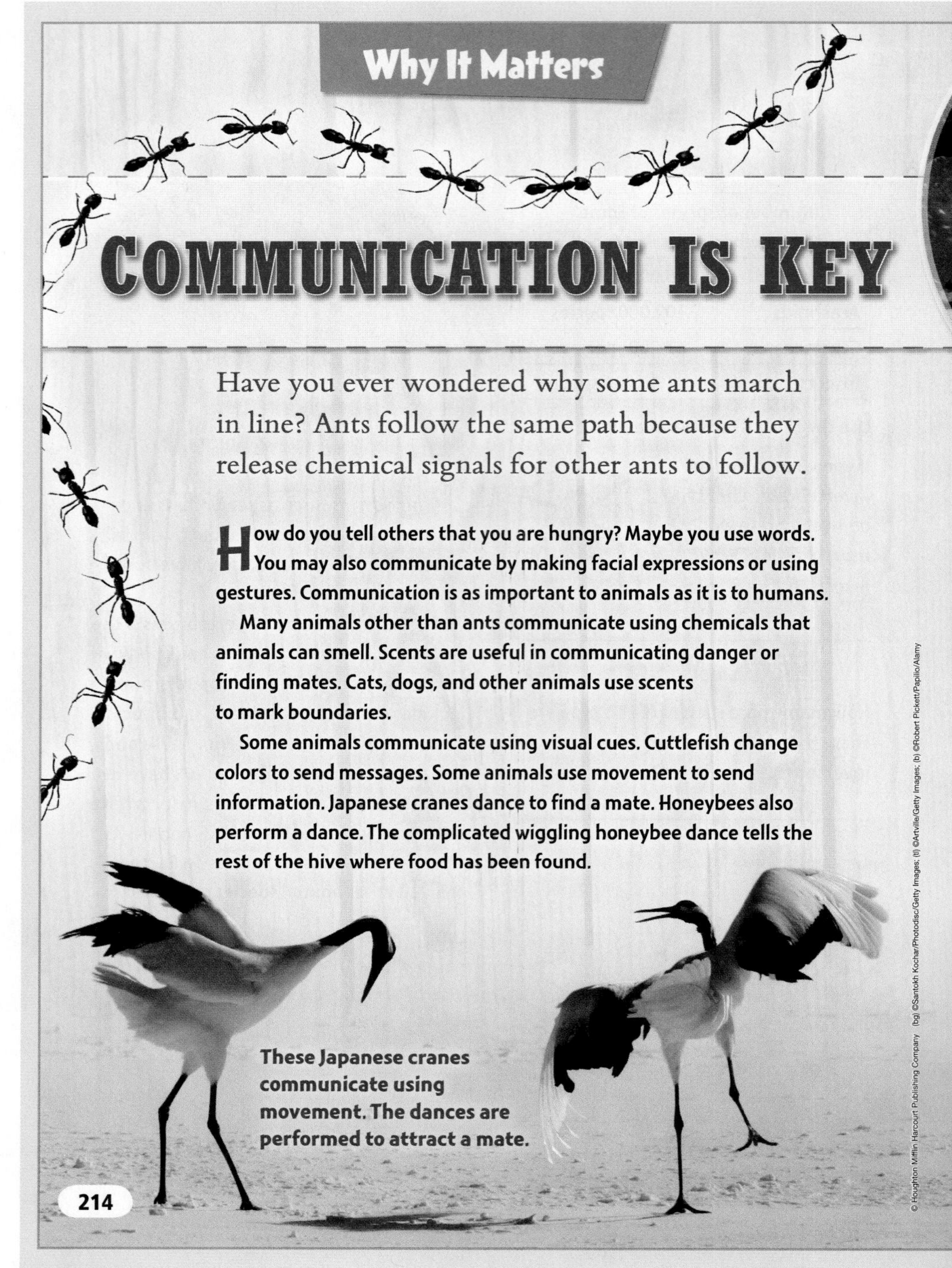

Why It Matters

COMMUNICATION IS KEY

Have you ever wondered why some ants march in line? Ants follow the same path because they release chemical signals for other ants to follow.

How do you tell others that you are hungry? Maybe you use words. You may also communicate by making facial expressions or using gestures. Communication is as important to animals as it is to humans.

Many animals other than ants communicate using chemicals that animals can smell. Scents are useful in communicating danger or finding mates. Cats, dogs, and other animals use scents to mark boundaries.

Some animals communicate using visual cues. Cuttlefish change colors to send messages. Some animals use movement to send information. Japanese cranes dance to find a mate. Honeybees also perform a dance. The complicated wiggling honeybee dance tells the rest of the hive where food has been found.

These Japanese cranes communicate using movement. The dances are performed to attract a mate.

214

Differentiation — Leveled Questions

Extra Support

What might happen if Japanese cranes lost the ability to dance? They might not be able to attract mates.

Challenge

Given that ants communicate by using chemicals, how might you keep ants from coming into your home? Sample answer: I could find a chemical that ants do not like. They would not follow that chemical into my home.

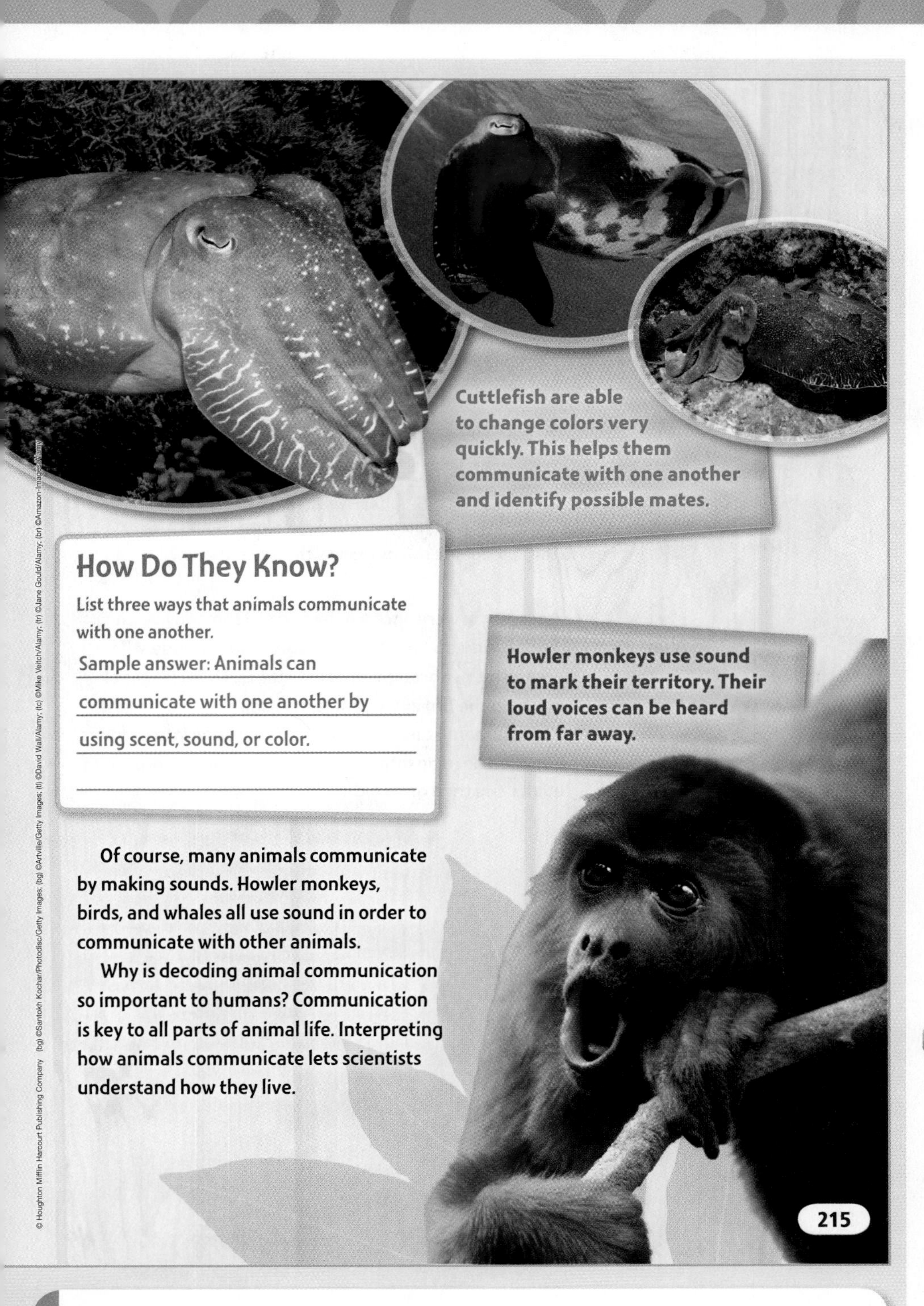

Cuttlefish are able to change colors very quickly. This helps them communicate with one another and identify possible mates.

How Do They Know?

List three ways that animals communicate with one another.

Sample answer: Animals can communicate with one another by using scent, sound, or color.

Howler monkeys use sound to mark their territory. Their loud voices can be heard from far away.

Of course, many animals communicate by making sounds. Howler monkeys, birds, and whales all use sound in order to communicate with other animals.

Why is decoding animal communication so important to humans? Communication is key to all parts of animal life. Interpreting how animals communicate lets scientists understand how they live.

215

English Language Learners

Nonverbal Communication Ask English learners to describe the ways they learn to communicate when they are having difficulty with language. Ask them to demonstrate some ways in which body language or facial expression can convey information.

Interpret Visuals

Direct students to the photos of the cuttlefish. **How might different colors be effective in cuttlefish communication?** Explain that cuttlefish will often change colors to show that they are ready to mate. Other cuttlefish will change color to signal that they do not wish to mate.

Look at the first cuttlefish photo. What other function might changing color serve? The cuttlefish is the same color as the algae that surrounds it. Changing to this color may serve a protective function.

How is the howler monkey communicating in the photo on this page? The howler monkey uses sounds to communicate.

What other animals use sounds to communicate? Sample answers: dogs, owls, whales, lions, songbirds, roosters, humans

Develop Science Concepts

If students are having difficulty completing the Interactivity, encourage them to reread the photo captions and use the examples as their answers.

Notebook Summarize Ideas

Have students review the concepts presented here by listing the different forms of animal communication and pointing out the examples of each shown. Then have students devise a statement that sums up the information on animal communication. Have them share their summary statements either orally or in writing.

2 Explain (continued)

Notebook Generate Ideas

Have students list the stages of life in the order in which they will experience them as humans. Write this list on the board. Brainstorm with the class whether all animals experience stages of life in the same way. Ask them to provide examples that justify their answers.

Active Reading

Remind students that sequence, or order, is important in text that describes the development of an idea or the steps in a process. Active readers stay focused on the sequence when they mark the transition from one stage of an idea or step in a process to another.

Interpret Visuals

Have students follow the human life stages shown on these pages. Return to the list students brainstormed in Generate Ideas. Have them match the stages they brainstormed to the photos shown here. **Even though the people shown here are not the same person, how could we show that these stages flow one into the other?** Sample answer: We could number the photos. **How could this cycle be completed?** If the adult had a child, the cycle would be complete.

Direct students to the photo of the scorpion at the top of the page. Explain that scorpions give birth to live young. The young are unable to protect themselves, so the mother scorpion carries her young on her back to keep them safe. **How do other organisms keep their young safe?** Sample answer: Many living things protect and feed their young until the young are able to live on their own.

STAGES OF LIFE

These young scorpions are different from their mother. How will they change over time?

Active Reading As you read this page, write numbers next to the appropriate stages to show the order of events.

Just as you were once a baby and will someday be an adult, other living things also grow and change. All organisms go through different stages. These stages all make up the **life cycle** of an organism.

All humans start off as infants.[1] They grow into toddlers[2] and then develop into children.[3] Finally, humans grow into adults[4] and then grow old.[5]

216

English Language Learners

Understanding Cycles *Life cycle* refers to the continuous repeating sequence of life stages. *Cycle* means "a circular series." Show students pictures of other terms that include the word cycle (bicycle, motorcycle). Point out that these devices have wheels, which turn around and around. Work with students to draw human and duck life cycles in the circular shape. Ask students to think of other things that have cycles (moon phases, the seasons). Present these cycles in a circular diagram as well.

Every life cycle begins with a fertilized egg. In some animals, like birds or reptiles, the egg may be enclosed in a hard or leathery protective shell, from which the young hatch. The eggs of most mammals develop inside the mothers' bodies. After a young organism develops from the egg, it will continue to grow.

The development of an organism can happen very quickly, or it may take many years. The organism grows larger and changes as it develops. When it is an adult, it is able to live on its own. Now the organism can reproduce, or make its own offspring. The organism will continue to age. Eventually, it dies.

From an egg to a hatchling, a duck changes as it grows.

▶ Draw a line from the young stage of each animal to its adult stage.

kitten	goose
puppy	cat
colt	human adult
gosling	horse
human child	dog
chick	chicken

Mature Adult

Writing Connection

Expository Text Ask students to choose an animal that is not shown on these pages. Have them research and draw a life cycle for that animal. Tell them to include a description of the sequence of events with their life cycle. Descriptions should be complete enough so that a person who had not read this lesson would understand the life cycle stages.

Develop Science Vocabulary

life cycle Have students look up the definition of *cycle*. It refers to a series of occurrences that repeats. Point out that in order to be complete, life cycles of living things involve more than one organism. Individual organisms are born, age, and die in a linear fashion.

Misconception Alert

Make sure students understand that the stages of animal development are not a sequence of distinct and dramatic changes. Between each of the stages shown, the organism undergoes subtle changes until it reaches the appearance of the next stage.

Develop Inquiry Skills

OBSERVE **How does size change as an organism moves through the life cycle?** Generally, organisms start off small and then grow larger. Eventually they reach an adult size and stop growing.

COMPARE **How is the beginning stage of a duck and a human the same and different?** Both start their life cycles as fertilized eggs. In ducks, eggs are enclosed in a shell from which the young hatch. In humans, eggs develop inside the mother, and the young are born live.

Notebook Summarize Ideas

Have students summarize this section by listing, either orally or in writing, the stages of a life cycle that could be applied to most organisms. Conclude by having students complete the Interactivity. Suggest that students first make the matches they are confident of, and complete the rest through the process of elimination.

2 Explain (continued)

Generate Ideas

Ask students to preview the two metamorphosis life cycles on these pages. Ask them to describe what they think is happening in the cycles. Point out that unlike the life cycles on the previous pages, the stages that these animals are experiencing are very different looking. Have students note any differences between the two graphics, and encourage them to write or draw notes on the graphics detailing these differences before they begin this section.

Active Reading

Remind students that signal words show connections among ideas. Words that signal comparisons, or similarities, include *alike, same as, similar to,* and *resembles*. Active readers remember what they read because they are alert to signal words.

Develop Inquiry Skills

CONCLUDE **What happens during metamorphosis?** An animal goes through different stages as it grows. The stages can be very different in form and function from one another.

Which type of animals undergo metamorphosis? Insects are the most common animals to undergo metamorphosis. However, frogs and some other animals also undergo metamorphosis as they grow.

Misconception Alert

Upon observing a small insect with wings, people tend to think it is a baby insect that is still growing. Explain that once an insect has wings, it is a fully developed adult, no matter what its size.

It's Time for a Change

Some animals don't just get larger as they grow. An animal may change so much that at different stages it doesn't even look like the same organism!

Active Reading As you read these two pages, draw boxes around the clue words that signal things are being compared.

Some organisms completely change form as they grow. This process is called metamorphosis. Insects are the most common animals that undergo metamorphosis.

In **complete metamorphosis**, an insect, such as this ladybug, goes through four different stages in its life cycle.

1. The insect begins life as an egg.
2. The egg hatches to produce a *larva*. The larva eats and quickly grows in size.
3. A larva develops into a *pupa*. Because the pupa does not move, this is often called the "resting stage." Although it is not moving in the pupa stage, the insect's body is undergoing dramatic change.
4. The adult emerges from the pupa. The adult insect can fly and reproduce.

Complete Metamorphosis

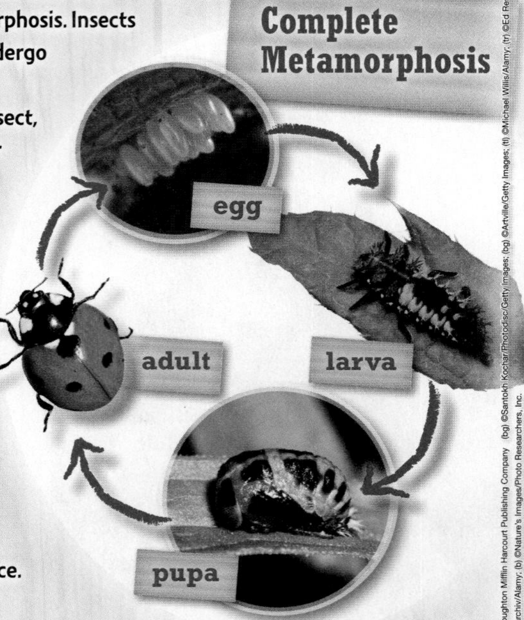

218

Differentiation — Leveled Questions

Extra Support

Which type of metamorphosis includes a nymph stage? incomplete metamorphosis

Which stages do both types of metamorphosis have in common? the egg and adult stages

Challenge

You find an empty shell on the ground in the form of an insect. What happened to produce this shell? The shell is the molting of a growing nymph.

Another type of metamorphosis that occurs in some insects is incomplete metamorphosis. **Incomplete metamorphosis** has three stages: the egg, the *nymph*, and the adult. The nymph stage looks like a smaller version of the adult, but a nymph cannot fly or reproduce. As the nymph grows, it *molts*, or sheds its hard outer shell. The nymph molts several times until it finally becomes an adult.

Metamorphosis is not limited to insects. Frogs also undergo metamorphosis as they go from egg to tadpole to adult. Can you think of any other animals that undergo metamorphosis?

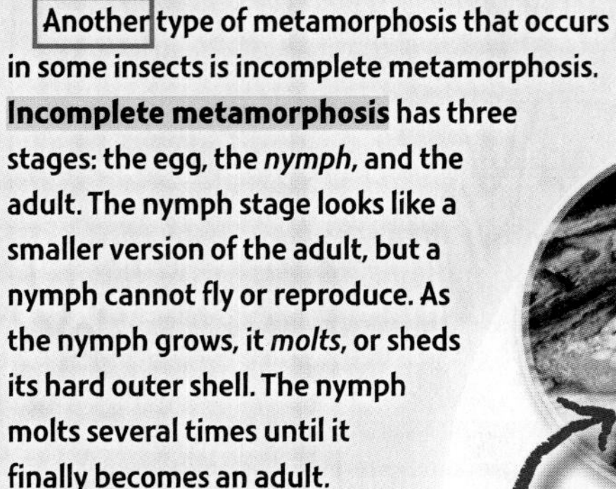

Incomplete Metamorphosis

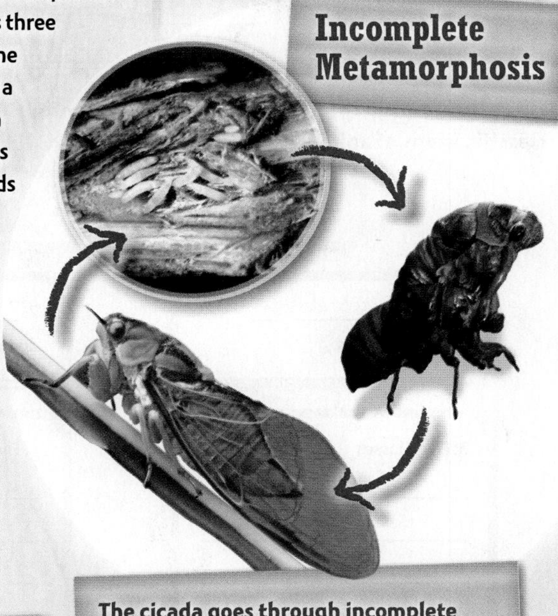

The cicada goes through incomplete metamorphosis. A small nymph emerges from the egg. The nymph grows and molts until it becomes a mature adult.

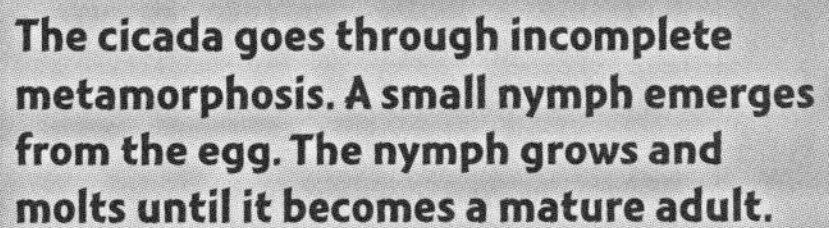

Insect Life Cycles

You see an insect egg lying on a leaf. Which stage is next? Name or describe the stage you would expect to see come out from the egg if the insect undergoes:

a. incomplete metamorphosis: nymph

b. complete metamorphosis: larva

Writing Connection

Diagrams with Extended Captions Ask students to research and choose an insect that is not shown on these pages that undergoes metamorphosis. Direct students to make a life cycle diagram specifically for that insect. Diagrams should include informative captions that describe each stage of metamorphosis shown.

Develop Science Vocabulary

complete metamorphosis Ask students to think about what the term *complete* means. Students may look up the definition, which is "to have all the parts." Use the graphics to show students that complete metamorphosis includes all the different parts or stages possible. These stages include egg, larva, pupa, and adult.

incomplete metamorphosis Contrast the definition of *incomplete metamorphosis* with that of *complete metamorphosis.* When something is incomplete, it lacks some parts or elements. Insects undergoing incomplete metamorphosis do not go through larva and pupa stages. Since these stages are missing, the metamorphosis is incomplete.

Develop Science Concepts

Tell students that during the larva, pupa, and adult stages of complete metamorphosis, insects typically eat different kinds of foods. **How would eating different foods during the stages of metamorphosis be an advantage to an insect?** Because they eat different foods, younger insects are not competing for food with the adults.

Develop Inquiry Skills

INFER **Why do you think that some insects are considered pests only during the larva stage?** The larva may eat crops or other plants that humans desire.

Notebook Summarize Ideas

Have students look again at the diagrams for complete and incomplete metamorphosis. Have them summarize the two processes orally or in writing. Have students use their summaries to complete the Interactivity box.

3 Extend/Evaluate

Sum It Up!

- Help students to understand the organization of the graphic organizer before they complete it. For example, the top box indicates the main idea of the organizer: animals. The next two boxes divide animals into two main groups: those with backbones and those without backbones. When completed, the bottom boxes indicate additional details about each of the main groups.
- Refer students to the pages in which the different classifications of animals are illustrated with descriptions and examples. Encourage students to use this information to complete the boxes.
- Students will need to be familiar with the stages of both types of metamorphosis in order to complete the Summarize exercise. Encourage them to try and complete the exercise using only memory first. Then have them check their work and make any corrections using lesson material.
- Remind students to check their work against the Answer Key and revise incorrect answers so they can use Sum It Up! to study for tests.

When you're done, use the answer key to check and revise your work.

Fill in the graphic organizer below with information about the classifications of animals.

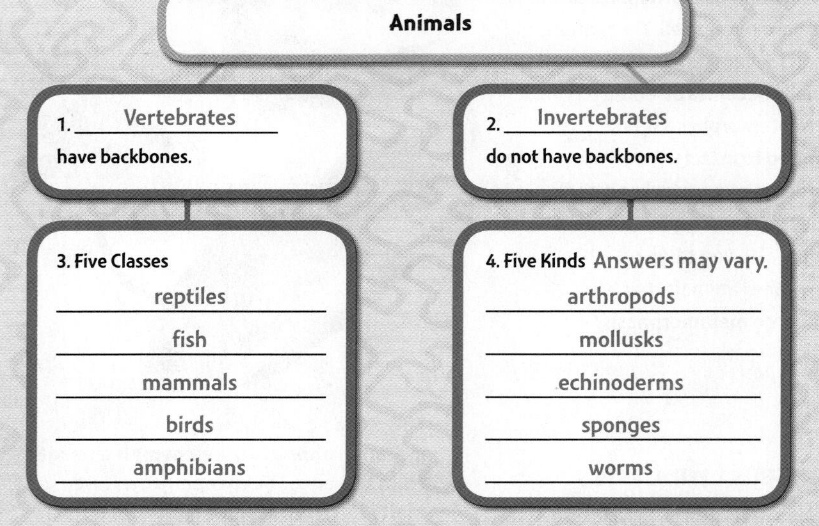

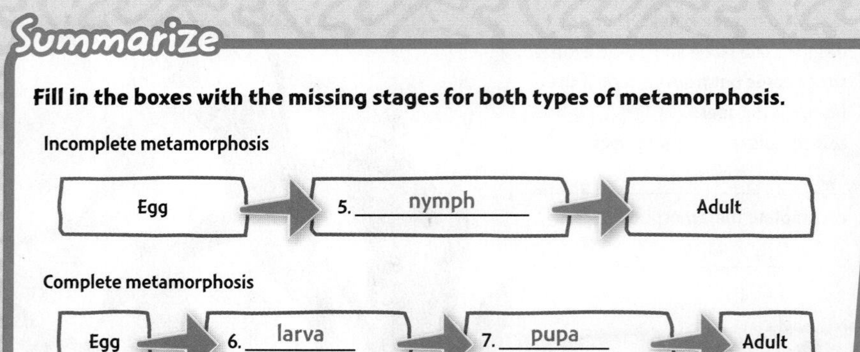

220

Answer Key: 1. Vertebrates 2. Invertebrates 3. Answers may vary: reptiles, fish, mammals, birds, amphibians 4. arthropods, mollusks, echinoderms, sponges, worms 5. nymph 6. larva 7. pupa

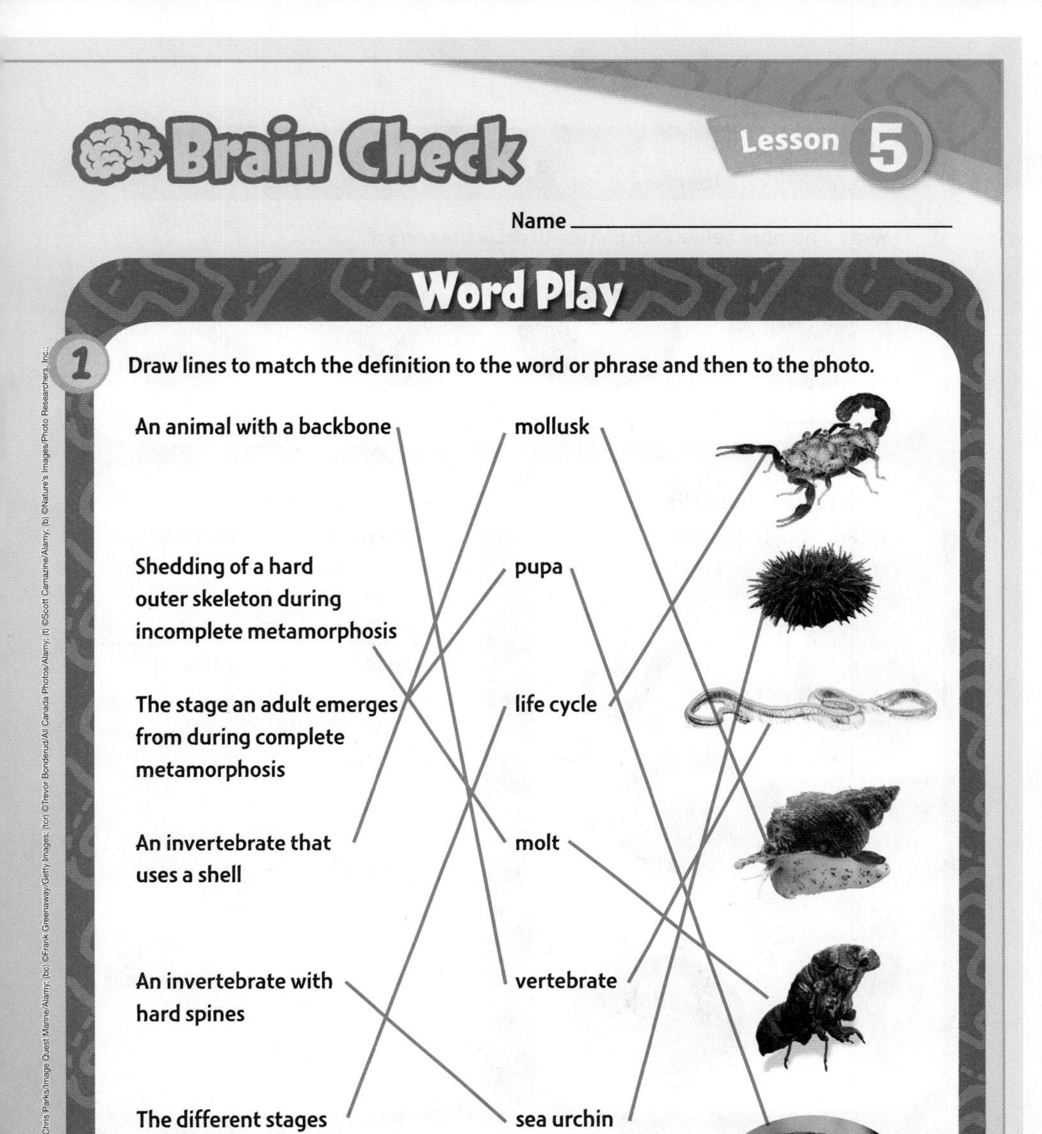

Brain Check

Lesson 5

Name ____________________

Word Play

1. Draw lines to match the definition to the word or phrase and then to the photo.

An animal with a backbone	mollusk
Shedding of a hard outer skeleton during incomplete metamorphosis	pupa
The stage an adult emerges from during complete metamorphosis	life cycle
An invertebrate that uses a shell	molt
An invertebrate with hard spines	vertebrate
The different stages of development of an organism	sea urchin

221

Answer Strategies

Word Play

1. If students are having difficulty matching the definitions/descriptions with the words and photos, have them look through the lesson for the photos shown here. Then have them compare the information on those pages with these definitions and descriptions. As an additional activity, have students make a game in which they write terms and descriptions on two separate cards and draw a picture on a third card. Working with a partner, students must pick the three cards that go together.

Assessment

Suggested Scoring Guide

You may wish to use this suggested scoring guide for the Brain Check.

Item	Points
1	30 (5 points per item)
2	20 (5 points per item)
3	20 (4 points per item)
4	30 (6 points per item)
Total	100

Lesson Quiz

See Assessment Guide, p. AG 42.

3 Extend/Evaluate (continued)

Answer Strategies

Apply Concepts

2. If students are having trouble, suggest that they label the images first, before trying to number them. If they are still struggling, refer them to the complete metamorphosis diagram in the lesson.
3. Review the definitions of vertebrates and invertebrates with the class as a whole. You may wish to run through several examples of both types of animals before having students complete this exercise.
4. Encourage students to try to complete this exercise by first reading the descriptions and then answering without looking at the choices. After going through the descriptions and writing their guesses, have them match up as many as they can. Then have them complete any remaining matches by selecting from the terms that were not used.

Take It Home!

Suggest that students write down their code before communicating with their partner. Encourage students to revise their code to improve communication.

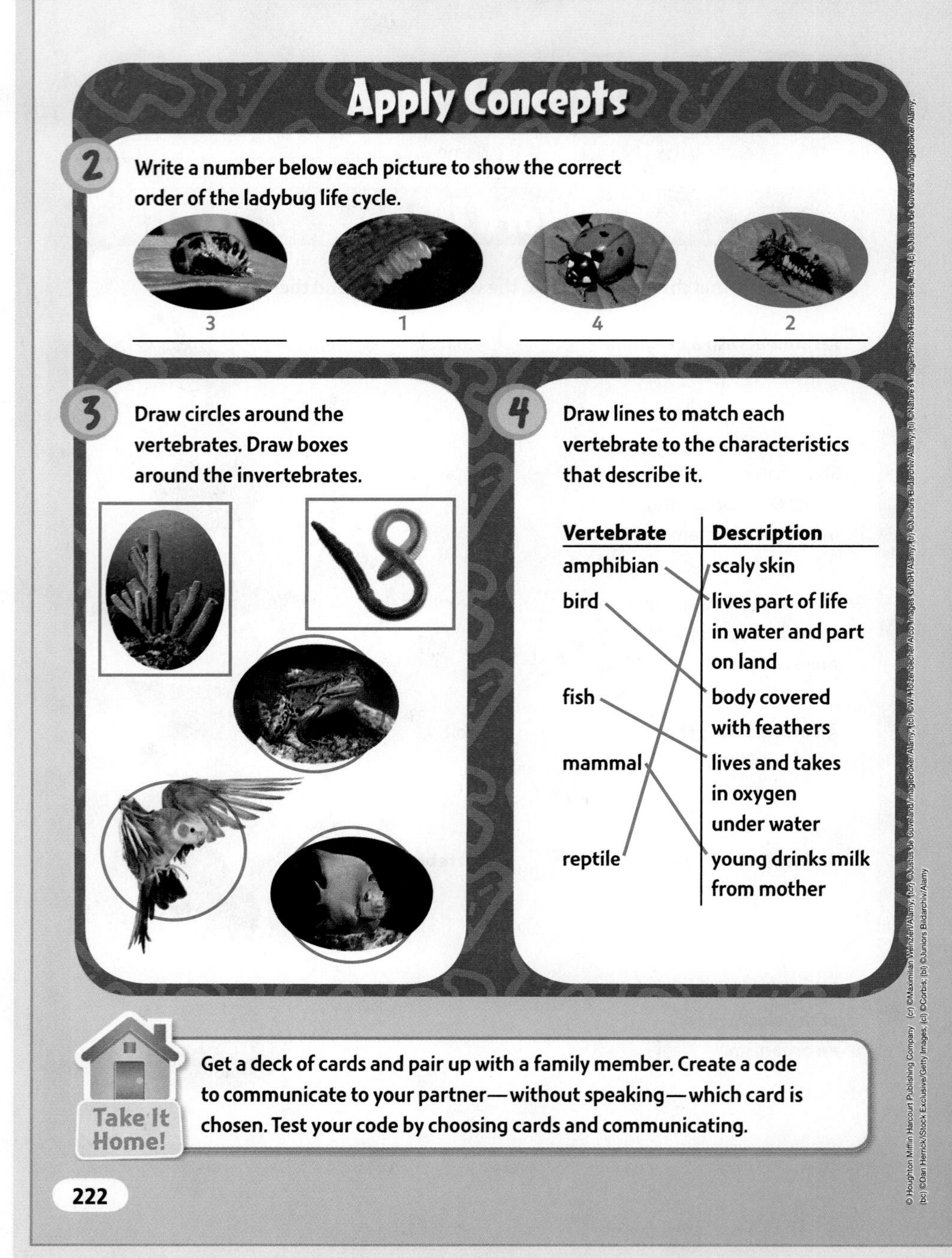

Apply Concepts

2 Write a number below each picture to show the correct order of the ladybug life cycle.

3 | 1 | 4 | 2

3 Draw circles around the vertebrates. Draw boxes around the invertebrates.

4 Draw lines to match each vertebrate to the characteristics that describe it.

Vertebrate	Description
amphibian	scaly skin
bird	lives part of life in water and part on land
fish	body covered with feathers
mammal	lives and takes in oxygen under water
reptile	young drinks milk from mother

Take It Home! Get a deck of cards and pair up with a family member. Create a code to communicate to your partner—without speaking—which card is chosen. Test your code by choosing cards and communicating.

222

Make Connections

Easy

Music Connection

Animals in Song

Ask students to find or think of a popular or childhood song that mentions or features an animal. Have students write the lyrics that describe the animal. Then have them classify the animal according to the information they have learned in the lesson.

Average

Writing Connection

A Bug's Life

Ask students to imagine that each of them is an insect undergoing metamorphosis. Have them write a story from the point of view of the insect as it goes through the different stages. Their story should include descriptions of how the appearance and lifestyle of the insect differs at each state. Encourage them to be creative.

Average

Language Arts Connection

Metamorphosis

Explain that *metamorphosis* means "change." Challenge students to find other uses of the term *metamorphosis*. Tell them to list the other examples that they find, along with descriptions of the change involved. Have them compare and contrast these examples of metamorphosis with the biological process that they have studied.

Challenging

Social Studies Connection

Ape Society

Students have learned about animal communication. Provide information to them about Jane Goodall's research with chimpanzee society and communication. Ask students to summarize in an oral presentation what Dr. Goodall learned.

People in Science

Objectives

- Describe the role of scientists.
- Describe that scientists come from all backgrounds.
- Determine the role of technology in the work of scientists.

Notebook Generate Ideas

Have a volunteer read the title of the feature. Then direct students to look at the photos. Ask them what conclusions they can draw about the work of Lisa Stevens and Raman Sukumar without reading the paragraphs.

Background

- Lisa Stevens is Assistant Curator, Primates and Pandas, in the Department of Animal Programs at the Smithsonian National Zoological Park in Washington, D.C. She received a Bachelor's of Science degree in zoology and pre-veterinary medicine.
- Raman Sukumar is an ecologist from India who was a Fulbright Fellow at Princeton University in 1991. He received various awards in conservation and currently teaches classes in ecological science at the Indian Institute of Science.
- The golden lion tamarin is an endangered species with approximately 1,000 individuals in the wild and 490 living in captivity. The animal became endangered because of deforestation. It was first listed as endangered in 1982 and was placed on the critically endangered list just 14 years later.

People in Science

Meet the Animal Activists

Lisa Stevens

Lisa Stevens is a zoologist. She has worked with animals for most of her life. Stevens manages the giant-panda exhibit at the National Zoo in Washington, D.C. As part of her job, she teaches people about this endangered species. When the panda cub Tai Shan was born at the National Zoo, Stevens took care of him. There are only 1,600 giant pandas living in the wild today. About 250 live in zoos around the world.

Raman Sukumar

Raman Sukumar grew up in India, where he loved studying nature. His grandmother called him *vanavasi*, an Indian name for "forest dweller." He has studied Asian elephants in the wild for more than 30 years. Sukumar wants to find a solution to the problem caused by people and elephants using the same land. He has taught many people why it is important to preserve the habitats of this endangered species.

223

Writing Connection

Write a Report Ask students to consider the work of a zoologist or an ecologist. Have them think about the types of knowledge that each of these careers might require. Remind students that both careers involve working with animals and understanding their needs. Invite students to do research to find out what kinds of classes and training are necessary for people who work in these fields. Have them summarize their findings in two paragraphs.

Golden lion tamarins are an endangered species. Read the story about the golden lion tamarin. Draw the missing pictures to complete the story.

Golden lion tamarins live in the rainforests of Brazil.

Logging and building have broken up the tamarins' habitat into small areas cut off from each other.

Drawing should show logging and building.

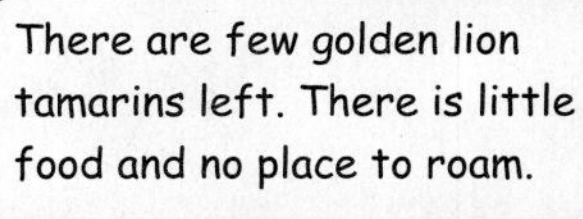

There are few golden lion tamarins left. There is little food and no place to roam.

Solution: People can set aside land as the tamarins' habitat.

Over time, the number of tamarins increases. They will have the food they need to live.

Drawing should show many tamarins together.

Science, Technology, and Society

Lisa Stevens helps provide a safe home for giant pandas at the National Zoo in Washington, D.C. Ask students to suppose that they have been asked to write a proposal about other ways in which humans can help protect the endangered giant panda. Have them include as much information as possible in their proposals about the giant panda and the dangers it faces in its own habitat.

Develop Science Concepts

Explain to students that animals can become endangered for various reasons. The golden lion tamarin became endangered because of deforestation and destruction of its habitat. **What happened to the tamarins when their homes were destroyed?** Sample answer: They did not have enough room to roam and meet their needs for food and water, so they began to die.

Why is it a good idea for people to help tamarins meet their needs? Sample answer: People are the only organisms who have the resources to help the tamarins.

Develop Inquiry Skills

COMPARE **How are the work of Lisa Stevens and that of Raman Sukumar similar and different?** One scientist works with animals in captivity, while the other works with animals in the wild.

What kind of information can be gained by observing animals in each environment? Sample answer: Observing animals in captivity helps scientists understand animal behavior because the animals can be observed often and in the same conditions. Observing animals in the wild helps scientists understand how animals survive in their natural habitats, but it may not be possible to observe them at all times.

Notebook Summarize Ideas

Have students summarize, orally or in writing, why protecting endangered species is important and how the work of Lisa Stevens and Raman Sukumar helps accomplish this.

Lesson 6

1 Engage/Explore | 2 Explain | 3 Extend/Evaluate

Options for Inquiry

FLIPCHART 

Students can conduct these optional investigations at any time before, during, or in response to the lesson in the Student Edition.

Directed Inquiry

A Gobbling Up Your Greens

20–40 minutes | small groups

Prep and Planning Tips

If time is short, you may want to have students start this activity with plants that are already growing instead of having students grow the plants from seed.

If you do start the activity with seeds, soak the seeds overnight in water or a liquid seed starter so that the seeds will germinate more quickly.

Expected Results

Students will most likely find that the grass plant is best adapted for grazing. Most grasses will become thicker and grow faster after they have been trimmed, as long as they are not trimmed too close to the roots.

Independent Inquiry

B Animal Adaptations

30–60 minutes | individuals

Prep and Planning Tips

Before students begin, have the class brainstorm a list of local animals that would be safe and easy for them to observe. Remind students about wildlife-viewing safety rules. Tell students that they should stay as far away from the animal as possible so that their presence does not affect the animal's behavior.

Science Notebook

Students can use the sample Science Notebook page as an example of how to organize their observations. Tell students to observe the animals for as long as possible. The more observations they make, the easier it will be for them to identify adaptations.

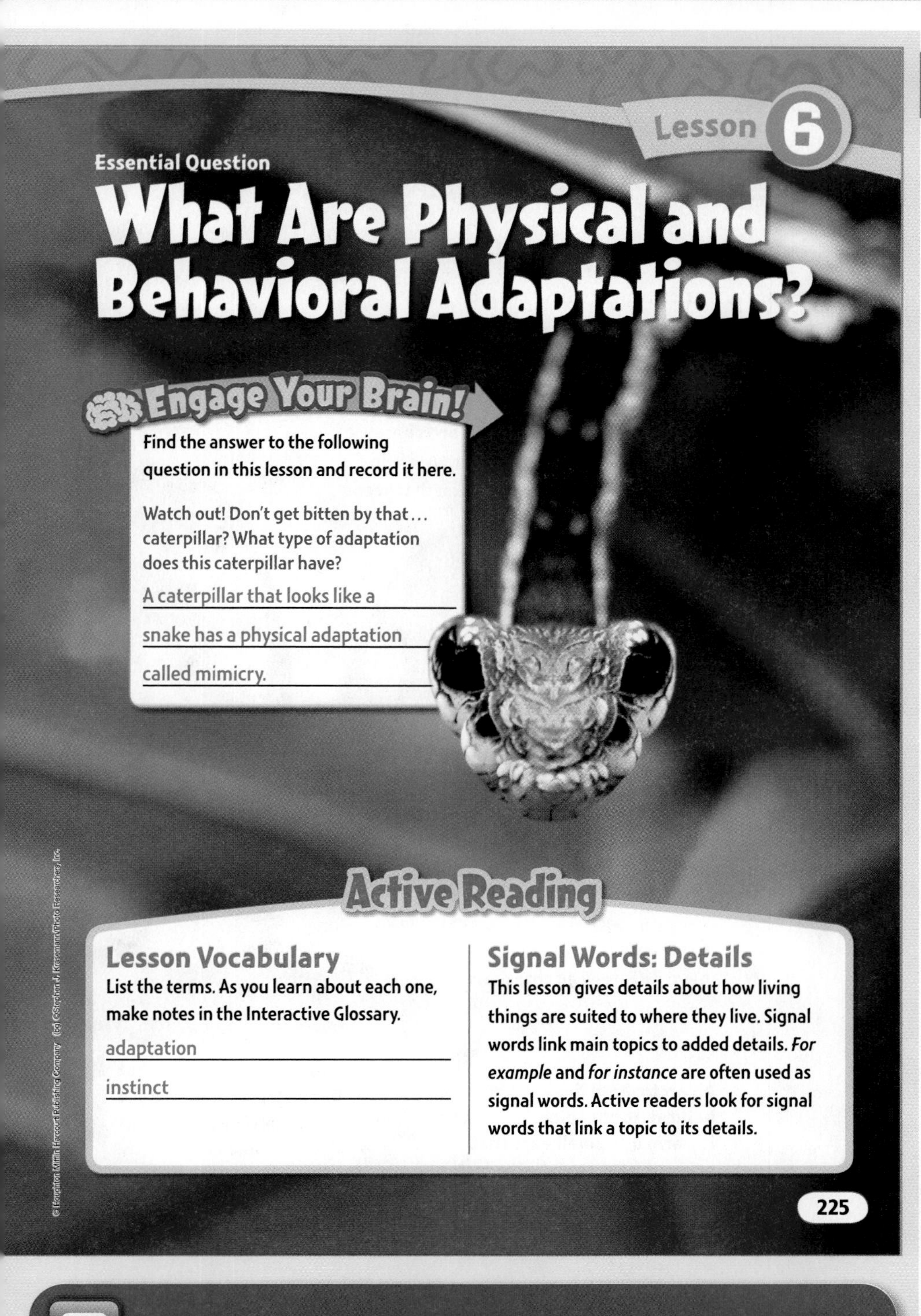

Lesson 6

Essential Question

What Are Physical and Behavioral Adaptations?

Engage Your Brain!

Find the answer to the following question in this lesson and record it here.

Watch out! Don't get bitten by that... caterpillar? What type of adaptation does this caterpillar have?

A caterpillar that looks like a snake has a physical adaptation called mimicry.

Active Reading

Lesson Vocabulary

List the terms. As you learn about each one, make notes in the Interactive Glossary.

adaptation

instinct

Signal Words: Details

This lesson gives details about how living things are suited to where they live. Signal words link main topics to added details. *For example* and *for instance* are often used as signal words. Active readers look for signal words that link a topic to its details.

225

Go Digital

An interactive digital lesson is available in the Online Resources. It is suitable for individuals, small groups, or may be projected or used on an interactive white board.

1 Engage/Explore

Objectives

- Define adaptation.
- Explain what physical and behavioral adaptations are.
- Describe how a life cycle variation could help an organism survive in a particular habitat.

Engage Your Brain!

Have students brainstorm answers to the question *Why might a caterpillar look like a snake?* Suggest that students think about different ways animals avoid predators.

Remind them to record their final answer to the question when they find it on the third spread of the lesson.

Active Reading **Annotations**

Remind students that active readers "make texts their own" by annotating them with notes and marks that help with comprehension. Encourage students to use pencil, not pen, to make annotations and to feel free to change their annotations as they read. The goal of annotation is to help students remember what they have read.

Vocabulary and Interactive Glossary

Remind students to find and list the yellow highlighted terms from the lesson. As they proceed through the lesson and learn about the terms, they should add notes, drawings, or sentences in the extra spaces in the Interactive Glossary.

2 Explain

Notebook Generate Ideas

Direct students' attention to the pictures of the rabbits on this page. Ask students to describe different features the rabbits have. For example, students might point out the rabbits' fur and long ears. Record the features that students list on the board. Then, for each listed feature, encourage students to brainstorm how they think that feature helps the rabbit survive.

Active Reading

Remind students that lesson vocabulary is defined once and then used as needed throughout a lesson. Active readers pause to be sure they recall the meaning of a new term as they encounter it in the text.

Develop Science Vocabulary

adaptation Make sure students understand that an adaptation can be physical, such as a long tongue to catch insects, or behavioral, such as a bird calling out a warning when it sees a predator. Ask students to think about their own adaptations. For example, you could ask students: **What is an adaptation you have that helps you stay warm in winter?** Sample answer: shivering

Develop Inquiry Skills

INFER **The arctic hare shown on this page has white fur in the winter and brown fur in the summer. How does the arctic hare's changing fur color help it survive?** Brown fur helps the rabbit blend into its surroundings during the summer, and white fur helps it blend in with snow during the winter.

Adaptations

Living things have many similarities. They also have many interesting differences.

Active Reading As you read this page, underline the definition of *adaptation*.

Deserts are home to many kinds of snakes. This is because snakes have characteristics that help them survive in a desert. For example, snakes have tough, scaly skin that keeps them from drying out.

A characteristic that helps a living thing survive is called an **adaptation**. Suppose an animal is born with a new characteristic. If this characteristic helps the animal survive, the animal is likely to reproduce and pass on the characteristic to its young. As long as the animal's habitat doesn't change, the young that have this characteristic are also likely to survive and reproduce. Over time, the adaptation becomes more common in the population. In this way, populations of plants and animals become adapted to their habitats.

These rabbits live in very different habitats. Because of this, they have different adaptations.

An arctic hare lives in a cold habitat. It has thick fur to keep it warm and small ears that prevent heat from being lost.

A jackrabbit lives in a hot habitat. Jackrabbits have large ears that help keep their blood cool.

226

English Language Learners

Words Easily Confused Discuss the spelling, pronunciation, and meaning of each of the following:

DEZ•ert (very hot or very cold dry land): The Sahara, in Africa, is the largest hot *desert* in the world.

dih•ZERT (to leave a place empty) As the hurricane approached, people began to *desert* the island.

dih•ZERT (sweet food eaten at the end of a meal): Do you want fruit or pie for *dessert*?

Ostriches, rheas, and emus all live on different continents. Even though they live very far from each other, they look almost the same! Their habitats are very similar, and so they share similar adaptations. These birds are all adapted for running fast. Ostriches are the fastest flightless birds on Earth. They can reach speeds of 72 km/hr (45 mi/hr)!

▶ Vines and trees are both plants, but they are very different from each other. What adaptations can you see in these plants, and how do you think these adaptations help them survive?

Sample answer: Trees have strong trunks that allow them to grow high above other plants and reach light. Vines also need light. Their flexible stems allow them to grow up the rigid stems of other plants.

227

Develop Science Concepts

Why don't all animals have the same adaptations? Animals live in different places and have different ways of living, so they need different adaptations to help them survive.

What does it tell you if two animals that live in different places have very similar adaptations? This would indicate that the animals probably have very similar ways of living and/or live in similar habitats. For example, both of the animals may live in forests or both might eat grasses.

Like animals, plants also have adaptations for surviving in certain habitats.

Which kind of habitat do you think most vines are adapted to live in? Explain your answer. Most vines are adapted to live in forest habitats where there are many trees that they can twine around and grow on. Vines are relatively rare in habitats without many trees, because it is difficult for vines to grow up plants that have flexible (herbaceous) stems, such as grasses and wildflowers.

Students can use this information as they answer the question in the Interactivity box.

Notebook Summarize Ideas

Return to the list of animals and adaptations students made as part of the Generate Ideas that kicked off this lesson. Have students review the list to determine whether they would add or change anything listed. Have them use their corrected list and the information they have learned on these pages to summarize the main idea orally or in writing.

Differentiation — Leveled Questions

Extra Support

Why do animals that live in different habitats have different adaptations? An animal's adaptations help it survive the conditions found in the environment where it lives.

Challenge

Ostriches, rheas, and emus live in grasslands. What are some adaptations they have to survive in a grassy habitat? Sample answer: They have long legs to wade through tall grasses and run from predators.

2 Explain (continued)

Notebook Generate Ideas

Have students preview the photos on these two pages. Ask students to think of some structures and behaviors they have observed in plants and animals that are unique. Invite students to consider how these structures and behaviors help the plant or animal survive. Allow students to discuss these examples and present as many ideas as they can. Then have them read the text.

Active Reading

Remind students that informational text contains many facts. Active readers process informational text with deliberate speed that enables them to focus on and retain the facts presented. Underlining facts helps active readers focus more readily.

Develop Inquiry Skills

INFER **Penguins and bison live in very different places. Yet these animals have a similar adaptation. Bison develop a thick layer of fat under their fur. Penguins have a thick layer of blubber under their feathers. What do these adaptations tell you about the environments where these animals live?** The fat and blubber help protect the animals from cold. So both environments must have cold temperatures, at least part of the time.

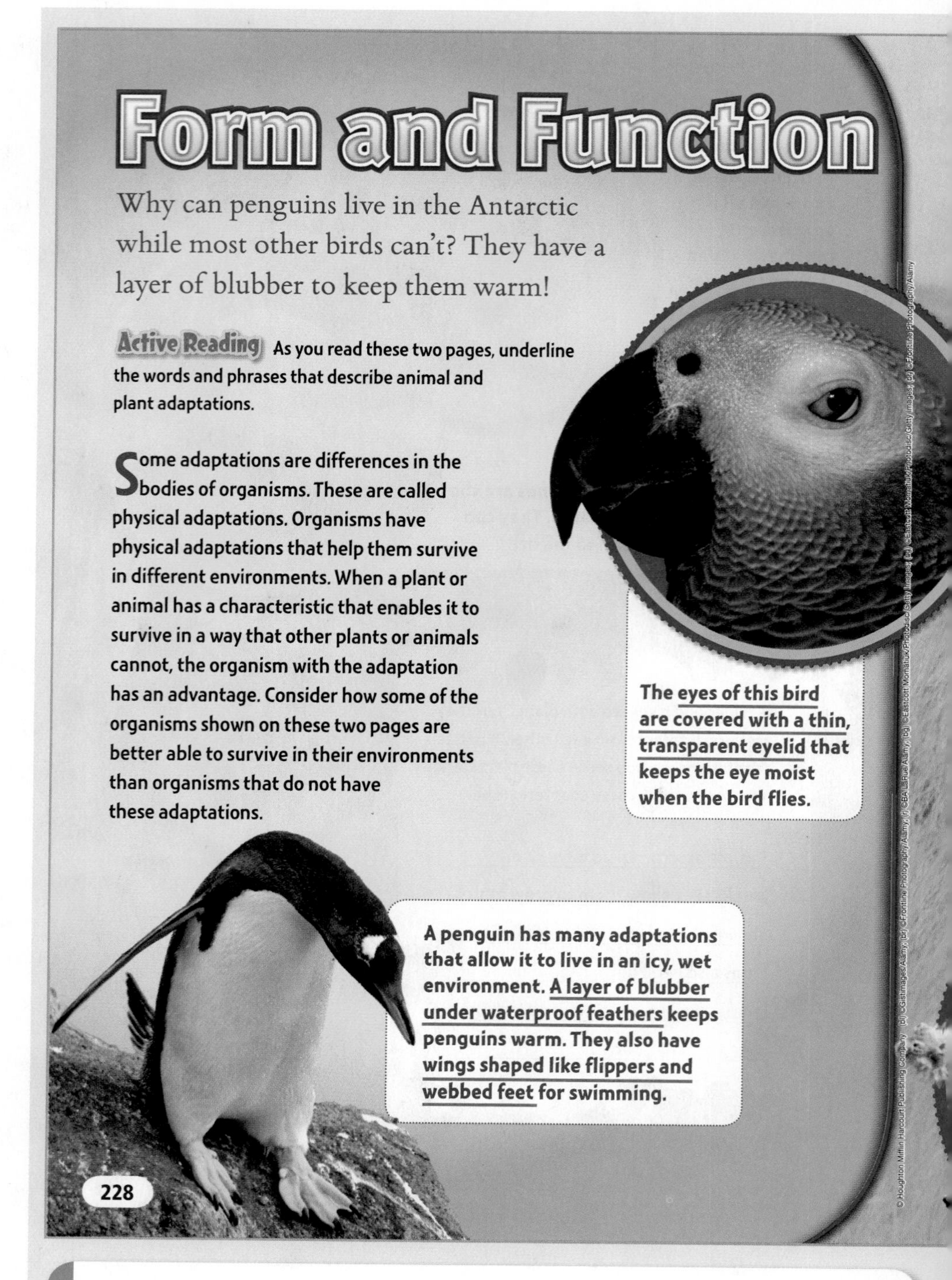

Form and Function

Why can penguins live in the Antarctic while most other birds can't? They have a layer of blubber to keep them warm!

Active Reading As you read these two pages, underline the words and phrases that describe animal and plant adaptations.

Some adaptations are differences in the bodies of organisms. These are called physical adaptations. Organisms have physical adaptations that help them survive in different environments. When a plant or animal has a characteristic that enables it to survive in a way that other plants or animals cannot, the organism with the adaptation has an advantage. Consider how some of the organisms shown on these two pages are better able to survive in their environments than organisms that do not have these adaptations.

The eyes of this bird are covered with a thin, transparent eyelid that keeps the eye moist when the bird flies.

A penguin has many adaptations that allow it to live in an icy, wet environment. A layer of blubber under waterproof feathers keeps penguins warm. They also have wings shaped like flippers and webbed feet for swimming.

228

English Language Learners

Science Terms Write *adaptation* on the board. Underline *adapt.* Explain that this word means "to adjust to conditions." Draw a double underscore under the suffix *–ation.* Share that this suffix means "action or process." So an adaptation is the process of adjusting to changes in the environment. Explain that the process they are going through to learn a new language is an adaptation.

Bison have adaptations that allow them to live on prairies. They have horns they may use for protection and fur that keeps them warm during cold winters. Bison also have wide hooves that allow them to run very quickly on grasslands.

The sharp spines of a cactus are actually modified leaves. The spines have a small surface area that minimizes water loss. This cactus shown has a thick stem that holds water, which is another important adaptation in a dry desert environment.

▶ Choose an animal or imagine a new animal. Write a description of the environment in which the animal lives. Then describe the adaptations that allow the animal to live in that specific environment.

Sample answer: A dolphin lives underwater. It has smooth skin and flippers so it can swim fast. A dolphin can also hold it's breath for a long time.

229

Writing Connection

Write a Short Story Have students write a short story about two animals or plants that live in the same environment. One organism has an adaptation that makes it well-suited for the environment; the other organism does not have this adaptation. For example, students could write about two desert plants—one has spines and the other does not.

Misconception Alert

Make sure students realize that the different characteristics, or adaptations, that plants and animals develop in response to their environments occur very slowly over hundreds of thousands of years.

Interpret Visuals

Have students look at the photos and read the captions on these pages. Suggest that they circle the adaptations described in the captions. Reinforce with these questions.

How do a penguin's adaptations reflect its environment? Sample answers: Webbed feet indicate that it spends time in water. Insulating blubber and waterproof feathers help the bird stay warm when it swims in the icy water.

What might happen to a cactus plant if it did not have sharp spines? It would be more easily eaten by animals.

The bird on this page has a membrane that protects its eyes when it is flying. What item have people invented to protect their eyes from the wind? goggles

Notebook Summarize Ideas

Have students summarize these two pages by making a T-chart with the column headings *Form* and *Function*. Direct students to list four or five physical adaptations of plants or animals and describe them in terms of form and function.

After students compile their charts, suggest they review the charts for ideas to complete the Interactivity. You may wish to extend the Interactivity by having students make a drawing of their organism in the environment it inhabits. Instruct students to use labels to point out adaptations.

2 Explain (continued)

Notebook Generate Ideas

Before students read the text, have them examine the pictures on these two pages. Instruct students to identify at least one physical adaptation displayed by the organisms in each picture. Then have students discuss how they think that physical adaptation may help the organism survive.

Active Reading

Remind students that signal words show connections among ideas. Words and phrases that signal examples include *for example, such as, for instance,* and *including.* Active readers look for signal words to help them identify examples and remember what they have read.

Develop Science Concepts

Organize students into pairs. Instruct each pair to choose an animal that is not shown on these two pages that is an example of camouflage.

Direct each pair to find or draw a picture of their chosen animal in its environment. Underneath the picture, students should write a caption that explains how camouflage helps the animal survive.

Allow time for each student pair to share their picture with the rest of the class. If possible, post pictures on a bulletin board in the classroom.

Eat or Be Eaten

Whether blending in or standing out, physical adaptations help organisms survive.

Active Reading As you read the next two pages, circle signal words that alert you to details about the main idea.

Some physical adaptations protect living things from being eaten. For example, roses have sharp thorns that help keep their stems from being eaten. Other physical adaptations help to keep an animal hidden. This type of adaptation is called *camouflage* [KAM•uh•flazh]. When green lizards hide in green grass, they are camouflaged.

Animals that hunt, such as eagles, have adaptations that help them catch food. Eagles have very good eyesight. They also have sharp claws on their feet, which they use to capture their food.

Many plants have adaptations that help spread their seeds. Some seeds can be carried by the wind. Other seeds are inside berries. When the berries are eaten, the seeds are carried to a new location.

Can you see the owl in this picture? The owl is camouflaged to look like bark.

The bright color of this rose attracts pollinators, but the thorns keep plant-eating animals away.

230

Writing Connection

A Rose by Any Other Name William Shakespeare, in his play *Romeo and Juliet,* said "a rose by any other name would smell as sweet." Have students brainstorm other common phrases about roses. (Sample answers: Roses are red, violets are blue; every rose has its thorn.) Then have students write their own poem or song about roses that incorporates some of the adaptations of roses and some of the common phrases they've heard.

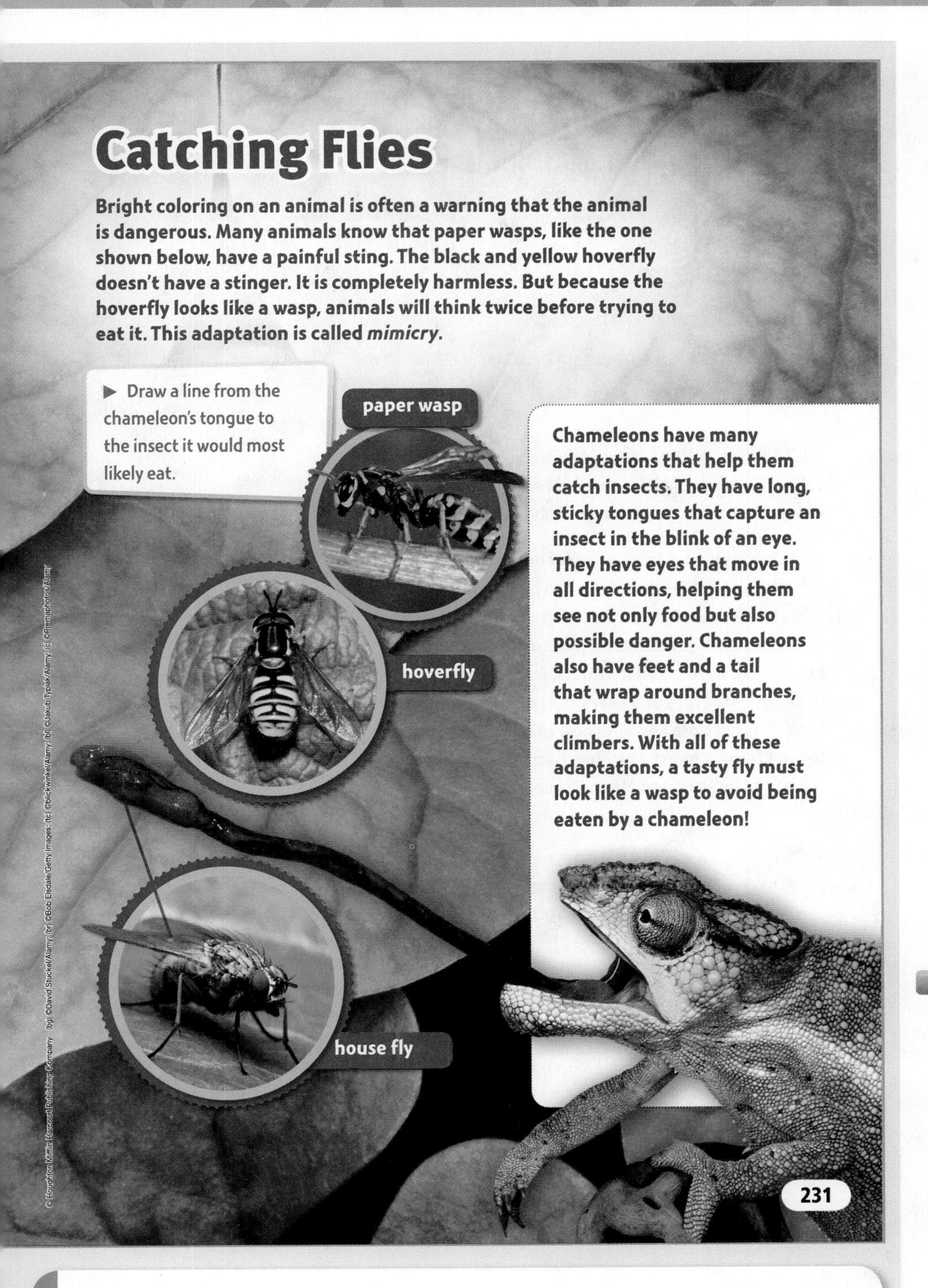

Catching Flies

Bright coloring on an animal is often a warning that the animal is dangerous. Many animals know that paper wasps, like the one shown below, have a painful sting. The black and yellow hoverfly doesn't have a stinger. It is completely harmless. But because the hoverfly looks like a wasp, animals will think twice before trying to eat it. This adaptation is called *mimicry*.

▶ Draw a line from the chameleon's tongue to the insect it would most likely eat.

paper wasp

hoverfly

house fly

Chameleons have many adaptations that help them catch insects. They have long, sticky tongues that capture an insect in the blink of an eye. They have eyes that move in all directions, helping them see not only food but also possible danger. Chameleons also have feet and a tail that wrap around branches, making them excellent climbers. With all of these adaptations, a tasty fly must look like a wasp to avoid being eaten by a chameleon!

231

Develop Science Concepts

Draw students' attention to the "Catching Flies" Interactivity on this page. Before students read about the Interactivity in their books, ask: **How many wasps do you see?** Students may answer that they see two wasps. However, only one wasp is shown. The other insect that looks like a wasp is actually a fly.

Have students turn back to the lesson opener and examine the picture of the caterpillar that looks like a snake. Help students relate the caterpillar's adaptations to those of the hoverfly shown on this page.

Develop Inquiry Skills

OBSERVE Show students various pictures of plants or animals displaying camouflage, mimicry, warning coloration, or other physical adaptations described on these two pages. Challenge students to identify the adaptation illustrated by the picture.

You may wish to award students extra credit based on the number of adaptations they are able to identify.

Notebook Summarize Ideas

Have students draw a picture of a plant or animal that is not shown on this page or the previous page. Have them circle and label the physical adaptations the organism has that help it survive in the environment in which it lives. Then have them summarize the main idea of these pages orally or in writing.

English Language Learners

Understanding Idioms Explain that the idiom *to blend in* means "to be similar to the things or people in one's surroundings." An animal that blends in with its environment can hide from predators. A fawn with spots blends in with its forest environment. A green insect on a green leaf blends in and can't be seen. Then define the word *camouflage* and use it in context: The Arctic fox's white fur is good winter camouflage.

2 Explain (continued)

Notebook ▸ Generate Ideas

Tell students that a behavior is a way that an animal acts. Behaviors can help animals survive and stay healthy. Ask students to think of behaviors that they engage in that help them stay healthy. Examples may include brushing their teeth, putting on warm clothes in winter, eating healthy food, and looking both ways before crossing the street.

Active Reading

Remind students that authors may use examples to illustrate a concept, such as a specific animal's behavior to exemplify animal behavior. Active readers focus on these examples as a way to deepen their understanding of the concept and remember its most important characteristics.

Develop Science Vocabulary

instinct Make sure students understand the difference between instincts and learned behaviors. Instincts are behaviors that animals are born knowing how to do. Learned behaviors must be taught to an animal in some way, even if it is only through observing other animals engaging in a similar behavior.

What is an example of an instinct? Sample answer: a spider spinning its web

Misconception Alert

Many people think that plants do not respond to stimuli. Plants have many responses to their environment. For example, plants turn in response to the movement of the sun, and they change direction of growth in response to gravity. Currently the term *behavior* is reserved for organisms with nervous tissue, but many botanists would like to expand the definition to include plant responses.

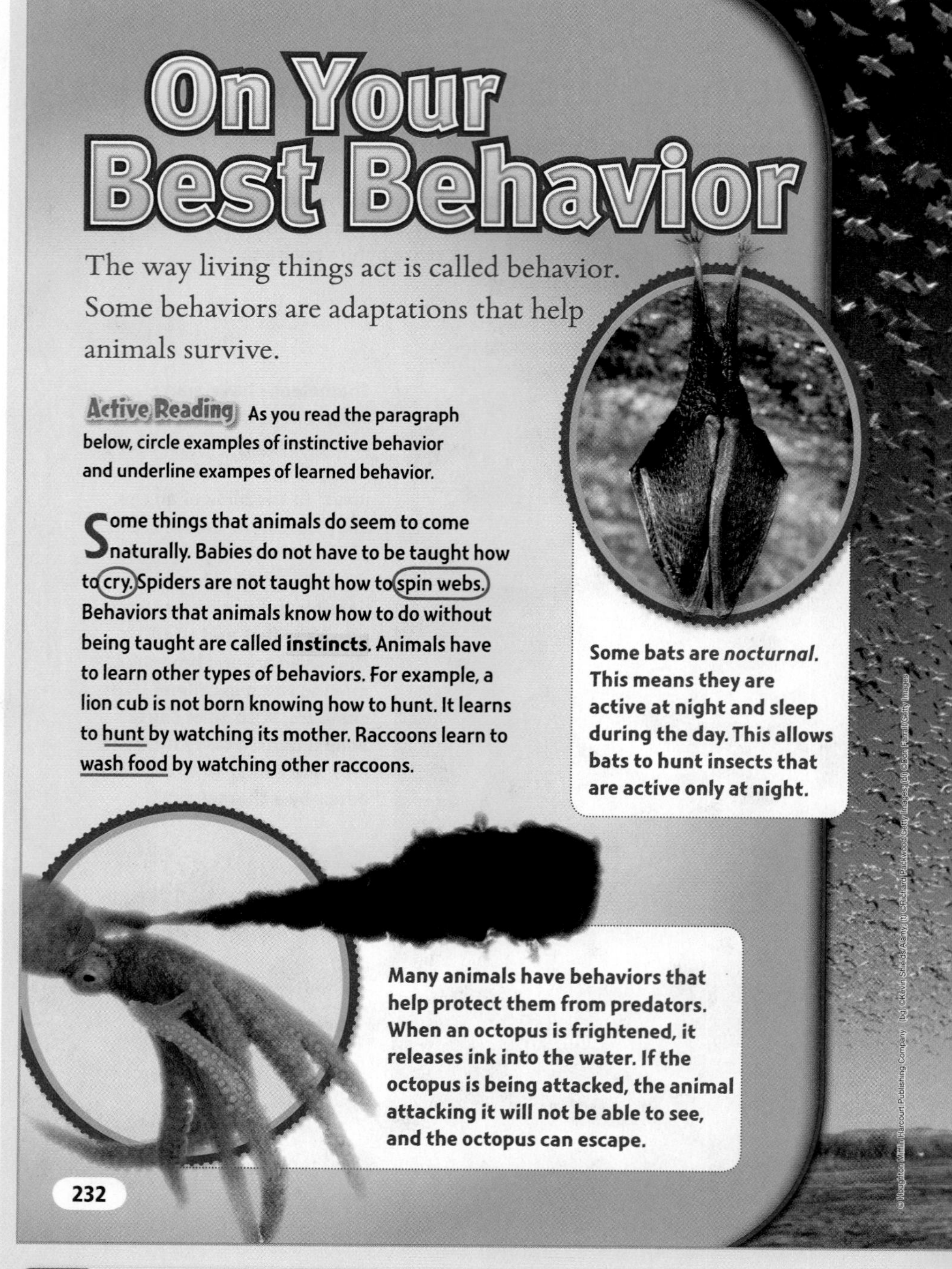

On Your Best Behavior

The way living things act is called behavior. Some behaviors are adaptations that help animals survive.

Active Reading As you read the paragraph below, circle examples of instinctive behavior and underline exampes of learned behavior.

Some things that animals do seem to come naturally. Babies do not have to be taught how to cry. Spiders are not taught how to spin webs. Behaviors that animals know how to do without being taught are called **instincts**. Animals have to learn other types of behaviors. For example, a lion cub is not born knowing how to hunt. It learns to hunt by watching its mother. Raccoons learn to wash food by watching other raccoons.

Some bats are *nocturnal*. This means they are active at night and sleep during the day. This allows bats to hunt insects that are active only at night.

Many animals have behaviors that help protect them from predators. When an octopus is frightened, it releases ink into the water. If the octopus is being attacked, the animal attacking it will not be able to see, and the octopus can escape.

232

Differentiation — Leveled Questions

Extra Support

How is a behavioral adaptation different from a physical adaptation? Behavioral adaptations involve how an organism acts. Physical adaptations are parts of an organism's body.

Challenge

In your own words, define the term *behavior*. Sample answer: Behavior is an action in response to something in the environment. Behavior is something that an organism does.

Each year, millions of snow geese migrate south in autumn and north in spring.

Some animals move to different locations at certain times of the year to find food, reproduce, or escape very cold weather. This instinctive behavior is called *migration*. Many birds, butterflies, and some bats migrate long distances.

Other animals hibernate. *Hibernation* is a long period of inactivity that is like sleeping. But hibernation is not the same as sleeping. When an animal hibernates, its body processes slow down and it stays inactive for months. Can you imagine taking a three-month nap?

The way that animals act toward other animals of the same type is called *social behavior.* Honeybees have very complex social behavior. They communicate using movements called the "waggle dance." A bee that finds food will return to the hive and do a waggle dance. The pattern of the dance gives other bees a lot of information! The dance communicates which way to go, how far away the food is, how much food there is, and even what kind of food it is!

Do the Math!

Interpret Data in a Bar Graph

Ground squirrels hibernate. They must eat a lot during the spring, summer, and fall to store up enough energy to survive hibernation. Study the graph below.

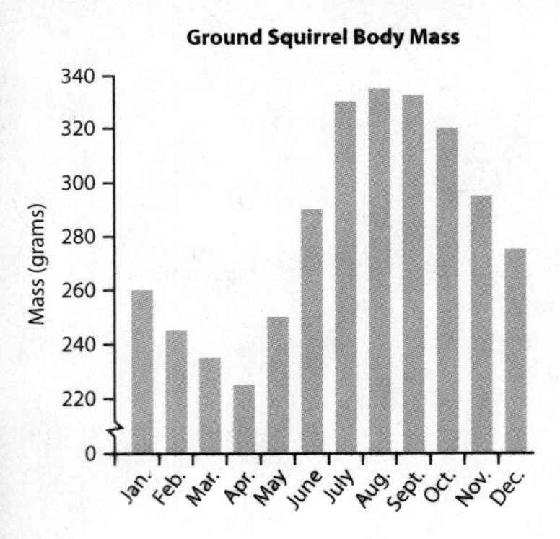

About how much mass does a ground squirrel have in March?

about 235 g

During which month do ground squirrels start to hibernate? How do you know?

They start hibernating in September, when body mass starts to decrease.

233

Math Connection

Graph Data Tell students that migrating animals can travel thousands of kilometers during a single migration. Give students the following data about the distances migrated by different animals in a year, and have them use it to make a bar graph.

Arctic tern: 71,000 km
Caribou: 1,500 km
Gray whale: 10,000 km
Monarch butterfly: 4,000 km

Share with students that the arctic tern is a small bird that has the longest migration pattern of any animal.

Do the Math!

Interpret Data in a Bar Graph

Before you have students complete this Interactivity, ask them to spend a few minutes studying the graph. **What does the graph show?** The graph shows how the mass of a ground squirrel changes over the course of a year.

How do you think an animal can gain mass? An animal gains mass by eating.

What is hibernation? Hibernation is a dormant or inactive state.

Do you think animals are able to eat while they are hibernating? Explain your response. No, animals are not able to eat while they are hibernating, because they are inactive.

Where do you think an animal gets its energy from while it is hibernating? During hibernation, an animal gets its energy from fat and other nutrients stored in its body.

Do you think an animal would weigh more before hibernation or after hibernation? Explain your response. An animal would weigh more before hibernation. Much of its mass would be used for energy while the animal was hibernating.

Notebook Summarize Ideas

Instruct students to make a T-chart titled *Behavioral Adaptations.* On the left side of the chart, students should list all of the behavioral adaptations discussed or shown on these two pages. On the right side of the chart, students should list how these behavioral adaptations help the animal survive. Have them summarize these pages by stating the main idea, either orally or in writing.

2 Explain (continued)

Notebook Generate Ideas

Write the term *life cycle* on the board. Review with students what this term means. Tell students that on these pages of the lesson, they will learn how different life cycles can be adaptations for plants and animals.

Active Reading

Remind students that authors may use examples to illustrate a concept, such as a specific animal's life cycle to exemplify life cycles. Active readers focus on these examples as a way to deepen their understanding of the concept and remember its most important characteristics.

Interpret Visuals

Have students examine the photo of salmon on this page. Have a volunteer read the caption aloud. Then ask:

Why might it be easier for young salmon to survive in a stream rather than in the ocean? Sample answers: There might be fewer predators in a stream than in the ocean. There may be more places to hide in a shallow stream. Food for young salmon may be more readily available and closely spaced in a stream than in the ocean.

How do you think salmon know when they should migrate upstream in order to lay their eggs? instinct

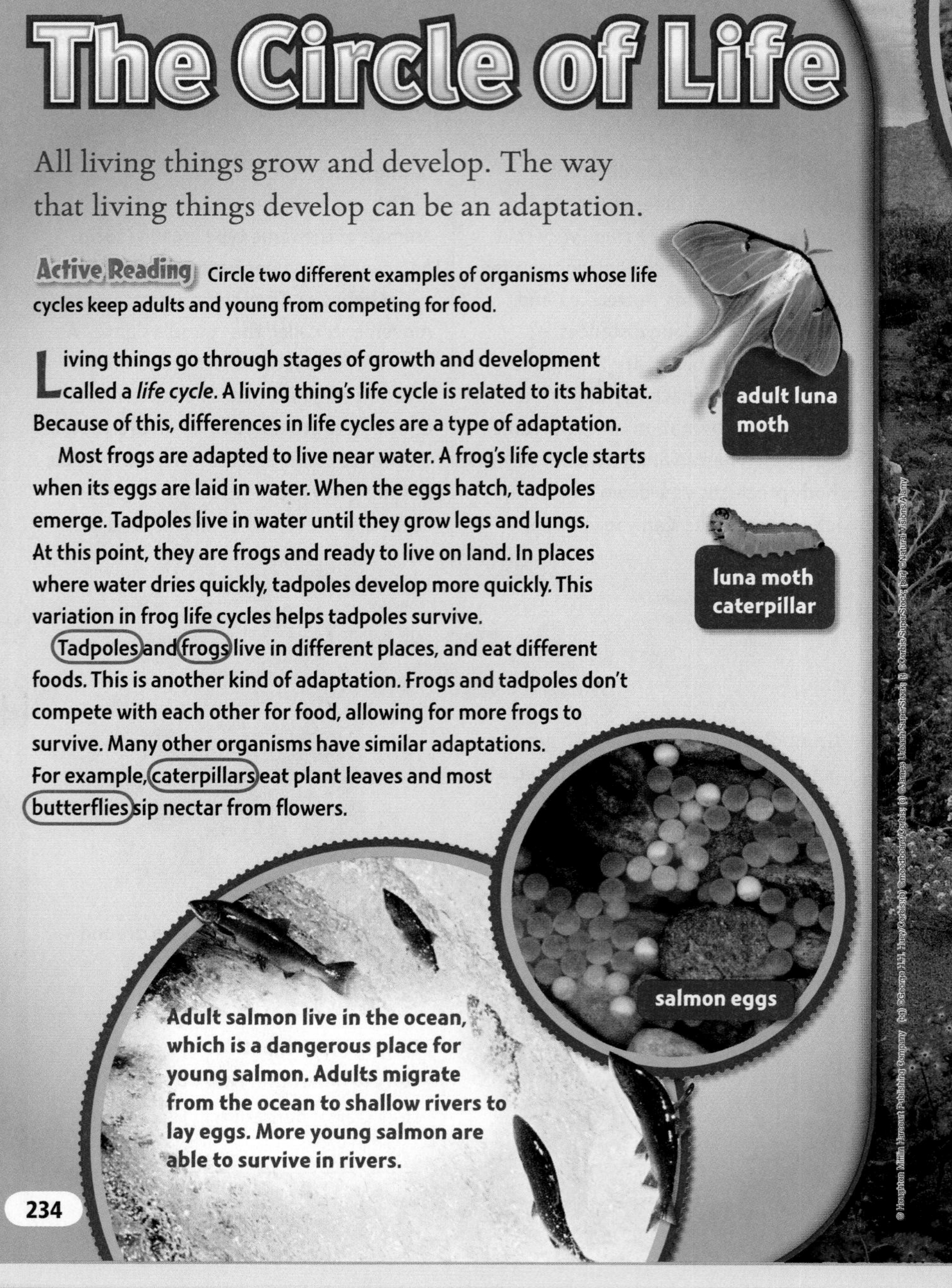

The Circle of Life

All living things grow and develop. The way that living things develop can be an adaptation.

Active Reading Circle two different examples of organisms whose life cycles keep adults and young from competing for food.

Living things go through stages of growth and development called a *life cycle*. A living thing's life cycle is related to its habitat. Because of this, differences in life cycles are a type of adaptation.

Most frogs are adapted to live near water. A frog's life cycle starts when its eggs are laid in water. When the eggs hatch, tadpoles emerge. Tadpoles live in water until they grow legs and lungs. At this point, they are frogs and ready to live on land. In places where water dries quickly, tadpoles develop more quickly. This variation in frog life cycles helps tadpoles survive.

Tadpoles and frogs live in different places, and eat different foods. This is another kind of adaptation. Frogs and tadpoles don't compete with each other for food, allowing for more frogs to survive. Many other organisms have similar adaptations. For example, caterpillars eat plant leaves and most butterflies sip nectar from flowers.

Adult salmon live in the ocean, which is a dangerous place for young salmon. Adults migrate from the ocean to shallow rivers to lay eggs. More young salmon are able to survive in rivers.

234

Differentiation — Leveled Questions

Extra Support

How would a frog's life cycle help it survive in places where water is plentiful only part of the year? Sample answer: When water sources dry up, the adult frogs that live on land may still survive.

Challenge

What is one advantage that the life cycles of butterflies and frogs both provide? Sample answer: Both life cycles keep the young and the adults from competing with each other for food.

▶ A female impala has one or two calves and then spends months feeding and protecting them. A female salmon lays thousands of eggs and then returns to the ocean. What are some advantages of each type of life cycle?

The young impala is very likely to survive because it is cared for by its parent. The mother salmon does not have to spend a lot of energy caring for the young, because there are thousands of them. Even if some die, many may survive.

Some animals can adjust their life cycle to changes in their habitat. In a very dry year, a pregnant impala can wait up to a month, until rain falls, to give birth. This life cycle variation helps make sure there is enough food and water for the young impalas to survive.

▶ It does not rain very often in the desert. When it does rain, the seeds of desert wildflowers, such as those shown below, immediately begin to grow. The plants bloom, make new seeds, and complete their whole life cycle within a few weeks! Explain how the life cycle of desert wildflowers helps them survive in the desert.

Desert wildflowers are adapted to take advantage of rainwater when it is available. The plants grow and make new seeds very quickly before the habitat becomes too dry again.

235

Develop Science Concepts

Before students complete the first Interactivity box on this page, have them recap what they have learned about the life cycles of salmon and impala. Ask:

How many offspring can a salmon have at one time? A salmon can have thousands of offspring at one time.

How many offspring does an impala have at one time? An impala has only one or two offspring at one time.

Which animal, a salmon or an impala, spends more time caring for its young? an impala

Do you think offspring that are cared for by adults are more likely to survive? Explain. Yes, offspring that are cared for are more likely to survive, because their parents help to protect and feed them.

Before students respond to the second Interactivity, make certain they understand the scenario that is being described. If they need additional help, ask:

What does the sun's energy cause water to do? evaporate

Students should be able to conclude that flowering desert plants must complete their life cycles while sufficient moisture remains in the soil.

Notebook Summarize Ideas

Lead students in a class discussion in which you have them compare and contrast some life-cycle adaptations with physical and behavioral adaptations. You may wish to have students take notes during the discussion and then produce a graphic organizer, such as a Venn diagram, that summarizes the main points of the discussion.

Writing Connection

Write a Fact Sheet Have students choose a local animal and find out how its physical and behavioral adaptations help it survive in its environment. If possible, take students to a place where they can observe their chosen animals, such as a local nature preserve. Ask students to put together a fact sheet about their animal's adaptations. The fact sheet should include at least one picture of the animal. Discuss some sources they can use for their research, such as encyclopedias, field guides, and local park webpages.

2 Explain (continued)

Notebook Generate Ideas

With students, brainstorm the answer to the question in the introduction. After students respond, ask questions to get them thinking more broadly. Invite students to imagine that they are hawks. **What would make you notice prey in a field of grass?** Students should say that they would notice movement or a color that was different from the grass.

Active Reading

Remind students that signal words show connections among ideas. *For example* and *for instance* signal examples of an idea. *Also* and *in fact* signal added facts. Active readers remember what they read because they are alert to signal words.

Develop Science Concepts

Show students pictures of ornamental goldfish. Explain to students that the varieties of ornamental goldfish were bred by people who noticed variation in natural goldfish populations. People selectively bred goldfish with certain characteristics to enhance that characteristic, such as large eyes, frilly tails, and bubble-shaped scales. **Why is variation in a population beneficial?** Students should recognize that variation in a population helps to increase the likelihood that at least some of the individuals will be able to survive if their environment changes.

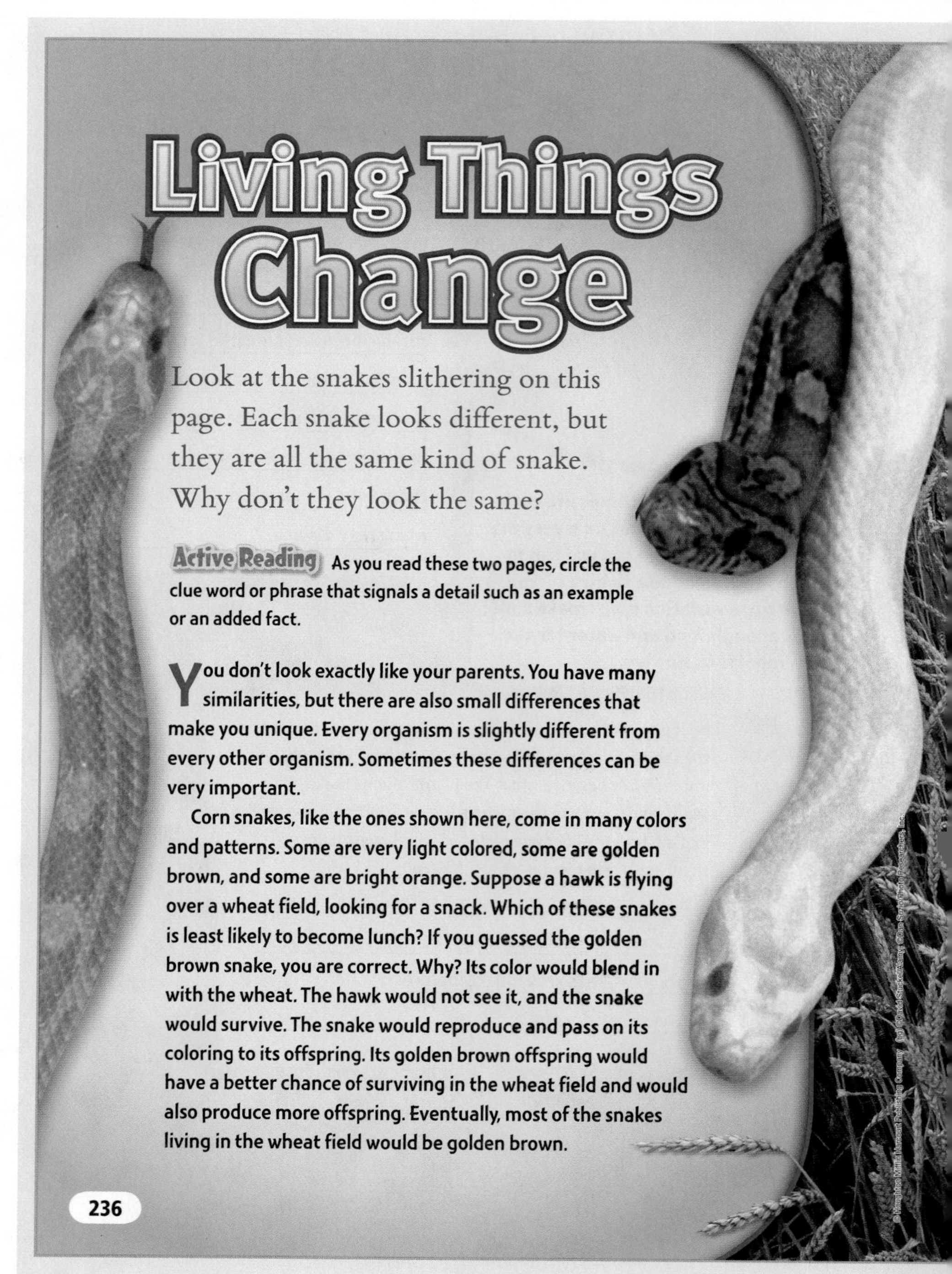

Living Things Change

Look at the snakes slithering on this page. Each snake looks different, but they are all the same kind of snake. Why don't they look the same?

Active Reading As you read these two pages, circle the clue word or phrase that signals a detail such as an example or an added fact.

You don't look exactly like your parents. You have many similarities, but there are also small differences that make you unique. Every organism is slightly different from every other organism. Sometimes these differences can be very important.

Corn snakes, like the ones shown here, come in many colors and patterns. Some are very light colored, some are golden brown, and some are bright orange. Suppose a hawk is flying over a wheat field, looking for a snack. Which of these snakes is least likely to become lunch? If you guessed the golden brown snake, you are correct. Why? Its color would blend in with the wheat. The hawk would not see it, and the snake would survive. The snake would reproduce and pass on its coloring to its offspring. Its golden brown offspring would have a better chance of surviving in the wheat field and would also produce more offspring. Eventually, most of the snakes living in the wheat field would be golden brown.

236

Differentiation — Leveled Questions

Extra Support

When an environment changes, why do some individuals survive while others die? Individuals have differences. Some individuals have characteristics that are better suited to the new environment than others are.

Challenge

Suppose less rain fell than normal. Which plants would be more likely to survive? Sample answer: those that can store water or with a root system that reaches deeper underground

Sometimes living things change because their environment changes. For example, bacteria have changed as a result of their changing environment. Since the discovery of antibiotics, people have learned how to kill bacteria. The first antibiotic, penicillin, saved many lives by killing bacteria that cause disease.

But in a very large population of bacteria, a few are not affected by penicillin. These bacteria survive and multiply. Over time, they produce large populations of bacteria that are not affected by penicillin.

Researchers have had to find new antibiotics to kill these bacteria. But, again, some bacteria are not killed. These bacteria continue to multiply.

While different types of antibiotics have been developed, bacteria have become resistant to many of them. Now there are bacteria that are resistant to almost all known types of antibiotics. These bacteria are extremely difficult to kill.

Do the Math!

Find Median and Mean

Length of Corn Snakes	
Snake 1	3.5 m
Snake 2	5.5 m
Snake 3	4.6 m
Snake 4	5.1 m
Snake 5	4.8 m
Snake 6	3.9 m
Snake 7	5.3 m

Adult corn snakes vary not only in color, but also in length. The table shows the lengths of several adult corn snakes. Study the data, and then answer the questions.

1. The median is the middle number of a data set when the numbers are placed in numerical order. Find the median of the data set. 4.8 m
2. The mean is the average of a data set. Find the mean of the data set. 32.7 m ÷ 7 = 4.67 m or 4.7 m

Antibiotics in soaps and cleaners kill many bacteria. However, when not all of the bacteria are killed, the ones that survive multiply. Little by little, bacteria are becoming resistant to antibacterial soap and cleaners.

237

Develop Inquiry Skills

INFER Do you think that all variations that individual organisms have can be seen? Why or why not? Students may say that the variations in the colors of corn snakes are visible, but the variations in the bacteria that allow them to survive an antibiotic (a change in the environment of the bacteria) are not visible.

Do the Math!

Find Median and Mean

Find the Median Show students how to find the median for a group of data with the following values: 8.9, 3.7, 5.7, 2.3, 7.4, 9.1, 4.8. Have students list the numbers in increasing order. Explain that the middle value in a range of numbers is called the median. In this set of values, 5.7 is the median.

Find the Mean Have students find the mean by adding all of the values and dividing the sum by the number of values. Remind students to round the quotient to the same number of places as the values in the list. In this set of values, 6.0 is the mean, or average. Have students complete the Interactivity on the student page.

Notebook Summarize Ideas

Invite students to summarize these two pages by sequencing how differences in individual organisms can lead to changes in a population. Students may summarize either orally or in writing.

Math Connection

Make a Bar Graph Have students make a graph of the data on this page. Begin by discussing the type of graph students will make. Help them to understand that this is discrete rather than continuous data, so a line graph wouldn't be appropriate. Instead, students should select a bar graph. Remind them to title their graph and label their axes. Then have students compare and contrast the kinds of information they can get from a graph, a table, the median, and the mean.

3 Extend/Evaluate

Sum It Up!

- As students examine the outline, encourage them to identify which pages in the lesson are covered by the two main sections of the outline. Tell students that as they fill out each section of the outline, they should refer to the correct portions of the lesson.
- Students will likely benefit from reviewing the illustrations and photographs in the lesson before working on this activity. You may wish to review the images with the class as a whole by having volunteers identify what each of the lesson's main images illustrates.
- If students have trouble completing part of this exercise, have them review the lesson before continuing on to the Brain Check activities.
- Remind students to use the Answer Key to check their answers. Students should revise incorrect responses so they can use the Sum It Up! page to study for tests.

When you're done, use the answer key to check and revise your work.

The outline below is a summary of the lesson. Complete the outline.

Summarize

I. Instincts: A behavior that a living thing does without being taught to do.

A. Example: spiders spin webs

B. Example: babies cry

II. Adaptations: A characteristic that helps a living thing survive is called an adaptation. Kinds of adaptations include:

A. Physical Adaptations

1. Example: camouflage

2. Example: thorns that keep plant-eating animals away

B. Behavioral Adaptations

1. Example: migration

2. Example: hibernation

C. Life Cycle Adaptations

1. Example: controlling when offspring are born

2. Example: having young that don't eat the same food as adults

Answer Key: Your answers may vary. Sample answers: I.A. spiders spin webs I.B. babies cry II.A.1. camouflage II.A.2. thorns that keep plant-eating animals away II.B.1. migration II.B.2. hibernation II.C.1. controlling when offspring are born II.C.2. having young that don't eat the same food as adults

Lesson 6

Name ______________________

Word Play

1 Use words from the lesson to complete the puzzle.

```
1C A 2M O U F L 3A G E
    I         D
    G         A
    R         P         4H
    A   5I    T         I
    T   N     A         B
    I   S     T         E
    O   T     I         R
    N   I   6N O C T U R N A L
        N     N         A
   7C Y C L E S         T
        T               I
                        O
                        N
```

Across

1. What type of adaptation helps a living thing hide in its environment?
6. An animal that is active at night is described as being ______________.
7. Stages that living things go through as they develop are called life ______________.

Down

2. An example of ______________ is birds flying south in winter.
3. What are characteristics that help an animal survive?
4. What behavior causes an animal to be inactive for a long period of time?
5. A behavior that an animal doesn't need to learn is a(n) ______________.

239

Answer Strategies

Word Play

1. If necessary, have students refer back to the pages on which each term is defined or discussed. As a challenge activity, ask students to construct their own crossword puzzles using the same or other relevant terms.

Assessment

Suggested Scoring Guide

You may wish to use this suggested scoring guide for the Brain Check.

Item	Points
1	28 (4 points per item)
2	18
3	18
4	18
5	18
Total	100

Lesson Quiz

See Assessment Guide, p. AG 43.

3 Extend/Evaluate (continued)

Answer Strategies

Apply Concepts

2. Refer students to the section of the lesson in which the cactus plant is shown and described. Ask students to think about how the cactus plant contrasts with other plants. Then have them use this information to make their drawings and labels.
3. Before students answer this question, review what the term *camouflaged* means.
4. You may wish to have students review the text under the *On Your Best Behavior* heading before answering this question.
5. If students are having difficulty answering this question, have them compare and contrast the life cycle of a narrow-mouthed frog with that of most other frogs. Point out that the eggs of most frogs hatch into tadpoles, which live in water. Students may also want to review the text under the *The Circle of Life* heading.

Take It Home!

Encourage students to take pictures of or make drawings of some of the plants and animals they saw on their walk. They can then share the images with their classmates.

Apply Concepts

2 Draw a picture of a cactus. Next to the cactus, draw a plant that is found in a non-desert environment. Label three adaptations that help the cactus plant survive in a desert.

Cactus plant should have a thick stem and spines instead of leaves. Labels or illustrations should show that these adaptations help protect the plant from animals and store water. A comparison plant should not show these characteristics.

3 Circle the camouflaged animal.

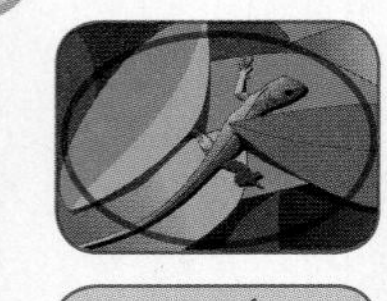

4 In winter, ground squirrels retreat into burrows and do not come out until spring. Circle the term that best describes this behavior.

Communication | (Hibernation) | Migration | Nocturnal hunting

5 A narrow-mouthed frog's eggs hatch directly into tiny frogs. The environment where narrow-mouthed frogs live is very dry. How is this adaptation helpful?

Because the habitat is dry, tadpoles won't have access to water to swim in. By hatching directly into a tiny frog, a narrow-mouthed frog is more likely to survive because it can move around on land.

Go for a walk through your neighborhood or a local park with your family. Look at different plants and animals, and point out different adaptations that the plants or animals have.

Make Connections

Easy

Art Connection

Comic Book

Tell students to think of an interesting or unique animal adaptation. For example, bats can find food in the dark using echolocation. Instruct students to draw a comic book story about a superhero that has a special adaptation and uses it to help people. If time allows, encourage students to share their comic books with each other.

Average

Math Connection

Word Problem

Adult male black bears weight about 300 pounds, but during the winter, they lose about 1/5 of their total body weight. After hibernation, about how much would a male black bear weigh? (The bear would most likely weigh about 240 lb.)

Average

Writing Connection

Form and Function Fill in the Blank

Remind students that plants and animals have structures with special forms to perform specific functions. These structures are useless or worse when applied in the wrong situation or environment. To illustrate this point, write this sentence frame on the board: *Yesterday I used ____ to ____*. Pass out two index cards to each student and have them complete the sentence by writing a term or phrase on each card to describe an activity that they did. For example, a student may write "*a shovel*" and "*dig a hole*." Students can take turns reading their sentences aloud. Students can trade cards and read the results aloud. Ask them to explain how having the proper tools is important to fulfilling a function.

Challenging

Health Connection

Adaptations and Basic Needs

Explain to students that adaptations help a plant or animal meet its needs. Organize students into small groups. Each group should discuss the following questions: **What do humans need to stay healthy? How do humans' adaptations help them to meet these needs?** Afterwards, have a representative from each group present an oral summary of the group's answers to these two questions.

Enduring Understandings

Revisit the Big Idea and Essential Questions

Big Idea **All living things have observable characteristics that allow them to be classified. Plants and animals pass these characteristics on to their offspring.**

To explore the Big Idea, post the lesson topics on the board one at a time, and have students explain how the content of each lesson relates to the Big Idea. Examples:

- Lesson 1: This lesson is about the classification of living things. This connects to the Big Idea that all living things have observable characteristics that allow them to be classified.
- Lesson 3: This lesson is about how plants grow and reproduce. It is through reproduction that plants pass on their observable characteristics to their offspring.

Essential Questions

Post the Essential Questions and use the following prompts to guide a discussion.

Lesson/Essential Question	Prompts
L1 **How Are Living Things Grouped?**	• List the six kingdoms and their basic characteristics.
L2 **What Is a Dichotomous Key?**	• Tell what a dichotomous key is and how it is used.
L3 **How Do Plants Grow and Reproduce?**	• Describe the role of flowers in angiosperm reproduction.
L4 **What Factors Affect Germination Rate?**	• Describe the factors that can affect germination.
L5 **How Do Animals Grow and Reproduce?**	• Draw the stages of complete and incomplete metamorphosis.
L6 **What Are Physical and Behavioral Adaptations?**	• Explain the difference between physical and behavioral adaptations, and give an example of each type.

Notebook Science Notebook

You may use the following strategy after students complete the unit or after each lesson.

- Have students review and edit the responses to Essential Questions they drafted at the beginning of the unit. Suggest they cross out sentences or ideas that are unnecessary or inappropriate.
- Have students draft Flashcard Facts in their Science Notebooks to prepare for a game of Q&A. Students can then write a question on one side of an index card, and the answer on the other. Have students use the cards to devise a variety of games played in pairs, small groups, or teams.

Science Notebook

Essential Questions	Answers
How Are Living Things Grouped?	
What Is a Dichotomous Key?	
How Do Plants Grow and Reproduce?	
What Factors Affect Germination Rate?	
How Do Animals Grow and Reproduce?	
What Are Physical and Behavioral Adaptations?	

Unit 4 Review

Name ______________________

Vocabulary Review

Use the terms in the box to complete the sentences.

adaptation
classification
dichotomous key
germinates
life cycle
spore

1. A seed that begins to grow into a plant starts to sprout, or ___germinates___.

2. A single reproductive cell that can grow into a new plant is a(n) ___spore___.

3. When scientists organize living things according to similar characteristics, they are using ___classification___.

4. The different stages that an animal such as an insect goes through as it grows and reproduces is called its ___life cycle___.

5. Any characteristic that helps an organism survive is considered to be a(n) ___adaptation___.

6. A chart with many choices that guide you to the name of the organism or object you want to identify is called a(n) ___dichotomous key___.

Science Concepts

Fill in the letter of the choice that best answers the question.

7. Ramon wants to classify an organism. The organism can be seen without a microscope. Its cells have cell walls but no chloroplasts. The organism gets food by breaking down dead organisms. Which kingdom does this organism likely belong to?
   - Ⓐ animal
   - Ⓑ fungi (filled in)
   - Ⓒ plant
   - Ⓓ protist

8. During the life cycle of a plant, pollen comes in contact with the stigma and an embryo forms. What is the name of this process?
   - Ⓕ fertilization (filled in)
   - Ⓖ germination
   - Ⓗ hibernation
   - Ⓘ migration

Item Analysis

Items	Depth of Knowledge	Cognitive Complexity
1–6	Level 1	Low
7	Level 2	Moderate
8	Level 1	Low

Unit Review

Answer Key

Vocabulary Review (4 points each)

1. **germinate**
   Challenge students to describe the sequence as a plant germinates. Refer them to Lessons 3 and 4 for more review.

2. **spore**
   Ask a volunteer to name plants that reproduce using spores. Students can review Lesson 3 if needed.

3. **classification**
   List a group of objects, and challenge students to classify them. For a review of classification, refer students to Lesson 1.

4. **life cycle**
   Have students review complete and incomplete metamorphosis in Lesson 5.

5. **adaptation**
   Challenge students to name an adaptation and identify it as physical or behavioral. For more review, refer to Lesson 6.

6. **dichotomous key**
   Refer students to Lessons 1 and 2 for review of how a dichotomous key is used.

Science Concepts (5 points each)

7. **B**
   Refer students to Lesson 1 to review the different kingdoms.

8. **A**
   Direct students to the flower image in From Flower to Fruit to Seed to differentiate germination and fertilization.

Assessment

Unit 4 Test and Performance Assessment

See Assessment Guide, pp. AG 44–AG 50 for Unit Test and Performance Task with Long Option rubric.

Unit Review *continued*

Answer Key

Science Concepts (5 points each)

9. B

The structure shown is a cone with seeds. Gymnosperms and angiosperms use seeds to reproduce.

10. C

An animal's color is a physical trait and, thus, a physical adaptation. Direct students to Lesson 6 to review physical and behavioral adaptations.

11. D

Have students compare and contrast the animals shown in the first two sections of Lesson 5 to review vertebrates and invertebrates.

12. C

Have volunteers list all of the variables in the experiment (light, soil, water, type of seed, type of container, temperature). Then discuss which of the variables were the same and which changed (temperature). The changed variable is the one being tested.

13. C

Suggest that students make a two-column chart in which they can list the stages of complete and incomplete metamorphosis. Direct them to Lesson 5 for additional review.

14. D

Review the two types of adaptations—physical and behavioral—discussed in Lesson 6. Point out that the description in the question says nothing about the animal's body part but instead describes how it behaves. Thus, it is describing a behavioral adaptation.

15. D

After identifying the characteristics that Alam noted, have volunteers tell why each choice could or could not be correct. Of the organisms listed, only bacteria are microscopic, single-celled, and have no cell walls.

Science Concepts

Fill in the letter of the choice that best answers the question.

9. Some plants have a structure like the one shown here.

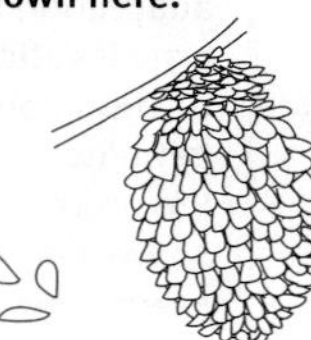

What function is carried out by this structure?

Ⓐ anchoring
Ⓑ reproducing (filled)
Ⓒ making food
Ⓓ transporting water

10. The coloring of the rough green snake allows it to blend in with its background. What type of adaptation is the rough green snake's color?

Ⓐ behavioral adaptation
Ⓑ life-cycle adaptation
Ⓒ physical adaptation (filled)
Ⓓ reproductive adaptation

11. Animals can be classified as vertebrates or invertebrates. Which structure must be present in order for an animal to be classified as a vertebrate?

Ⓐ a tail
Ⓑ a brain
Ⓒ a wing
Ⓓ a backbone (filled)

12. Manuel did a science fair project on seed germination. Here is the procedure he followed:

Step 1: Place equal amounts of moist soil into two 1-gallon glass jars, and plant 10 radish seeds in each jar.

Step 2: Cover both jars.

Step 3: Place one jar in the refrigerator. Place the other jar in a dark closet.

Step 4: Observe both jars at the same time every day. Record any differences observed in the germination of the seeds.

What was the purpose of Manuel's project?

Ⓐ to determine whether moisture affects germination
Ⓑ to determine whether seeds need oxygen for germination
Ⓒ to determine whether temperature affects germination (filled)
Ⓓ to determine how long it takes different types of seeds to germinate

13. Vanessa is observing an organism undergoing metamorphosis. Which stage must she observe in order to conclude that the organism undergoes incomplete metamorphosis?

Ⓐ adult
Ⓑ larva
Ⓒ nymph (filled)
Ⓓ pupa

Item Analysis

Items	Depth of Knowledge	Cognitive Complexity
9	Level 2	Low
10	Level 2	Moderate
11	Level 2	Low
12–13	Level 3	High

Name ______________________

14. The diagram below shows how an ant lion catches its food.

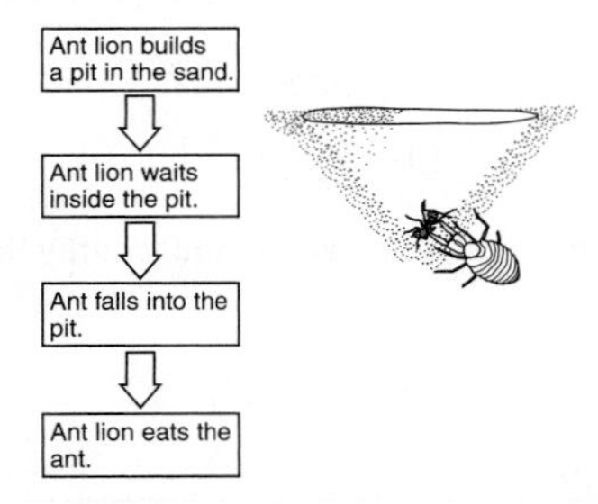

What does the diagram suggest about the ant lion?

Ⓐ The ant lion is not adapted to its habitat.

Ⓑ The ant lion has a diet of both plants and animals.

Ⓒ The ant lion survives by hunting and chasing food.

Ⓓ The ant lion has behavioral adaptations for its environment.

15. Alam is classifying organisms into different kingdoms. When he observes one group of organisms under a microscope, he sees that they are each made up of one cell with no cell wall. Which kingdom do these organisms **most likely** belong to?

Ⓐ plant kingdom

Ⓑ fungi kingdom

Ⓒ animal kingdom

Ⓓ bacteria kingdom

16. Scientists use classification to group living things. What is likely about living things that are placed in the same group?

Ⓐ they are all the same age

Ⓑ they are all the same color

Ⓒ they are all the same size

Ⓓ they all have similar characteristics

17. The picture below shows a structure found on one type of plant.

Which type of plant produces this structure?

Ⓐ ferns

Ⓑ mosses

Ⓒ angiosperms

Ⓓ gymnosperms

Item Analysis

Items	Depth of Knowledge	Cognitive Complexity
14	Level 2	Moderate
15	Level 3	High
16–17	Level 2	Low

Unit Review *continued*

Answer Key

Science Concepts (5 points each)

16. D

Scientists classify organisms by grouping them together according to shared characteristics. The more closely two organisms are grouped, the more characteristics they share.

17. C

Only angiosperms produce seeds in flowers. Gymnosperms produce seeds on cones, and ferns and mosses do not produce seeds or flowers.

Short Option Performance Assessment

Task

Sort It Out
Have students work in small groups to make rules for classifying items in their desks. They should sort items into several "kingdoms" and sort the members of each kingdom into as many smaller groups as they can.

Rubric

Preparation Provide adequate time for students to display and observe the characteristics of the items in their desks prior to making rules for classification. To save time, students might consider the content of only one desk rather than of all the group members' desks.

Scoring Rubric—Performance Indicators

___ Groupings are based on objective and observable criteria.

___ Simple criteria are used to establish different "kingdoms" of objects.

___ Additional classifications are added to enable objects to be sorted into smaller groups that show more similarities.

Observations and Rubric Scores

3 2 1 0

Unit Review *continued*

Answer Key

Apply Inquiry and Review the Big Idea (7 points each)

18. Sample answer shown on student page.

Suggest students use a process of elimination to first determine what these organisms are *not.* It is obvious that none of these are simple organisms (protists, bacteria, or Archea). All of these organisms can move around, so they are not fungi. They do not make their own food, so they are not plants. Thus, they are all animals.

19. Sample answer shown on student page.

Remind students that in a scientific investigation, all conditions are kept the same except for the one being tested. Suggest that students make a list of what would be needed to grow seeds (water, correct temperature, container of soil, same type and number of seeds) and then identify the one thing that will be changed to meet the requirements of the investigation (amount of water). Then they can describe how they will test and measure the effects of differing amounts of water in order to come to a conclusion.

20. Sample answer shown on student page.

Remind students that living things are adapted to their environment. Discuss how the environment would be different if the snow melted (it would no longer be white) and how that would affect the white rabbits' ability to hide from predators.

Apply Inquiry and Review the Big Idea

Write the answers to these questions.

18. These organisms are very different, and yet they are all classified in the same group.

Identify the two characteristics that allow them to be classified together, and identify the group to which they all belong.

Sample answer: All three organisms are made up of many cells. None can make its own food through photosynthesis and must obtain food by eating other organisms. They would therefore be classified together in the animal kingdom.

19. Lily wants to learn how changing the amount of water that she gives a pumpkin seed will affect its germination rate. List the steps she could take in a scientific experiment to determine whether water affects the seeds' germination.

Sample answer: Lily should add the same amount of soil and the same number of pumpkin seeds to each of four pots that receive the same amount of sunlight and experience the same temperatures. Only the amount of water added should vary. Pot 1 remains dry. Pot 2 gets a normal amount of water. Pot 3 gets half the normal amount, and Pot 4 gets twice the normal amount. Lily can then observe and take measurements as the seeds germinate to learn how differences in water affect germination.

20. A population of white rabbits lives in a snowy mountain environment. Hawks that fly high in the air hunt for the rabbits. Describe how the population of white rabbits might change if the climate of the mountain changed and the snow melted for a long period of time.

Sample answer: It is likely that the population of white rabbits would decline rapidly if the snow melted. The white fur is an adaptation that allows the rabbits to blend in with the snowy background and avoid being seen and eaten by hawks. If the snowy background disappeared, the rabbits would become easier to spot, and it would be harder for them to avoid the predators.

Item Analysis

Items	Depth of Knowledge	Cognitive Complexity
18	Level 3	Moderate
19	Level 3	High
20	Level 3	Moderate

Teacher Science Background

Concise science background for all the major topics and concepts in this program is provided in the Teacher Edition Planning Guide. This background is provided for this unit only.

Additional background information is provided in Online Resources. The online content, appropriate for teachers and students, provides the following benefits:

- Free up-to-date web content to extend and expand student understanding
- Lessons, assessments, and deeper exploration of content for teachers
- Content that is constantly reviewed and vetted by experienced NSTA educators (National Science Teachers Association)
- Activities to bring science alive in the classroom

Animals

Adaptation

An adaptation is a characteristic of a plant or an animal that allows the organism to survive in a particular environment. Some adaptations have developed over many generations. Some, however, occur within a single generation. The key to adaptation is variation, or difference, within a species. In order for a species to survive, it must be able to adapt, or change, to better fit new circumstances that arise within an environment. Adaptations can take the form of changes both in an organism's body (physical adaptation) and in its behavior (behavioral adaptation). An example of the former is the long, pointed beak of the hummingbird, which is designed to fit inside tubular flowers. An example of the latter is the nest-building and courting-dance activity of the male bower bird that helps him attract a mate. These adaptations do not happen during one animal's lifetime, but over many generations. The shape of a bird's beak, the placement of a fish's eyes, and the shape of a mammal's teeth are just a few adaptations that help animals survive.

How Animals Are Born and Grow

All animals produce offspring in one of two ways. Some animals hatch from eggs, while others develop inside the mother before she gives birth. Some animals look like their parents when they are born and others do not. Some need a lot of parental care; others need little. All need food, water, air, and shelter to survive. Either the parent helps the young meet these needs, or the young are equipped to meet them. In species where there is little or no parenting, the adults produce many offspring to compensate for those lost to predators. An animal's body covering also changes as the animal grows. Young animals that have to fend for themselves tend to develop mature body coverings faster than animals that receive parental care.

Protective Body Coverings

An animal's body covering protects an animal from the harmful elements of its environment. The hard outer shell of an insect and the sharp quills of a porcupine act as shields around these organisms. Body coverings also protect animals from extreme temperatures. Thick hair traps an animal's body heat to insulate it in a cold environment. Thin porous skin enables an animal to release body heat and keep cool in a warm environment.

Animal Classification

Living things can be grouped into domains and kingdoms. Two of the kingdoms are the plant kingdom and the animal kingdom. To organize the thousands of different species in the animal kingdom, zoologists group animals into categories according to their genetic makeup and their physical similarities and differences. Zoologists divide the animal kingdom into smaller and smaller groups called *subkingdoms*, *phyla*, and *subphyla*. This classification system is called a *taxonomy*. Animals can further be divided into smaller groups. The science of animal classification has been developing for more than 300 years. Because contemporary scientists can study the genetic makeup of animals, scientists can now group them in more ways. They have even found some new groups. Some animals may seem to belong to one group but actually belong to another. For example, a whale lives in water like a fish, but it is a mammal. It feeds milk to its young, and it has lungs instead of gills.

Vertebrates and Invertebrates

The terms *vertebrate* and *invertebrate* are used by scientists as a matter of convenience. The terms do not indicate a natural division in the animal kingdom because the divisions do not indicate the real relationships among the animals in the groups. Some invertebrates are more closely related to the vertebrates than they are to other invertebrates. For example, echinoderms (the group that includes sand dollars, sea stars, and sea urchins) belong to a group of animals called *deuterostomes*. The term describes the animals' embryonic development. All vertebrates are deuterostomes. Most other groups of invertebrates, however, belong to a group called *protostomes*. Thus, echinoderms are inferred to be more closely related to vertebrates than to other invertebrate groups.

Heredity

Nature Versus Nurture

- Behavior is the response of an organism to its surroundings.
- Behavior may be inherited—passed from parent to offspring—or learned.
- Instincts are behaviors that are inherited responses to stimuli and do not require learning. In newborn humans, instincts include crying.
- Some instinctive behaviors are influenced by learning. For example, a tiger is born with the instinct to hunt, but it must learn skills to hunt effectively.
- Learned behaviors are acquired completely as a result of experience. In humans, reading is a learned behavior.

Plants

Flowers

The blossoms of flowers are often arranged in groups. They appear in tightly packed clusters, broad clusters, or along a single stalk, such as the puya. The *puya* is an ancient treelike angiosperm that grows in the Andes Mountains of South America. Its flowers form spikes of up to 8000 bright-green blossoms. This plant, classified as a bromeliad, forms flowerstalks that can be nearly 5.4 m (18 ft) tall.

Roots

The two basic root systems found in plants are a taproot system and a fibrous root system. In a taproot system, such as in a carrot, a large root grows down into the soil, producing smaller lateral roots. A fibrous root system, such as in grasses, begins with a primary root that is shortly replaced by many roots that form from the stem. Both root systems have adaptations to perform certain functions. For example, taproots of beets and carrots are modified to store food. In mangrove trees, large, woody prop roots develop from adventitious roots on horizontal branches.

Tropism

The response of a plant to stimuli in its environment is called *tropism.* This response is triggered by plant hormones called *auxins.* A plant that grows toward a stimulus is said to display a positive tropism, while one that grows away from a stimulus displays a negative tropism. Most plants show tropisms to light, or phototropism, and gravity, or gravitropism. The root displays a positive gravitropism and a negative phototropism. As the stem grows upward, it shows a negative gravitropism and a positive phototropism.

Unusual Pollinators

The tiny Australian honey possum feeds on pollen and nectar from desert flowers such as the *Banksia* and, in the process, pollinates the plants. The South American creeper is a plant that gives off a bad odor that attracts flies. When a fly enters the flower, it becomes trapped overnight. During its "incarceration," the fly pollinates the plant. The flower fades by morning and the fly escapes.

Photosynthesis

Photosynthesis is a series of chemical reactions that plants and some protists and bacteria use to convert solar energy into chemical energy. The basic photosynthetic reaction converts six molecules of water and six molecules of carbon dioxide into one molecule of glucose (sugar) and six molecules of oxygen. Chlorophyll and other pigments enable the chemical reaction by absorbing energy from different wavelengths of sunlight. Additional chemical reactions convert and store the glucose as complex sugars and starches.

Plant Adaptation

An adaptation is a characteristic of a plant or an animal that allows the organism to survive in a particular environment. Some adaptations have developed over many generations. Some, however, occur within a single generation. The key to adaptation is variation, or difference, within a species. In order for a species to survive, it must be able to adapt, or change, to better fit new circumstances that arise within an environment.

Types of Plants

Plants can be divided into two groups—flowering plants and nonflowering plants. Flowering plants have special parts that make seeds. Seeds are the first stage of growth for many plants. Roses and lilies are kinds of plants that have flowers. A conifer is one type of nonflowering plant. Conifers are plants that have cones instead of flowers. The seeds are made inside of cones, which hold and protect the seeds. After some time, the seeds will be ready to grow into new plants. When this happens, the cone will open and the seeds will fall out. Most conifers have needle-shaped leaves that stay green all year. Many conifers do not shed their leaves like other plants. Pines, spruce, firs, cypress, and yews are kinds of conifers.

What Plants Need

Plants need light, water, and air to produce food through a process called *photosynthesis*. This process takes place in a plant's leaves and green stems. These parts contain chlorophyll, which enables the plant to use water, carbon dioxide from the air, and light energy from the sun to make sugars. Plants then use the sugar to grow and to form flowers, seeds, and fruit, which enables them to reproduce. Soil supplies nutrients, which are certain chemical elements that plants need to live. Plants grown hydroponically, or in a growing solution, get these nutrients from the solution. Plants that grow aeroponically, or in air, get the nutrients and moisture they need from air.

Plant Nutrients

All plants need certain chemical elements to live. Elements they need in large amounts, called macronutrients, include carbon, hydrogen, oxygen, sulfur, phosphorus, nitrogen, potassium, calcium, and magnesium. Nutrients needed in smaller amounts, called micronutrients, include copper, zinc, iron, nickel, and other minerals. Plants get oxygen and carbon through their leaves and absorb other elements through their roots. Most root absorption takes place from the soil; however, plants grown hydroponically, or in water, obtain the minerals they need from a mineral-rich growing solution. Plants grown aeroponically, or in air, have their roots sprayed with a mineral-rich solution.

Plant Parts

Plants have parts that are adapted to get what the plant needs. Most roots grow underground and absorb water and nutrients. Roots also anchor the plant. Some roots, called taproots, are thick. Other roots, called fibrous roots, are thin and spread out. Stems support a plant's leaves and flowers and improve the plant's ability to absorb water and nutrients. Some stems, such as tree trunks and limbs, are woody. Leaves make most of the food that the plant needs in a process called photosynthesis. The leaves contain chlorophyll, which enables them to use light energy to combine water and carbon dioxide to make the plant's food. Some plants reproduce from seeds. Seed plants are divided into two main groups. In flowering plants, the fruit protects the seeds. In conifers, such as pines and firs, seeds are made in cones.

Seeds

Seeds contain the food they need to start the growing process, but they have three other requirements for continued growth—warmth, oxygen, and water. The roots are necessary for further plant development. Seeds use their stored food to initiate sprouting. They absorb water through their covers from the soil. They get oxygen from air, which is trapped between soil particles. Warmth is usually provided by the sun.

Parts of a Seed

Seeds come in many different sizes, shapes, and colors. The outside of a seed is the seed coat. This covering protects the seed. Some seeds, such as those of the coconut palm, have additional protection in the form of shells or husks. The fleshy part of the seed, called the cotyledon, is food for the embryo, which is the beginning of a new plant. The radicle is the first part of the plant to grow from the seed. It is the root of the plant embryo. The radicle holds the seedling in the soil and absorbs water that the seedling needs for growth. The shoot, which consists of both stems and leaves, emerges after the root.

Fruit

Most fruits contain seeds. Through fruits, plants are able to disperse their seeds with the help of various animals. Oranges, cherries, and tomatoes are all considered a type of berry. Blackberries and strawberries are a different type of berry. Both types ripen into a sweet, moist fruit, which is attractive to the animals that eat them. Then the seeds pass, unharmed, through the animal's digestive tract and are deposited on the soil in a new location. Fruits are an important part of the human diet because they provide the body with vitamins, such as vitamin C, and dietary fiber. Humans eat fruit in the forms of fresh fruit, jams, jellies, and pickles. Fruits can be packed in cans or jars or frozen to preserve them or transport them.

Teacher Notes

SQUIRRELLY
the Squirrel

Dana Keone O'Banion

Illustrated by Sean Winburn

AuthorHouse™
1663 Liberty Drive
Bloomington, IN 47403
www.authorhouse.com
Phone: 1-800-839-8640

Published by AuthorHouse 10/27/2014

ISBN: 978-1-4969-3128-3 (sc)
ISBN: 978-1-4969-3129-0 (e)

This book is printed on acid-free paper.

For my wonderful sons Devin and Dixon
and children *everywhere*
—D.K.O.

Mommy and daddy squirrel had wanted a child of their very own for a long time. They were very happy when their little blessing came as a baby boy squirrel. They named him "Squirrelly." He was a very tiny fellow. His fur was kind of ragged. His tail was long and thin like a rat's tail not bushy like all the other squirrels. Also, his eyes were small and squinty and he needed to wear glasses. His parents didn't mind his appearance. They were ecstatic to have a child of their own. They loved him with all of their heart and unconditionally.

When they first took Squirrelly home and showed him to their friends and neighbors, most were polite and said "what a boy." However, when mommy and daddy encountered strangers, the looks they received and comments made were not so kind. Many strangers said things like "what a strange looking child." Generally, mommy and daddy would just smile or say "he's our son and we love him just the way he is."

As Squirrelly began to grow or get older as that was a more accurate description, he tried to play with other children. The other children often teased and called Squirrelly "rat tail" or "four eyes" among many other nasty names. At first, Squirrelly would run home and cry. His mommy would calm him with his favorite walnut cookies and a glass of milk. She told him that he was special and his beauty was inside. She instructed when the other children teased him that he should not get upset and just say "so" in response to their taunts.

Each night as his dad would tuck Squirrelly for bed, his daddy would tell him how special he was and would teach Squirrelly through stories how to be the best squirrel he could be.

One summer Squirrelly was old enough to leave his parents' home so he left and took all the lessons his parents had taught with him. He did not move very far though. He lived in a nice home just across the park from his parents.

All summer squirrels were told and knew that the winter would be very cold and snowy. So Squirrelly began collecting nuts and berries so that he wouldn't have to leave his home to find food in the winter. He collected twigs and leaves to keep his place warm.

Other squirrels about his age who were playing all summer noticed Squirrelly diligently collecting food for the winter. One squirrel named Milton teased "old rat tail" all summer long. "Hey look at old rat tail collecting all that junk. He has always been weird. Why would anyone rather collect food and junk than play?" Milton would say. Squirrelly paid Milton no mind and continued his diligent efforts. His mother and father had taught him to complete the things he set out to do no matter what others thought about him.

As the fall came, Squirrelly was just about set. He bought several books to read over the winter and snuggled in near his fireplace to begin reading. He stopped by to see his parents and let them know that he was prepared for the winter.

Milton and the rest of the gang continued to play through the fall. Milton had convinced everyone that it wasn't necessary to collect food. There would be plenty of food when winter came. "I know of an old man who always comes to our park with nuts and candy each winter to make sure we don't starve", he said.

Winter came roaring in like thunder. The once autumn colored landscape was covered in white. The snow was very deep and very cold and hard to move around in. After the initial blizzard ended Milton and the other squirrels went to a spot near a bench where the old man would sit and feed the squirrels. There was no old man. Little did Milton know that the old man who always came to the park in the winter had moved and would be feeding squirrels in another park this winter.

"Well, I am sure he'll be here tomorrow," Milton exclaimed. All the little squirrels went back to their homes hungry but anxiously awaited the next day. After several days all the squirrels including Milton began to worry. They spread out all over the park to try to find the old man. They had no luck finding him and were all getting very hungry. Many of the squirrels had moved to this park from far away and had no family they could go to for help.

Meanwhile, Squirrelly was enjoying his warm fireplace and the book he had been reading. He periodically poked his head out and saw the other squirrels in the park. He would invite them in but they were not interested. They were too busy now trying to find food.

One day Squirrelly looked out and saw Milton. Milton looked cold and hungry. Squirrelly invited Milton inside to share some of his food and get warm, but Milton refused. He was too proud to eat with Squirrelly.

Days became weeks and weeks became months. Squirrelly was sitting happily by his fireplace when all of the sudden—"Crash" he heard at his door. It was one of the other squirrels, Sammy. He was out of breath because he had rushed over. Sammy said "I need help with Milton." "Milton crossed the street to retrieve some crumbs from a garbage can and fell in." Milton was too weak to climb out. Squirrelly raced out of his front door with Sammy. They both grabbed Milton and brought him back to Squirrelly's home. Fortunately, Milton was not hurt bad and as his body began to thaw and his eyes opened he saw a blurry vision of Squirrelly smiling at him. "W-w-what? Where am I?" asked Milton. "You are here at Squirrelly's home" exclaimed Sammy who was warm sitting by the fireplace and stuffing his mouth with nuts and berries. Squirrelly helped me bring you here because you were hurt.

Squirrelly? Milton asked. But why? I have never been nice to you. Squirrelly just smiled and said "you are right because you never got to know me."

Anyway, don't worry about it. Get something to eat and get some rest.

As Milton felt better he thanked Squirrelly. Milton noticed that Squirrelly had enough food to feed hundreds of squirrels.

He explained to Squirrelly that "there are several squirrels who have been starving and cold outside because all they did was play late into the fall and listen to me about how we were going to get food this winter." "Do you think you could find it in your heart to share with them also?" "Of course," said Squirrelly, "I have offered all winter long but each of you said you were doing just fine and didn't need anything from me."

Milton exclaimed "what a nice person you are, I'm sorry I never got to know you before."

Squirrelly said, "don't worry about it, now call your friends so no one else attempts to cross that busy street just for a crumb."

Milton poked his head out of Squirrelly's house and called to all the other little squirrels wandering in the park. They could not believe their eyes but all rushed to Squirrelly's house to find out what was happening. They arrived to see a smiling Squirrelly and more food than they had ever seen in their lives. Squirrelly invited them into his home. Some huddled near the fireplace to get warm. Others sat at the table filled with fruits and nuts and ate until their hearts' content.

They all were happy. Another squirrel named Shirley, stood up and claimed "we were all wrong about you Squirrelly. We judged you and never took the time to know you. You are truly special and have shown us all the benefit of hard work and compassion.

Squirrelly just smiled.

When the spring came, all the squirrels went out to play again. Squirrelly wasn't with them. He sat prepared to watch the game from his home as he always had. But this time just before the first pitch, Milton called to Squirrelly and said "hey buddy, get down here and throw out the first pitch."

Squirrelly was happy to and made a very good pitch too.

The End

CPSIA information can be obtained at www.ICGtesting.com
Printed in the USA
BVOW07s1822100216

436212BV00025BA/464/P

9 781496 931283